# CASTING
*for*
# MURDER

ALSO BY MIKEL DUNHAM

*Stilled Life*

# CASTING *for* MURDER

## Mikel Dunham

ST. MARTIN'S PRESS     NEW YORK

*for Margaret*

~

Design by Judith A. Stagnitto

Library of Congress Cataloging-in-Publication Data

Dunham, Mikel.
    Casting for murder / Mikel Dunham.
        p.    cm.
        "A Thomas Dunne book."
        ISBN 0-312-06924-3
        I. Title.
    PS3554.U4684C37   1992
    813'.54—dc20                    91-40925
                                      CIP

First edition: March 1992
10 9 8 7 6 5 4 3 2 1

Special thanks to Jason LaPadura, Natalie Hart, Gary Murphy
and
Dr. L. Savina, Chief of Police, Venice, Italy.

# 1

". . . and they have no idea how he was killed? I see. Well, I don't know. It's not so easy for me to just drop everything and fly over there but . . . yes, I understand. I'll do what I can. Thank you for calling me. Good-bye."

Rhea Buerklin was no stranger to murder.

Several years before, her partner, Emil Orloff, mixed up in the SoHo drug scene, had been brutally dispatched in the basement of their mutually owned art gallery on Prince Street. Time passed. Little by little, she managed to free herself from the sharpest edges of that memory; the Press found new sensations to cover, the NYPD no longer invaded her privacy, she returned to a normal routine and came to believe that, finally, surely, it was someone else's turn to be mortified by unavoidable violence.

Then the news came from a complete stranger—a static-ridden overseas phone call at six o'clock on an airless, Saturday September morning—a man with a pinched businesslike voice informed her that Jodie Rivers, one of the artists she represented, had been murdered in Italy.

She absorbed the information. She somehow managed to indicate to the stranger that she comprehended. She hung up.

Still half asleep, she rose from her bed in T-shirt and panties. She walked into her closet, pulled down a suitcase and returned it to her king-size bed. She snatched a pack of Lucky Strikes from her bedside table. She padded down the hallway and into the kitchen. She switched on the coffee machine. She retraced her steps back into the hallway and entered the open expanse of her living room. She crossed over to the tall elbowed windows overlooking the corner of Spring and Greene Streets, empty this time of morning. She ignored the ebullient, wet-nosed advances of Crunch, her Jack Russell terrier. She stared out the window, vaguely contemplating the angular display of a drab city sunrise. Sinking down to the window seat, she went through the motions of smoking a cigarette.

Grief was out of the question, of course.

She was stunned. She was baffled. She was outraged.

First, Emil.

Now, Jodie Rivers, the son-of-a-bitch.

What had she done to incur *double* wrath from the hands of Fate? Murder meant sensationalism, sensationalism meant the Press, and the Press meant Rhea Buerklin was a sitting duck for the inevitable public mess that followed.

There was something else: How do you get even with a dead man?

An hour passed.

Fortified by two cups of coffee, she began to move about her loft in a purposeful manner, self-imposed activity designed to keep her mounting anger at bay. She packed her bag. She made a list of all the things to be taken care of. There was so little time! She'd have to call a staff meeting the minute the gallery opened. There were appointments to be canceled, a dozen phone calls to be made, especially to Ornella and Henry. She'd have to bribe Anne, her administrator/ bookkeeper, to house-sit for her and to take care of Crunch. She'd have to go to the bank, of course. . . .

Rhea took a shower, made a fresh pot of coffee and, finally, prepared to impart the complicated news. As prepared, in any case, as she ever would be, she called John Tennyson.

Tennyson was with Homicide. He had been in charge of the murder investigation of her partner. In the intervening years, she and

Tennyson had become more than friends, just dodging the kind of companionship that fell into the snug pattern of lovers. Not a smooth alliance. There was an age difference of ten years—she, approaching forty and he, approaching fifty—the difference in their backgrounds was planetary. But it was a relationship that they both valued, clung to, like an oddball clock stubbornly positioned dead center on a mantlepiece, for all the world to see and no one to quite comprehend. . . .

"Thank God you're back, John!" she exploded over the telephone. "When I found out this morning, I . . . I can already see the headlines: JINXED SOHO GALLERY. Field day for the Media. You see what I'm dreading, don't you?"

Tennyson stifled a yawn and rubbed his eyes. He had been wakened by Rhea's call. Only the night before, he had returned from a month's fly fishing in Montana, his first extended vacation in years. His mind lingered in the mountains. He still hadn't unpacked. Next to his bed lay an open suitcase which he now regarded: those flaccid, folded rubber hip boots, so useless in New York, one of the most subjugated sights he'd ever seen.

"I'm not hearing a very charitable attitude," he managed to observe while readjusting his pillow. "No heavy heart? No 'poor Jodie'? I thought you were devoted to his work."

"Who's talking about his art?" Rhea answered, a little defensively. "You have no idea what he'd been up to. While you were merry-ass-deep in streams casting for trout—"

"Now, now, now. . . . I just woke up. Besides, you could have been casting too. You were invited, remember?"

"Yes," Rhea admitted, "I should have gone with you."

Indeed, there was no solid reason why she should have remained behind in New York during August. Overnight, SoHo had become an economic vacuum. Most galleries, including Rhea's, closed for the month. What was the point in staying open? The collectors who paid big bucks for contemporary art deserted New York in favor of country estates where they dwelled on golf swings and bucolic luncheons. Rhea could have decamped as well. In addition to Tennyson's invitation, she had turned down free use of the old Gruss estate in the

Hamptons (haven for social supernumeraries among the fragile dunes), a free chalet in Switzerland, a guest house cantilevered over a Sardinian grotto, even a very tempting ski trip to Chile—all because. . . .

It sounded so silly in retrospect. Since Emil's death, she had devoted her time and energy to taking full possession of the gallery, removing the tainted memory of his personality from the premises. She had never quite succeeded, had she? By being left behind, by having the gallery all to herself during August, by going through inventory in the basement storeroom and weeding out every last work that was left over from Emil's reign . . . squatter's tactics . . . it had been her intention to stake a claim once and for all and make the gallery entirely her own.

"It doesn't make a damn bit of difference now," she sighed. "John, the point is this: Jodie Rivers got himself murdered. His problems are over, while mine . . ."

If Rhea wasn't overly saddened by the news, John Tennyson was even less so. He never had liked Jodie and avoided him whenever possible. Intolerably cocky and self-promoting about his career, Jodie had been equally boring about his female conquests. A real skirt-chaser, Jodie. Used his looks as bait. His eyes had that lubricated sheen of a drug user and his self-absorbed attitude was one of a guy who found no value in what other people had to say. He was ambitious, overly coddled; a lady's man jostling for space in the artist community. All repellant characteristics, in Tennyson's humble opinion.

"Damn it! How could he have done this to me?" Rhea continued.

"To you?" Tennyson joked. "Sounds like you're blaming Jodie for his own murder."

Rhea thought a moment before answering. "I guess I am. I'm serious, John. Whatever happened, whoever killed him, Jodie asked for it."

"Hum. Any ideas who might have helped him in this enterprise?"

"That's your department."

"Okay, Rhea," John said, stretching. "You're going too fast for me. Let's have the particulars, first. How was he murdered? Do you know yet?"

"Strangulation. Someone throttled the bastard."

Bastard?

Tennyson could hardly have cared less what she called Jodie, and he was used to Rhea's lack of decorum but, still, her abusive tone didn't quite make sense. Among her stable of artists, Jodie had been one of her favorites. Tennyson scratched his neck and readjusted the telephone. "Just what did Jodie do to you while I was gone, anyway?" he asked.

"Plenty. I know how bitchy I sound but believe me, John, I'm in good company. There's a whole list of us who got stung. There's Ornella Saltzman, there's Jodie's brother, Henry Rivers, there's me, there's Crunch, there's—"

"Crunch?" Tennyson interrupted. "What did Jodie do to Crunch?"

"Long story. You'll see for yourself. Don't get me sidetracked. The point is, we were all victims. In the last few weeks of his life, Jodie betrayed every person who should have meant something to him. Burning bridges left and right—"

"Okay, we've got a lot of people—and one dog—pissed off at Jodie."

"That's right."

"Mad enough to kill him?"

"I haven't had time to think about—"

"Murder has a funny way of never giving you time."

"Yes," Rhea said ruefully. "I'm beginning to remember. And now that I'm supposed to fly over there, I'd better put it in high gear, hadn't I?"

"Over where?"

"Italy. Didn't I tell you? Jodie was killed in Italy. The plane leaves late this afternoon . . . if I do go. That'll put us in Venice by morning, local time. Jodie's father, Verle Rivers, is having his private jet flown in for us."

"Private?"

"You knew the old man was loaded."

"Well, you mentioned one time that he had money but—"

"Megabucks," Rhea clarified. "Circle of friends include the Swarovski family, the Baron Thyssen-Bornemisza—"

"Not on my Rolodex. Who are they?"

"Seriously rich rich-folks and world-class art collectors."

"If you say so. That's your department. And this Verle Rivers is in their league?"

"Plays cards at the big boys' table."

"So what was Jodie doing in Italy?"

"I don't know, except that that's where his father was . . . is."

"Verle Rivers lives in Venice?"

"No, I doubt it. He might have a place there, but I can't imagine it being home. He's too much in the center of things. Venice is a backwater."

"Let me get this straight. Jodie went to Venice to visit his father, is that the idea?"

"As far as I can work out. But, John, that's screwy. There was plenty of bad blood between Jodie and the old man. For all practical purposes, Jodie was disowned. When Jodie had his last one-man show, Verle Rivers, who happened to be in town, wouldn't even drop by the gallery to look at the paintings, let alone buy one. And now get this—"

"Wait a minute. The father is supplying *you* with a private jet."

"That's right."

"What's the point in your going over?"

"Not just me. Jodie's older brother, Henry Rivers. He lives here, in Manhattan."

"Oh. So the old man, who didn't get along with his son, is now closing family ranks, and you're to go along for the ride?"

"Something like that."

"I still don't get it."

"Neither do I," Rhea grumbled. "That's why I haven't decided whether or not to go."

"Rhea, this is not getting clearer for me. When you talked to the father—"

"I didn't actually talk to him. I talked to a lesser mortal who told me that Mr. Rivers would 'very much appreciate my presence as the two of us had some unfinished business to' . . . apparently, Jodie had struck a deal with his father over some of the paintings I was supposed to be representing in his upcoming show and—"

"Hold on. Jodie was in Italy selling paintings that you were representing here in New York?"

"See why I'm coming off as hysterical? And that's just the tip of the nasty iceberg. There's more, John, lots more. The last time I saw Jodie was ten days ago. He came to the loft. Are you ready for this? During his visit, he stole some jewelry."

Tennyson pivoted his hips and dropped his bare feet to the floor. "Jodie stole from you?"

"A very special diamond brooch with three hunka-munka jealousy-provoking sapphires set in platinum: Cartier's, Paris, circa 1937."

"Worth?"

"I haven't had it appraised for years, but I'd say we're talking fifty, sixty thousand. It's an important bauble, not that I ever wore it. And I don't give a damn about the money . . . well I do, of course, but . . . John, the brooch was my mother's. One of the few things I had of hers."

"You are pissed."

"You thought this was an act? And it hasn't helped matters that you were in Montana, unattainable in your log cabin or wherever the hell you were staying."

"Did you report it to the police?"

"Sort of. I called your Sgt. Lipski. I figured he'd be able to keep a lid on it. The problem was, it was two days before I discovered the theft."

"You weren't sure you wanted to press charges."

"Can you blame me? With Jodie's show coming up? If the media got hold of the story . . . I just wanted the brooch back. Anyway, Lipski came down immediately. Only, by then, well, Jodie had already disappeared."

"And you had no reason to believe he was on his way to Venice?"
"Nope. No idea."

"Was he mad at you? Did you have an argument or something?"
"We always had arguments."

"No particular reason why he would steal from you?"

"No! It goes against all reason. It's insane. If there's anyone on earth he should have been sucking up to, it was me. You know that.

I was giving him a one-man show in October. I made his career. There's not one damn thing about this that's straightforward."

"Strangulation is straightforward enough."

"What?"

"You said someone throttled him. Hard to envision it as an accident, isn't it? Premeditation unlikely."

Rhea paused, "How do you figure that?"

"You said 'throttle.' That's very different from using a rope or wire or whatever. If you were planning a murder, would you want to touch your victim? Or would you choose a gun or poison or something that was, you know, less intimate? Hands are not the standard modus operandi of premeditated murder."

Rhea objected, "There might be a certain personal satisfaction derived from using one's hands."

"Fortunately for you," Tennyson laughed, "strangulation also rules out a female perpetrator. Women don't strangle. Jodie was a pretty big guy in his, what? mid-thirties? It would take a good-sized man to bring him down. Time of murder?"

"Sometime last night, Venice time."

"Where?"

"I told you, Venice."

"But where? In a hotel? On the street? In a boat?"

"Oh . . . I didn't think to ask. Stupid of me, huh?"

"Might shed some light—might not—and you say that the bereaved father already wants to talk business."

"That's what I've been trying to tell you, John. Nobody in this mess is apt to be bereaved."

"But not everybody was angry enough to kill him. You mentioned a woman."

"Ornella. Ornella Marsh Saltzman. A woman I've known for years."

"Profession?"

"No profession, unless there's such a thing as professional divorcée. Ornella's a C.E.O. groupie, the kind of woman who goes through life with an impatiently hoisted Chanel handbag. Current husband made a fortune in food processing. Dreary man. Anyway, she's a serious collector of Jodie's work. Three major pieces to date. She was also a connoisseur of Jodie's more, uh, intimate talents."

"A little nuzzling going on?"

"And, believe me, she's no spring chicken. The point is, he turned on her like he turned on everyone else. Right around the time he stole my brooch, he stole a tiny, but very valuable, Redon drawing from her summer home on Martha's Vineyard."

"Jesus. Something was up, wasn't it? I wonder what he needed the money for? Drugs?"

"Your guess is as good as mine."

"And this Ornella woman . . . she was upset but she refused to bring in the police, right?"

"How did you—"

"A wealthy married woman? Not hard to figure out. Still, she must have been plenty pissed."

"Of course she was, but you're on the wrong track, John. I know what you're thinking. Forget Ornella. Ornella may be greedy but she's harmless. Ornella couldn't possibly be involved with . . . the only reason I brought up Ornella was . . . I'm just trying to explain to you what Jodie was up to while you were gone."

"Okay. What about the brother, Henry Rivers? You said Jodie betrayed him too."

"Yes. I've saved the worst for last. Jodie stole from him, like he did from the rest of us. Only the stakes were higher. Not only did he pinch Henry's American Express card—"

"Wait a minute. This is around the same time as the brooch and the drawing?"

"Yes, that's right. Same time. Not only did Jodie take his brother's plastic, he helped himself to Henry's woman as well."

"Oooo. Don't like the sound of that."

"Neither did Henry. I get the impression he was very much in love with this girl."

"What's her name?"

"Lisa Morris."

"You know her?"

"No. Supposedly, she's in Europe. She's a model. She went to Munich on a job about the same time as—"

"Same time as Jodie disappeared?"

"You got it."

"How far is Munich from Venice?"

"A half day train ride."

"Convenient. And you never met Lisa?"

"Not that I know of. Jodie was always sauntering into the gallery with a new specimen in tow. Lisa could have been one of them."

"You suspect the brother?"

"Christ, I don't know. I haven't had time to suspect anyone, have I? I just found out about it myself."

"Well, think about it now. Being buddy-fucked by your own brother—"

"Ugly expression, John."

"Not a very pretty act, either, especially if he's using your American Express card to do the buddy-fucking. A hard pill to swallow. Some people might even think it's a good enough reason to kill."

"Henry Rivers has been in New York all this time," Rhea objected. "Jodie was killed in Italy. That's an alibi the size of an ocean."

"Contracts can be transatlantic."

"Of course, I've only met Henry a few times, but no, it's very unlikely."

"Why?"

"Just a feeling. Henry's very different from Jodie. Total opposites. Comes off as a decent, quiet sort. Keeps a sense of proportion about his own importance. Quite likable, in a sad-faced kind of way."

Tennyson hesitated for a moment. "That's it? That's your reason for disqualifying him? And now you propose to goose-step onto a private jet with him—just like that—haul ass to a foreign country with someone you barely know and someone who, sad face or not, has a motive for murder?"

"For God's sake, Jodie was killed in Venice! Quit drumming up stateside motives and quit trying to discredit Henry! And anyway, what if he did have Jodie knocked off, which is pretty farfetched, why should I feel in danger?"

"Well, for one reason, you're the nosiest woman I ever met."

"Thanks."

"It's true. It's beyond your capability to just let go of something. And if you get wind of whose responsible for this, you'll represent a most unwelcome complication. Maybe you already do. You don't know a damn thing about Henry or his father who *wasn't* stateside. Why go over there half-cocked?"

"Why stay here and wait for the Press, half-cocked? Remember how they hounded me the last time?"

"Nothing you couldn't handle."

"What are you saying? That I shouldn't fly over to Venice with Henry? Or that I shouldn't fly to Venice, period?"

"You tell me. You're the one involved with all these strangers. Is it a threatening situation, or not?"

"What are you yelling at me for?"

"I'm not yelling."

"Why does it have to be threatening?"

"It doesn't. Calm down. I'm just playing catch-up, that's all. I haven't even had coffee. You call me before I'm awake and hit me with all this information and . . . Hello? Rhea, are you still there?"

"I'm thinking," she said irritably. "You're right. Talking over the telephone is no good. I'll cook you a big breakfast."

"What?"

"You could be down here in thirty minutes."

"Forget it. I've got to go to work this morning."

"I need your help, John. The plane leaves this afternoon. There's not much time."

"Not a hell of a lot I can do from this end," Tennyson grumbled. "Venice is beyond my jurisdiction."

"Am I beyond your jurisdiction?" Rhea countered.

"Most of the time, yes."

What *was* the hold that Rhea had over him? Tennyson liked to think he was old-fashioned when it came to women, though Rhea never gave him much of chance to be old-fashioned. There again, he was old enough and experienced enough (divorced after a long marriage) to roll with, if not always appreciate, new-fangled displacements of the heart. Rhea was well-off financially, a successful businesswoman independent of any man, especially a man on a cop's salary. She was of Brazilian–German parentage, which melded her methodical stubborn streak with a passionately spontaneous one, a combination that kept Tennyson off guard but equally whetted for the challenge. Although from a privileged background, she never used class as criteria for friendship. She was a loner keen on loyalty, a quality Tennyson found immensely attractive. She had an honest nature carefully hidden under a patina of cynicism; she was tough, all right, but it was the kind of toughness that often launched him (a fireman's son from Queens) into vigorous sparring. Her mental alacrity was inspiring. Her mind was all over the place and she spoke four languages, something Tennyson had no talent for and admired openly. And there was also this: Rhea Buerklin was as fine looking a woman as ever immigrated to American soil. When Tennyson watched her stride across a room with those long dark legs . . .

"Jodie's been murdered," Rhea said quietly, as if to remind herself.

"So you keep telling me."

"So brush your teeth, get dressed and come down to the loft. Please. I need to see you about this, to sort out my thoughts, to decide if I should get mixed up in this mess any more than I already am—"

"Horse shit."

"What?"

"I know how you are when you're cranked. It's like stopping a train. You keep describing Jodie's murder as a mess."

"What's that have to do with anything?"

"There's nothing more irresistible to Rhea Buerklin than a mess to clean up."

"*That's* horse shit."

"Is it? You want to avoid the Press, don't you? And what about your invitation to talk business with the old man, by your own admission a world-class art collector?"

"I admit that's tempting, but that could wait. And quit sounding like a detective."

"I thought that's why you called: to talk to a detective."

"I want to see *you*, John."

"And what about your mother's brooch?" Tennyson ignored her. "Don't tell me you're going to snooze while diamonds and sapphires disappear into thin air. Tell the truth, Rhea. You've already packed, haven't you?"

Rhea didn't answer.

"You *are* packed, aren't you?"

"What if I am? And I'm not saying that I am! Does it makes sense to rush around at the last minute in order to get to the airport? Listen, are you coming down here or are you just going to gall me to death?"

"Don't know. Did I hear something about a big breakfast?"

"Whatever you want. Cholesterol heaven."

"And lots of fresh coffee?"

"Buckets," she answered and hung up the kitchen phone before John could introduce further stipulations.

She hurried over to the long counter piled with art books. Using her forearm as a bulldozer, she cleared a path to make room for omelets.

Rhea was an excellent cook, though her expertise could be an unpleasant process to observe. The clanging of pans and slamming of drawers, the generous seasoning with expletives as she rifled her refrigerator—"What if I *am* packed, goddamn it! What's wrong with *that?*"—not to mention the hands bristling with dangerous-looking kitchen implements—all added to the portrait of a manic cordon bleu. Nevertheless, this aggressive behavior masked an inner state of equanimity. For it was when she disfigured raw food that Rhea settled into some of her most plangent deductions. As she reduced Porcini mushrooms to a stack of paper-thin slices, she pondered the nature of Jodie's betrayals and how best to amass them for John Tennyson's benefit. She'd botched her first attempt on the phone. He'd taken the wrong slant entirely . . . trying to talk her out of going to Venice. . . .

Verle Rivers. Chop chop.

Henry Rivers. Chop chop.

Ornella Saltzman. Chop chop.

Crunch. Quadruple chops.

How to calibrate the extent of their mistreatment?

And her own mistreatment?

People who betray: Is the behavior instinctual or learned, and if the latter is true, who had been Jodie's teachers in such a suicidal pastime? Who had fired up his most base instincts?

On one level, of course, Jodie had been betrayed by his own good looks. Any man that handsome is bound to get, sooner or later, snagged by the mirror. He was a looker, the bastard, and had sapped it for everything it was worth. He was tall, broad-shouldered, with shaggy dark blond hair, a flawless complexion, and moss-colored eyes that flooded over a woman's body. Those large expressive hands, flashing white teeth and big, ingratiating smile, as vain as it was photogenic—the kind of easy, disrespectful boyish grin that journalists liked to snap, and women, like Ornella Saltzman, stood in line to sample firsthand.

"My dear," Ornella had once confided to Rhea, "Jodie brings a certain puppy-dog athleticism to his bed, a kind of sandbox authority I haven't enjoyed for years. Positively yummy. And he calls me such naughty things!"

"No offense, Ornella," Rhea rolled her eyes, "but what do you suppose he calls the other five thousand women in his life?"

Ornella was unflappable: "Who am I to resent his concurrent conquests? I am a married woman."

"Yeah," Rhea reminded her. "Three times over."

"My point exactly! The more one tastes, the more malleable one's taste buds, don't you think? Which rather brings us to you: I'm surprised he hasn't seduced you. God knows you're attractive enough and don't try to deny it. Women would kill for a body like yours, tall and athletic and you never gain a pound. So why does Jodie swear your relationship is strictly business? I should think he would be all over you. Or is he just being discreet?"

"Jodie? Discreet?" Rhea laughed.

In truth, Jodie had flirted with Rhea—endlessly, though in an odd, self-deprecative manner—as if he were still exploring the best maneuvers to win over his "Boss," for that's what he always called Rhea.

She removed a package of bacon from the refrigerator.

In any case, the particulars of Jodie's virility remained hypothetical. Rhea had an iron-clad rule never to get involved with her artists. She had broken that rule only once and the results had been disastrous. No, as long as Jodie remained artistically seductive—that is to say, productive—and as long as he kept his hands off Anne and Catherine, the women on her staff, Rhea excused his sexual bravado as a minor annoyance.

Rhea separated the bacon and placed it into a skillet.

What stupidity! A Redon drawing might be worth a small fortune, but it certainly wasn't worth losing Ornella's patronage. What the hell had Jodie been thinking about?

A relatively harmless SoHo stud with a burgeoning career suddenly turns thief and traitor. Why? What had happened to Jodie in the last month or so to illicit such madness? What had wedged itself into his life that Rhea didn't know about? Lisa Morris, the model who hopped from one brother to the other? Was she behind this?

But why steal?

If Jodie had been desperately in need of a lot of money, and there was no reason why he should have been, couldn't he have gone to his father? Or was that estrangement so unconditional that . . . But, damn it, Jodie *had* gone to his father, to Venice. . . .

The bacon crackled. With a frown, Rhea used a long-tined fork to turn the slices.

Willful betrayal: Henry, Rhea, Ornella—it didn't make sense, especially in light of the staggering outpouring of his recent work. He had never seemed happier. He had never painted with such abandon, with such authority.

Rhea transferred the bacon onto a warming platter and shoved it into the oven. Satisfied that there was nothing else she could do until Tennyson's arrival, she lighted her fourth Lucky Strike of the morning.

Willful self-destruction.

But there again, what painter, in her stable of artists, was *not*, to some extent, a participant in willful self-destruction? It rather went with the territory, didn't it? Substance abuse, chaotic personal relationships and other forms of intrinsic sabotage—wasn't that the accepted backdrop for creativity?

Rhea stubbed out her cigarette, quit the kitchen, walked down the hallway and entered her living room.

She approached one of Jodie's most recent paintings, which was propped between two windows. She shook her head.

This, she reminded herself, staring at the painting, this is why I stay in this idiotic business. This is why I put up with the unpleasant vagaries of people like Jodie. And this is why, if Jodie walked into the room right now, I would embrace him, slug him in the stomach, then embrace him again.

It was a large work, standing eight feet tall. The first thing that caught one's attention was the sheer weight of the painting's frame: It was a welded construction of stainless steel spoons bent and bullied and bunched together to create a sense of twisted, almost suffocating flamboyance. Within this frame was yet another frame comprised of forty-eight aqua-colored plastic bottles of Mylanta, the over-the-counter antacid commonly taken by ulcer sufferers. The tight-fitting juxtaposition of these concentric perimeters—Baroque on the outside, Warholian on the inside—was frictive and unsettling. Even more startling was the actual painting, which was rendered in a clotted mixed-media of oil, emulsion, steel wool and razor-sharp metal shavings that glinted and jutted out from the canvas as if to warn the viewer, "Don't touch."

Ingredients of a toxic waste stew.

It was Jodie Rivers's signature, really, those metal shavings. One critic had described it as "a formidable disdain for sable brushes or anything else that might be construed as soft or compromising or forgiving or ingratiating or, heaven forbid, feminine. The whole point of his paintings *is* the points—a pun on the hackneyed phrase 'cutting edge'—for if you dared to graze your hand across the surface of his canvases, surely and quite literally, you would be lacerated. Jodie Rivers's paintings don't invite eyes. They invite blood."

Yes, Rhea thought to herself, but whose blood? And if, as the critic suggested, Jodie's work addressed itself exclusively to male sensibilities, what men did Jodie have in mind? All men? One particular man? Himself?

Rhea turned her attention to the actual subject matter of the painting, harshly rendered in bold clumpy strokes: Hurrying directly toward the viewer, out of a vaguely pastoral backdrop, was a boy carrying a smaller boy in his arms. The older child's face was tense. The younger child's face was dull, expressionless, his limbs dangling as if to suggest either sleep or death. Two forlorn figures trying to escape the painting itself—an ambulatory pietà.

But in what context? Boys fleeing a hellish childhood? Were they brothers? Was that it? Was it a portrait of Henry and Jodie Rivers?

Jodie never explained his subject matter, though he enthusiastically squelched anyone's attempt to attach autobiographical intent. When Rhea had tried to press him on this particular painting, Jodie had raised his hands in exasperation: "Why must the image go beyond itself? It is what it is, isn't it?"

Not surprisingly, the title of the piece, *Wall Street, Here We Come*, did nothing to clarify.

"But this isn't a painting about money!" Rhea objected.

"Isn't it?" Jodie challenged.

"Jodie, the subject matter is human. Spoons and antacids and a relationship between two boys that . . . they're linked by a common male—"

Jodie's smile turned into a sneer: "I'll slash the goddamn thing if you say male bond. Mutual bonds, marketing and selling bonds, joint control of financial interests bonds—those are the only bonds I know about."

"But the bottles of Mylanta," Rhea had persisted.

"Let's just say I'm interested in side-effects."

"But—"

"Quit hounding me, Boss. I don't need to put words up on the wall to make a visual statement. I'm no goddamn Jenny Holzer. I do what an artist is supposed to do. I make images. If I wanted to annotate my work, I'd write the fuckers instead of paint them. Words are irrelevant."

For a moment, Rhea stared blankly, as if transfixed. Then she checked her watch. Tennyson should be in his car by now, sweating bullets in hot, muggy, September morning rush-hour traffic, probably cursing, edging his way down toward SoHo.

For a moment, Rhea had the unpleasant sensation of compression. Somewhere in Venice, for some reason, a pair of strong, eloquent hands had intervened, had put a stop to all of Jodie's mad behavior, had made Jodie's internal struggling, his talent, his cockiness, his treachery, his handsome features, his womanizing, his reluctance to talk about his own work—all of it—irrelevant.

For the first time, Rhea felt a sense of loss, a kind of sad weight she could almost feel just hovering above her shoulder blades. A growing body of work was suddenly a *completed* body of work. And for this, Rhea now realized, she was deeply sorry. And just as she began to juggle this unexpected moment of tenderness, out of the corner of her eye, she saw Crunch trot into the room.

Her body stiffened.

Three weeks before, it had been closing time at the gallery. Crunch, who spent his days lazing in Rhea's inner office, suddenly stirred, sensing that a pee-break was imminent. Rhea couldn't find his leash. She always put it in the top drawer of her $200,000 Wendell Castle "Egyptian" desk, but it wasn't there. She was already late for an appointment uptown. Crunch scampered impatiently.

Giving up on her search, she and Crunch left the gallery without it. Crunch tore down the sidewalk ahead of her.

Just as Crunch rounded the corner of Greene and Prince, he encountered a sociopathic rottweiler who suddenly, without provocation, fifty-percented Crunch's left ear. Rhea kept her wits about her. She maced the bully dog, refrained from doing likewise to its lax owner, and retrieved the amputated flap. (If there was one thing Rhea despised more than gratuitous violence, it was gratuitous waste.) She dusted off the bloody ear—size and shape of an oversized postage stamp—packed it in her purse and rushed to a Park Avenue veterinarian who, for a small fortune, reattached the appendage to its rightful owner.

She didn't mind the money so much but, one week later, when the vet removed the bandages, it was discovered that Crunch's reimplantation had been botched: The vet had sewn Crunch's ear on backward, furry side forward.

And what about the missing leash?

Jodie Rivers, of course. He had visited the gallery the same day as the dogfight. While Rhea had attended to business elsewhere, Jodie had idly rifled her desk and, without bothering to ask, appropriated the leash in the name of High Art. An old gnawed dog lead was just the thing for one of his new canvases!

Later, when confronted with his transgression, Jodie's tone was less than apologetic: "I'm sorry Crunch got hurt but the effect of a flipped ear is pretty striking, don't you think? Botched surgery: not a bad concept. Adds character. The montage look. Yes, I could grow to like it."

"Enough to pay the vet bill, asshole?" Rhea said and smiled wanly. "Because that's exactly what you're going to do the next time I sell one of your paintings."

"You don't really hold me responsible for—"

"Damn right I do."

"I won't pay," Jodie sniffed.

"You have no choice!"

Crunch followed the mounting argument with a patchwork ear.

"And what," Rhea continued, "in that drug-soaked mind of yours, makes you think that you've the right to go through my desk?"

"The same thing," Jodie said and laughed, "that makes you think that you've the right to go through my paintings finding deep, biographic meaning. Get off the high horse, Boss."

"If you didn't have a show coming up in October . . ."

Jodie released a dreamy smile and raised his expressive hands (cuticles stained with oil paint) in front of her face: "It's going to be a great show, Boss. Right now I have such a . . . a tight grip . . . paralyzing . . . I might even say exhilarating . . . the rest doesn't matter."

Crunch barked.

*Tight grip?*

*Exhilaration?*

*To have the life choked out of you?*

Rhea checked her watch again. She gazed down at Crunch, whimpering and wagging profusely, no doubt in reference to the fried bacon, or the pressing need for his morning walk, or both.

With a shudder, she turned away from the painting.

"A fucking mess," she said aloud.

Crunch wagged even harder.

Rhea entered the hallway, then froze. "Where the hell did I store my passport! Out of my way, Crunch!"

Crunch gave her a wide berth as she stormed past him and disappeared into the bedroom at the end of the corridor.

He flopped to the floor with a petulant, periscopic ear. There was no use following her. He knew what her suitcase meant. Was he invited to go with her? Or would he be abandoned to that mild-mannered assistant who never gave him enough food?

Crunch listened to Rhea opening and slamming drawers. For a moment he deliberated on the ineluctability of abandonment. Then he got up, trotted into the living room and cocked a back leg against the edge of Jodie's painting.

# 2

"So there you have it," Rhea said, after breakfast. "Back-stabbed Anonymous. We all belong to the same pathetic club."

Tennyson rose to help with the dishes.

"No, keep your seat, John."

Rhea rinsed off the plates, placed them in the dishwasher, then returned to the table with more coffee. She refilled Tennyson's cup, kissed him on the cheek and sat down beside him.

"There's a couple of other things I should probably mention. Things that, even by Jodie's standards, were extreme. Red flags that I had no business taking as lightly as I did.

"First of all, at the beginning of August, he plucked out his eyelashes."

Tennyson cocked his head as if he hadn't heard correctly: "You mean his eyebrows?" he asked.

"No," she answered. "Eye*lashes.*"

"Why would he?"

"At the time, I just thought it was a bit of theatrical nonsense. You know, a way to get a reaction out of people. Part of his self-promotion, his myth-making. It was mildly shocking. It gave him a bald, startled kind of look. Anyway, when I invited him to supply a reason, he tore into a tirade about how eyelashes were for cowards. It was like, and I quote, 'watching life from behind venetian blinds.' His very words. It could be just a coincidence but I thought you ought to know.

"The second thing is that he failed to show up for an interview with Brock Callaway, a correspondent for *Details* magazine. I don't need to tell you how unlike Jodie that was. Jodie would undergo a heart transplant to get into print.

"The third thing is that, ten days ago, he got into a fistfight at 185 Wooster." 185 Wooster was a current high contempt, club-and-fashion restaurant for New York's downtown set. "His opponent, if you can call him that," Rhea continued, "was a sculptor—a much hyped artist, in my opinion—from the Mary Boone Gallery. The story goes that Jodie had knocked him to the floor and was in the process of actually urinating on him, a gesture intended to illustrate what he thought of the artist's work. (I should add here that the victim was half Jodie's size.) In any case, Jodie whipped it out and, before he could actually do the dirty deed, he was collared and removed from the scene.

"As a matter of fact, that's why Jodie was at my apartment the night he stole my brooch. I'd gotten a call from the owner of the restaurant. The only reason he didn't have Jodie arrested was out of deference to me. He could have thrown the book at him. Assault and battery, destruction of property, committing an obscene act in a public place. . . . So I called Jodie up and told him to get his worthless ass down to my loft. I read him the riot act. Show or no show, I'd had it and I wanted it to be very clear how close I was to dumping him. More coffee?"

Tennyson shook his head. "What did Jodie say?"

"That the artist deserved to be pissed on which, figuratively, is probably true. I just can't figure it out, John. By that night, he seemed to be impervious to what he was doing to himself."

"Well," she concluded, "that's about it. What I Did on My Summer Vacation. Do you still think Jodie's death places me in mortal danger?"

"I never said you were in danger," Tennyson grumbled. "I just know your potential for courting danger, that's all. You hardly know Henry. You've never met Lisa Morris. You only know Verle Rivers by reputation. I'm not so sure you even knew Jodie that well. Why barrel into it?"

"Here we go again."

"Well, goddamn it, there's too many unknowns. All I'm saying is that flying over there lacks prudence."

"Prudence?" Rhea laughed as if she had never heard the word.

"Yeah." Tennyson leaned back, looking her square in the eye. "Did you ever try it?"

"Not intentionally."

"I didn't think so."

"Since when is prudence so great . . . unless you happen to live in a vacuum . . . which I don't. Was I being imprudent when Emil got himself killed three years ago? Was I being imprudent when Jodie stole my brooch? Standing still never prevented me from getting my shoes scuffed. And if I don't fly over today, what do you propose I do with myself in the meantime?"

Tennyson stretched his legs. "Well, for starters, we could have dinner tonight. A nice bottle of wine, good food, heated arguments over candlelight. . . ."

"Sounds tempting," she said and sighed, taking Tennyson's hand in her own.

He started to move his chair, crab-wise, toward her but, just then, the telephone rang. Rhea dropped his hand and hurried over to the wall extension next to the refrigerator.

"Henry!" she exclaimed, turning her back to Tennyson. "I've been trying to get in touch with you all morning but your line's been busy. I know. One of your father's lackeys called me. It's awful, isn't it? In spite of everything, I'm sorry. Yes, yes I agree. Listen, Henry, I think you should know that your father wants me to go over with you. No, there's no problem from this end. I can go, that is, if you're sure I won't be in the way. You're sure? Um-hum. Un-hum. Is that right? Why? Um-hum. . . ."

Tennyson began to loose track of the conversation but, as he went through the motions of sipping his coffee, he gave way to the certainty that Rhea was going, a certainty that left an acrid taste in his mouth.

He looked up. Rhea was now jotting down something on a piece of paper. Jesus, look at her—forward ho! For all practical purposes, Rhea was already in Venice.

"I might be able to help," she was saying. "Yes, I've got a friend in the police. I told you about him. Um-hum. He's back now. Oh, and Henry, do you know *where* he was killed? La what? La Fenice! Yes, I know it. God! What was he doing there in the middle of the night? Um-hum. No. No thanks. It'll be easier to catch a cab from down here. Okay, Henry. See you at four."

She hung up the phone and returned to her chair.

"That was the brother with a motive," she said.

"So I heard," Tennyson answered, trying to remain impassive. "You found out where Jodie was killed."

Rhea nodded: "La Fenice, the Venice opera house. Actually, outside the opera house, on the steps leading up to the building. They don't have a clue as to what he was doing there."

"Was he an opera buff?"

"Don't think so."

Crunch jumped onto her lap. Without looking down, absorbed in thought, she massaged the dog's neck.

"John," she said, "what if the murder has nothing to do with the rest of us? I mean, I've been dwelling on Henry and Ornella and myself because . . . What if the murderer doesn't even know the rest of us? What if the killer is from Venice, for instance, a complete stranger?"

Tennyson shrugged. "At this point, that would be the obvious supposition."

"Well . . . it has to be pursued, doesn't it?"

"By someone. Not necessarily you."

"Could you just indulge me for a minute? Jodie was a jerk, right?"

"He never won my heart."

"A loose cannon always inviting trouble."

Tennyson offered no objection to the description.

"Well? What's to keep him from making *new* enemies in a new country?"

John nodded his head. "It could have gone down like that: Jodie gets taken out by an unknown Italian." He looked up, his eyebrows knitted. "How well do you know Venice?"

"I used to know it very well. When I was a schoolgirl, I'd meet my father there on holidays. It was one of his favorite haunts."

"What are the people like?"

"In Venice? Cosmopolitan. A little jaded. Not gushingly friendly, but they're cordial enough, especially if you speak their language. Proud of their town, their past glory . . . as they should be."

"Violent?"

Rhea made a face. "Pussycats compared to New Yorkers. Argumentative, yes. Violent, no."

"You like the place."

"It reminds me of Papa," Rhea said simply. "It was always a tremendous release to escape from school and . . . no doubt, it had something to do with me being in the gallery business today. Venice is like a warehouse for masterpieces . . . a repository for centuries and centuries of great art." Rhea shook her head and laughed.

"What's so funny?" Tennyson asked.

"Nothing, really. I was just thinking what a scrawny kid I was back then . . . I must have been pretty idealistic too."

She sighed and lowered Crunch to the floor. "How did we get onto *this* topic?"

"You were telling me about Venice. What's it like, this time of year? Lots of tourists?"

"In early September? Yes. There's always tourists in Venice— though it would be less crowded than during the summer months."

"Jodie was killed at night. And Jodie was a night person, right? Liked to rock-and-roll after midnight. What do people do in the evenings? Where do they go?"

"Venice goes to bed early. You go out to dinner and that's about it. After ten or eleven o'clock, the streets are fairly empty."

"Is it dangerous?"

"No, not at all. You can walk down any alley at three o'clock in the morning and feel perfectly safe. It's spooky, very spooky with the dark canals going off in every direction, the echo of your own footsteps, but it's *safe,*" she emphasized with a barely disguised smile.

Rhea warmed to the subject in direct proportion to Tennyson's mounting interest, evidenced by his rapid line of questioning. As she spoke, she began to visualize, if not the actual murder, at least the backdrop in which the event took place.

"And Venice," she continued, "in spite of its labyrinth of dead-end streets, is really quite small. And since there are no cars in Venice, the sense of intimacy, of compression, is everywhere. Jodie was resourceful and, Lord knows, he wasn't shy. He would have had the town cased out in no time."

"Where would a guy like Jodie go at night if he wanted some action?"

"The Lido, probably. That's an island nearby. Fifteen minutes by speedboat. The Lido is where the casino is."

"And drugs? Where would he go to score?"

"On the streets, I guess, like everywhere else." Rhea's face suddenly registered doubt. "But in Jodie's defense, he wasn't all that caught up in drugs. Really, John. He was a lightweight . . . a pothead, maybe, but that was about it. He liked his booze. Bourbon was his drug of choice."

"Still, Venice is a port city, isn't it? There's bound to be drug traffic coming in from the Middle East or Southeast Asia or both. If Jodie had gotten a sudden yearning for some hash or something harder, he would have—"

"He would have found a way to get it," Rhea said in total agreement. "So, if it was a stranger who killed him, late at night, it could have been drug-related." Her chin jerked upward as if she had just remembered something. "Or woman-related," she added. "Jodie took women like drugs. So much of his ego was wrapped up in his ability to make good with the ladies, pitiful really, maybe he put the flam on the wrong skirt. He had no sense of morality or moderation, none that I ever saw. Maybe it finally caught up with him. Maybe some Latin with a hairy chest decided to teach pretty-boy Americano a lesson."

"Not impossible," Tennyson agreed. "Especially in light of the nature of his death. Hands around the neck indicates a confrontation of passion."

Rhea nodded but her face darkened. "I forgot to tell you something. When Henry called . . ." Rhea set down her coffee cup and handed Tennyson a piece of paper. "This is the number of Lisa Morris's modeling agency in Paris. Henry gave it to me over the phone."

"Why?"

"Henry found out this morning that Lisa never went to Munich. She was with Jodie, in Venice."

"Not too surprising."

"Yes, but . . . what's weird is . . . well, she left Venice the same day that Jodie was killed."

"Reason?"

"Supposedly, she was on her way to Paris for a shoot."

"What do you mean, 'supposedly'?"

"Henry called her Paris agency but they won't tell him anything."

"Routine policy, I would imagine," Tennyson said with a shrug, "to protect the girls. Oh! So that's what you two were talking about," Tennyson added, his shoulders slumping in recognition. "Let me guess. You offered Henry my services, right?"

"Well, you could get the agency to talk, if you wanted to, couldn't you?"

"No. Not directly. I would have to get in contact with the Paris police who, in turn, would call Lisa's agency. But it would be easier for Henry to give the number to the Italian police. If he's flying over today, let them take care of it."

"Damn it, John, Henry's not asking you to do this. I am. Don't you see? Henry's afraid that something might have happened to Lisa."

"Why should he be afraid?"

"I was about to explain. Lisa has a friend in Paris, another model, with whom she always stays. This morning, Henry called that girl but she hasn't heard from Lisa. She didn't even know that Lisa was in Europe."

"Did Henry tell her about the murder?"

"No. Only that it was an emergency and that he needed to talk to Lisa as soon as possible."

Tennyson regarded the floor for a moment, then looked up.

"When you were talking to Henry, did he use the word 'afraid'?"

"Yes."

"Did he sound afraid?"

"Well, I don't know. He sounded nervous, distracted, completely distraught—"

"What's to be afraid of . . . unless he knows something that we don't know?"

"It's just an expression. I don't see how you can draw any conclusion. . . . Henry's just upset, that's all. His brother's been killed and he's—"

"How did he react to that? Was he remorseful about his brother's death? What did he say?"

"Nothing, really. Neither one of us dwelled on it. It *is* rather embarrassing, considering how much we've been bad-mouthing Jodie. Henry was more interested in convincing me that I would be welcome company and that—"

"Why would you be welcome company?"

"Well . . . I don't know, John, am I that hideous to be around?"

John and Rhea exchanged a highly expressive glance.

"Why," Rhea continued, "are you being so suspicious of Henry?"

"Why," Tennyson countered, "are you being so nonsuspicious?"

"I don't think he wants to be alone right now. Given the circumstances, there's nothing terribly unusual about that, is there?"

"But he's not going to be alone," Tennyson objected. "He's going to be with his father, isn't he? That's why he's going to Venice."

"Why can't he be illogical at a time like this? Why are you being such a hardass?"

Tennyson mumbled something unintelligible.

"What did you say?"

"Just thinking out loud, Rhea. Something happened to Jodie, in the last month or so, to provoke an urgent need for money. Urgent enough for him to steal, to jostle the very people who were helping him the most. Right?"

"Right."

"He suddenly treats his friends like competition in a demolition derby. He plucks out his eyelashes, he blows off an interview, he tries, quite literally, to piss on the competition. He makes off with his brother's woman, sneaks over to Venice, where his father, with whom there's no love lost, just happens to be.

"Why is Jodie behaving like a certified lunatic? We don't know. And what about the sire of the gene pool? Why is Verle Rivers in Venice? We don't know. Why does Lisa say she's going to Munich when she's really going to Venice? We don't know. Why does Lisa leave Venice? Seems to be some doubt there too.

"In any case, Jodie is murdered on the steps of the opera house. What's the father's reaction? Let's talk business. What's the brother's reaction? His main concern is for the well-being of Lisa."

Tennyson fidgeted with the piece of paper, unable to disguise his agitation.

"Now, Rhea, listen to me. Listen to me very carefully. There's something wobbly as hell about this. Too many disparities. Too many colors. Something or someone supersedes all this. Maybe there's no connection between New York and Venice . . . but something or someone intervened in Jodie's life to propel him from New York to Venice. This isn't just an idle hitchhike. You see what I'm saying? Nobody, not even Jodie Rivers, was that much of a thumb-tripper."

He shook his head as if he were annoyed with himself. "My ex-wife had a theory on meat spoilage. You take the meat out of the refrigerator, shove the meat to your nose, take a big whiff and, if it honks back at you, then you know it's no good. This whole goddamn thing honks, Rhea. And if I'm coming across as a hardass this morning it's because . . ."

"Because you don't want me to go," Rhea said, cupping her coffee mug with both hands.

Tennyson shifted his chair away from the table and scratched his knee. "The father," he said irritably. "Everything seems to gravitate toward the father." He looked up. "What do you know about him, other than that he has big bucks and friends with fancy names?"

Rhea sighed. "Humble origins. Self-made man. Verle started out in Oklahoma. That's where Jodie and Henry grew up. He was as an oilman."

"Was?"

"He may still be in oil but he's also branched out into all sorts of things . . . clusters of radio and TV stations in the Southwest, God know's what all. My information gets pretty sketchy from this point on . . . just the few things that Jodie told me about him and hearsay from other people . . . an international conglomerateur, if there is such a word. In 1992, when the market blows wide open in Europe, there's going to be beaucoup booty amassed if you know how to bleed deregulations. Major turf battles. The whisper is, and, again, this is just hearsay, he's now into European communications takeovers."

"And Jodie wasn't getting any spill-over?"

"As long as I've known Jodie, he's always been short on cash."

"What about Henry? Is he cut off too?"

"I don't know."

"What's he do for a living?"

"Henry's a casting director."

Tennyson blinked as if he didn't understand.

"You know," she explained, "he selects actors for roles in shows . . . legitimate theater and TV stuff. . . . He's also cast a few movies."

"Is that big bucks?"

Rhea shrugged. "I doubt that he's getting rich. But if he's busy, he probably does all right for himself. He doesn't work for anyone. He has his own business."

"Ah," Tennyson grumbled skeptically. "Whatever his income, it's chump change next to his father's."

"Well, yes."

"Any other siblings?"

"No."

"What about the mother? Where's she?"

"Dead. For many years, I think."

"Is he good looking?"

Rhea was taken by surprise. She looked out of the corner of her eye.

"You mean Henry? Gee, John, is that relevant?"

Conversational logjam. They glared at each other. Rhea lighted a cigarette. Tennyson folded the piece of paper and stuffed it into his back pocket. He rose from the table and left the kitchen.

After a moment, Rhea and Crunch followed him into the living room where he was already sprawled across the length of the sofa, his tie askew, his forearm resting across his brow.

"Move over," she said gruffly and sat down beside him. She plucked up the tip of his tie. "Why are you so pissed off?"

"It's not you," he sighed. "Lots of things—how much I don't want to return to work this morning—how ineffective my job is in deterring crime—what it would be like to be filthy rich, to be a Verle Rivers, to do whatever you damn well please, whenever you damn well want to. Typical vacation blues stuff." He brought down his arm and lightly touched Rhea's waist. "If I were going to Venice today, instead of you, do you know the first thing I'd check out? Verle Rivers's will. Always begin by excavating the artifacts. What provisions has he made for his sons? Where's all that money going to, once he dies? You can study families until you're blue in the face but wills . . . will-making is one of the few activities in life in which there's no percentage in lying."

Rhea nodded and rested her hand on Tennyson's belt buckle. "And how," she asked, "am I supposed to get hold of his will?"

"You won't," Tennyson laughed. "I just meant that it would be illuminating if you could. But now that I think about it . . . ." He gave her waist a quick squeeze as if to get her attention. "When you get over there, bend your ears a little. You might pick up some gossip in that direction. You have one very valuable advantage that I've never had—access—carte blanche access to people in high society."

"Verle Rivers is not exactly high society. High money, maybe."

"See what I mean? You make that distinction. I don't. I've seen you around them. They don't talk down to you like they do to me."

"I'll keep my ears open," she said with a shrug.

Tennyson gave her another squeeze. "You never answered my question about Henry."

Rhea measured her words: "Henry is not bad-looking. He has a solidly constructed male body. Tall . . . about your height. He lacks your confidence, your profile and your distinguished gray hair."

"In other words," Tennyson said, "he's younger than me."

"By at least a decade."

"And, unless we find out otherwise, he's the heir apparent to a major fortune."

"Yes."

"Some women would consider that kind of man extremely attractive."

"Yes."

"Like this Lisa Morris, wherever she is. Or maybe even a woman like you."

"You trying to bait me again?"

"You're a damn fool for flying over there with him."

"I never said I wasn't."

"Fuck it. I'll see what I can find out about Lisa. But I want the name and address of Henry's business. And while you're at it, give me Ornella's phone number. That's about all I can do from this end."

Rhea leaned forward, as if to kiss him, but Tennyson held her back: "Just tell me one thing," he said. "All that talk about you and your dad in Venice . . ."

"What about it?"

"If there were no private jet, if there were no Verle Rivers at the end of line, if Jodie had been killed in Des Moines, Iowa, would Rhea Buerklin be so hell-bent on flying to the scene of the crime?"

Rhea's eyes narrowed imperceptibly. Slowly, purposefully, she put her hands around Tennyson's neck and exerted considerable pressure.

Tennyson responded by pulling her closer to him. He took possession of her lips. It felt great to be strangled.

# 3

Rhea had traveled on private jets before, but nothing had prepared her for the size and somber opulence of Verle Rivers's arena in the sky. A commercial airline could have crammed in a hundred seats or more, but Verle Rivers's floor plan called for negotiating elbow room and entrepreneurial largess—a board of directors' aerie suitable for a modern-day doge—which, when Rhea thought about it, was no doubt the point. An airborne power play. To enter Verle's jet was to invite suspension of one's personal identity.

Starting at the fore of the cabin was a communications deck blinking erratically and looking as if it had been lifted from NASA. Beyond this was a sleek, wraparound bar flanked by a long, imposing conference table of black, silken wood. Farther astern were four seating nooks, presumably, to host Verle Rivers's more elite and intimate leveraged buy-outs.

The color scheme, if you could call it that, gave no relief. It was steadfastly monochromatic, from black to light gray, with only an occasional glint of chrome, pearl or crystal. The arched walls, turning over on themselves in a kind of self-parody, were covered with gray pinstripe flannel. Rhea wondered if this last detail was some interior decorator's little joke. In any case, she now regretted her outfit, a gray linen suit which, though in her own gallery carried weight, conspired against her in the present environs and threatened to render her completely invisible. It was then that Rhea realized what was wrong with this plane. The decor was an elaborate lie, garishness disguised as sobriety. If there was ever a place that called for a red dress, Verle Rivers's jet was it.

Moments after stepping aboard, a bespectacled man of indeterminate age and diminutive stature presented himself with a smile that was nothing less than fiduciary. It seemed that the little man didn't possess a smile of his own, and lacking the natural reflex, had been loaned one—standard issue, germ free—by Verle's corporation.

His attire was immaculate. He modeled a navy suit of expensive material and superlative cut, a starched shirt of unnatural white, a perfectly knotted gunmetal gray tie and black shoes obsessively buffed. His close-cropped hair was parted to perfection.

Why did his look of approval put her on her guard?

"Ms. Buerklin," he intoned in a vaguely British accent. "Good afternoon Ms. Buerklin, and welcome aboard. I'm Wallace Darlington."

Rhea's nostrils flared unexpectedly. She never trusted a man who wore too much cologne. Darlington was doused—musk and chrysanthemums.

Even more off-putting was his handshake, which was like squeezing a damp clump of modeling clay.

"It was I who telephoned you this morning, Ms. Buerklin."

"Was it?" she said, her smile, like his, now twisted into a bogus concoction. "I thought I was speaking to someone from Venice."

"From midatlantic, actually," Darlington answered with tight lips, his glasses catching the overhead lights in flashes. "I was flying over with the plane at the time. I hope the connection wasn't too static, Ms. Buerklin."

"No, I . . . I just didn't realize you could make midatlantic phone calls."

"Mr. Rivers has his own satellite." Again, his trussed smile.

"He's so looking forward to meeting you, Ms. Buerklin. And he wished me to convey to you his hope that your trip will be a pleasant one. Well! As soon as young Mr. Rivers arrives, we will be taking off. Will you come with me, please?"

Traversing a tightly woven, dove-colored carpet, she followed in the wake of his scent to the back of the plane.

Darlington came to a halt. He made a mincing gesture with his arm. "Wherever you like, Ms. Buerklin," he said. "Please," he added, although the suggestion sounded more like an order.

Very irritating. And that awful fragrance! And that smile that made you want to smack him. And why did he keep repeating *Ms. Buerklin*? The man's excessive formality came off as an insult and, the more she thought about it, the more she suspected it was intentional.

Rhea, an old hand at trench warfare, chose the seating nook farthest astern. She moved over to the window seat and sank down into what was—undeniably, maddeningly—the most comfortable seat she had ever experienced: mole gray leather, as soft and squashy as mud. She plucked up one of the seat belts. Engraved on the buckle was the trident logo of Maserati.

"Cozy?" he asked.

"Um," she said, trying to lean away from his perfume. "Where are the gas masks?"

"I beg your pardon?"

"I said, what sort of plane is this, may I ask? Like most women, I'm mad for aeronautics."

If Darlington saw anything odd in this comment, he didn't display it. "We're riding in a BAC-1-11, Ms. Buerklin."

She looked around. Behind her was a narrow alcove with three closed doors. "And what's back there?"

"The left door is the rest room. The right door is storage. And the center door, Ms. Buerklin, is Mr. Rivers's bedroom of which, Mr. Rivers sincerely hopes, you will avail yourself, should you grow fatigued. Ah!"

The door to the left of the cockpit opened and through it came a young man with a fresh, handsome face.

"Here comes Matteo. I'm afraid I'll be occupied during the trip, Ms. Buerklin, but if there's anything you need, please don't hesitate to ask Matteo. Matteo, this is our passenger, Ms. Buerklin. See that her flight is a pleasant one."

Darlington looked down at Rhea with a commiserative expression: "There are various refreshments. Le Cirque prepared us cold suppers . . . whenever you're hungry, Ms. Buerklin. Also, Ms. Buerklin, there's a selection of videotapes in the cabinet over there and—"

"Thank you," Rhea interrupted, "just sneak me a jug of whiskey and I'll be fine."

Darlington opened his mouth as if to say something but changed his mind.

"The bar is opened isn't it, Mr. Darlington?"

"Yes, of course," Matteo said, taking up the slack with a smile that seemed, to Rhea's relief, genial enough.

Just then, Henry Rivers entered the plane.

"Good," Darlington said as if he had just been released from an unsavory task. "If you will excuse me . . ."

Rhea's curiosity went on red alert.

"What may I get you?" Matteo asked.

"Ah . . . let me think," she said, stalling for time and straightening up in her seat in order to get a better view of the exchange up front.

Henry was a big, broad-shouldered man with a friendly, reasonably presentable countenance. But today, Rhea barely recognized him. His features were drawn and, in spite of his stature, he looked small, out of place, even menaced as Wallace Darlington approached him. Darlington offered his hand in greeting but Henry didn't appear to notice. He clutched a battered briefcase with both hands.

A conversation ensued. Rhea couldn't hear from this distance but Darlington's gestures were overly deferential, while Henry's indicated extreme discomfort. The way in which Henry rubbernecked the interior of the plane strongly suggested that he had never been here before. And, although his mouth remained agape, he kept his chin tucked as if he were a child confessing to an act of disobedience. He kept eyeing the open portal. Was he having second thoughts about coming?

It was only when Darlington pointed to the aft of the plane and Henry spied Rhea, that Henry pulled in his stomach and grew a full two inches. He brushed past him and hurried back to Rhea.

"Whew," he said, ignoring Matteo and plopping down in the seat adjacent to hers.

"Hot as blazes!" he said in a twangy accent that perfectly duplicated his dead brother's. He extracted a handkerchief from his inside coat pocket and mopped his forehead. The handkerchief struck her as odd and old-fashioned. He hadn't shaved. A heavy shadow clung to his jaws. His eyes were bloodshot and deeply underscored with dark rings. Had he been crying?

"Some crop-duster, huh?" he joked, but his voice, normally low and resonant, was now pinched and slightly breathless.

Darlington started to return but—catching Rhea's eye—stopped, consulted his watch and, with a shrug, turned about-face and disappeared into the cockpit.

"Is Mr. Darlington the pilot?" she asked.

"Does he smell like one?" Henry asked.

"No. You thirsty, Henry?"

"Parched."

"Good. Have you met Matteo? Matteo, this is Henry Rivers. I'm going to have Dewar's and water. What would you like, Henry?"

"Oh," Henry fidgeted. "Seven-up would be fine . . . diet, if you have it."

"Very good, sir." Matteo spun on his heels and headed back toward the bar.

"Well," Rhea said, patting Henry's hand and smiling in an attempt to put him at ease. "At least the bar's stocked."

"Yes."

Darlington reemerged from the cockpit. Henry shifted in his chair uncomfortably.

"Matteo seems pleasant enough," she said, trying to deflect his attention.

"I guess so."

"Can't say I care much for Mr. Darlington."

Henry didn't respond. He was ordinarily such an easy, rhythmic conversationalist. In fact, once he got going, he was hard to turn off.

"Mr. Darlington's a bit snobbish for my taste," Rhea said, determined to talk Henry through his obvious discomfort. "And silly. Absurdly formal, or don't you agree?"

"What? Oh, yes, I agree. Formal," he repeated with a grimace. "Did you get a load of his accent?"

"I did, yes. Couldn't quite place it. Where do you suppose he's from? Australia?"

"An Okie trying to sound like an Oxonian don."

"How can you tell?" Rhea paused for a moment. "That's a precise reading for a first meeting."

"It's not my first meeting. Wallace has been with the company for years, for decades, for as long as I can remember."

"What is he, the court jester?"

"Nope, and you shouldn't dismiss him like that," Henry warned with a raised eyebrow. "He's a main player in these here parts. A man of many talents."

"Name one," she sniffed.

"Brilliant with numbers. Dad says he can juggle mathematical constructs that make investment bankers go weak at the knees."

"Okay. Valuable asset. But if he's so important, what's he doing playing host to us? Surely, your father could get anyone to bring us—"

"Whenever my old man is faced with an unpleasant task—like an underhanded business transaction or the necessity of being around his offspring—Wallace is there to intervene, to be the bad guy, to divert people's hatred. It's an old trick of Dad's. Darlington is a deceptively easy target." Henry smiled. "Jodie used to call him 'Uncle Wally.' "

"To his face?" Rhea said and laughed. "He had a gift for nicknames. Jodie called me 'Boss,' the sarcastic jerk. And now that I see your father's plane, I'm beginning to understand the extent of his sarcasm."

"He called me 'Hank,' " Henry confessed. "Anyway, just remember that Wallace is multitalented . . . what show business people call a triple threat."

"Triple? What's the third asset?"

"He's known Dad longer than any of us. Dad's not the kind of man to hang onto the past. Wallace is the only exception, and it gives him an edge."

Rhea was confused. "So it's just an act? . . . the bad accent, the bad cologne and all of that cordiality-on-loan stuff?"

Henry shook his head with a mirthless laugh. "Just the opposite, Rhea. Wallace is naturally pretentious. That's what makes him so fucking good. How old would you say he is?"

"I don't know now. Before, I would have said forty-five but if you say he's been with your father—"

Henry smiled triumphantly. "He's sixty-five-plus."

"Amazing. You could never tell—"

"Yes, you can. Next time you get a chance, check out his hands. He's had a face lift and a damned good one at that . . . but the hands, they never lie. Neither do the smile lines . . . not that he has any . . . nor the neck . . . though his is pretty well covered up. He also dyes his hair."

"Very observant . . . for a man," Rhea commented, openly impressed.

"I'm a casting person. I mean, even if I hadn't known Wallace all my life . . . well . . . itemizing physical illusion, phony accents . . . that's my job."

"Yes, I guess it would be," Rhea said, crossing her legs.

Had she detected the slightest hint of pride in his voice?

As if reading her mind, he added, "Not that it does me much good. Surface stuff. Doesn't necessarily make me a good judge of people."

"How old would you say I am?"

"Oh, no. I don't guess women's ages. Not to their faces."

"Go ahead. I'm not touchy."

"Well . . ."

For a moment they studied one another's faces. Although his eyes were of a darker hue than Jodie's, and more brooding, they had the same moist, aggressive quality. Was Henry a womanizer like Jodie? If he were, he played a much more subtle game. Jodie's aggressiveness had been cocky. Henry's was somehow bruised and, because of it, far more alluring. It was all a matter of taste, of course. . . .

"Go on. Guess."

"Well," he ventured. "You haven't yet succumbed to the knife—"

"And I never will. I have bad luck with surgeons. Even my dog has bad luck with surgeons."

"I'd say you are between thirty-seven and forty."

"Thirty-nine," she pronounced. "You're good. Pretend that you had never met me before . . . that you knew nothing about me. What else could you glean from my personal appearance?"

"Oh, lots of things. You don't wear makeup, except for lipstick, which means that you're either indifferent or at ease with your looks. I'd bet on the latter. What else? Your fingernails are short, well-manicured, with no polish . . . which probably means you don't regard yourself as a decoration. Your haircut, though a simple one, is expensive. Very expensive. It needs to be cut often and takes a small fortune to maintain. That little suit you're wearing didn't come off a rack. The way you sit, the way you handle Matteo, the way you comforted my hand a minute ago, the way you're chatting me up right now to put me at ease . . . everything suggests that you take certain trappings for granted. This jet, for instance," Henry said and laughed. "Dad's putting on a hell of a show, here. Aren't you impressed?"

"Not as impressed as you are. I'm sorry, Henry, I couldn't help but notice. This is your first time aboard, isn't it?"

He shrugged. "Does that surprise you? I would have thought you would have known, through Jodie, that—"

"I knew about Jodie and your father. Not you."

"Dad's always been democratic when it comes to his sons—equal distribution of deprivation. We were never led to the trough. Not very often, in any case."

"Why not? It's none of my business, of course, but . . ."

"Verle's a man of principle! Self-made. Expects everyone to be like him. Why let money bias a relationship? Climb up on your own, that sort of thing." Henry checked himself. "We're getting dangerously close to self-pity. To get back to your question: no, I've never been on this fucking showboat before. That's why I'm so grateful that you're here. You can be my buffer . . . protect me against mean old Darlington. You can hold my hand when we enter the rarified halls of the Gritti Palace."

Rhea turned with a start: "We're staying at the Gritti?"

"Didn't Wallace tell you?"

"No."

"Do you know the Gritti Palace?"

"Well, yes."

"Figures." Henry's eyes became distant. "I saw the Gritti Palace once. Way back when I was a college kid, I backpacked it through Europe one summer . . . youth hostels . . . that sort of thing . . . something you wouldn't know much about. Anyway, I was in Venice briefly. One day, I was on one of those water-buses that goes down the Grand Canal . . . crammed in like a sardine with hundreds of other peons. Someone pointed out the Gritti terrace as we passed by . . . at a discreet distance, of course . . . handsome people enjoying their drinks under the canopy, attended by waiters dressed in white . . . looked nice."

Matteo returned, expertly balancing a silver tray with one hand. The lead crystal tumblers were only half-full. Rhea immediately took exception to the stingy servings. The young man apologized, explaining in a thick accent that the aircraft had just been cleared for departure.

"He might spill," Matteo said, pointing to Rhea's glass.

"He wouldn't get the chance," Rhea assured him. "If you prefer, Matteo, we can speak in Italian."

"*Si, Signora . . .*"

"What did he say?" Henry asked, after Matteo left.

"He wants us to fasten our seat belts."

Within moments, the plane wheeled around and began its taxi toward the runway. Matteo sat down next to Darlington, who was preoccupied with a prospectus at the communications board.

Henry took a deep breath. His hands fumbled with the fastening hinge of his belt buckle. "Damn it," he said. "I can't seem to . . ."

"Are you okay?" she asked, reaching over and helping him with the apparatus.

"I don't feel much of anything," he grumbled.

It was an obvious lie. His fingers shook and he kept folding and unfolding his handkerchief and mopping his face. Henry was a man at the end of his tether, a man who had obviously gone through hell since the morning. His mood was slippery, continually shifting, without warning, from levity to cynicism to utter despair.

"Dazed," he continued. "Can't seem to . . . to catch up with myself. Murder. It's a very unreal thing to deal with."

"I'm sorry, Henry . . . but in a way, I *do* know what you're going though."

"Yes, you do, don't you?" Henry sounded grateful. "I remember when your partner was killed. It was in the papers—"

"That's the worst of it. The papers."

"Is that why you've come? To avoid the papers?"

"I don't know. My friend, John, has a different theory: Venice, itself."

"What do you mean?"

"He suggested that I wouldn't have been be so quick to board a plane bound for a less scenic destination. Des Moines was his example."

The idea seemed to cheer Henry up. "Neither would I. Did you give John the number of Lisa's agency?"

"Yes."

"So he'll help us."

"Well, to a point. I think you should know that he's not very keen about me coming . . . especially with you. This triangle between you and Jodie and Lisa: He says that, if you were in love enough—"

"Which I was . . . oh, I get it. He thinks I might have had Jodie killed."

"No, I don't think he really suspects—"

"But he hasn't ruled out anything. Good man."

"You didn't, did you?"

"Kill Jodie? Would I tell you if I had?" Henry grinned. "Look at the way he's got us scrambling."

"Who?"

"Jodie. After a lifetime of trying to become the center of things, he's finally succeeded. Right now, he's probably laughing his ass off."

Rhea measured her words: "I don't think he's in a position to be laughing."

"I can't very well feign sorrow."

"Of course not."

"Your cop friend has every reason to be suspicious. I could have killed Jodie. I'll never forgive him for . . . You must feel the same way . . . about your mother's brooch, I mean."

"Jodie wasn't my brother."

"Jodie wasn't anybody's brother. I bet he died with a nasty fucking grin on his face. Well, now I'm grinning. Here I am, ensconced in the back of a fancy jet, flying off to the Gritti Palace with a beautiful woman by my side. As far as I'm concerned, it's a fucking holiday." Henry picked up his 7UP and lifted it in her direction. "Cheers, to . . . to . . . to whatever is appropriate at a time like this. I'll be damned if I can figure it out."

"To the quick capture of Jodie's murderer," Rhea suggested.

"Not likely . . . but, yeah, that's a good one," he said and laughed, taking a thoughtful sip.

Rhea drained her scotch in one gulp.

The plane came to a full stop.

She looked out her window. The sun hung low in the west.

"Henry, about the Press . . ."

"What about it?"

"I don't want to sound like I'm lecturing but . . . your family is going to be under close scrutiny for a while. Jodie had become well known and he was colorful enough to make good copy. Add to that the fact that your father is an important businessman and that Lisa is a high-paid model . . . well, everyone will be dragged in. You see what I'm saying? The cops won't walk on egg shells either. It won't be amusing when they catch up with us. Complete invasion of privacy. We'll all be treated as public domain and it will only make matters worse if you come at them—the cops *or* the Press—with this off-the-wall attitude. Just . . . play it straight, okay? It'll save you a lot of trouble."

"Play it straight," Henry repeated. "And do you think the Press is going to play it straight when they find out what Dad was doing in Venice?"

Rhea looked up, puzzled.

"Well, come on," he continued, "you think they won't whoop it up over a woman half his age?"

A sudden expression of understanding washed over his face.

"Wallace *is* being mum today, isn't he?" he said and chuckled. "He didn't tell you, did he?"

"Tell me what?"

"My father is in Venice because, at the age of seventy-two, he's taken a new wife. The living legend is on his honeymoon."

Rhea bit her lip.

The engines roared. A few moments later, the jet rushed down the runway and into the afternoon sky. Rhea stared out the window and watched the aircraft gain altitude until there was nothing to observe but the monotonous hard sheen of the ocean below. From the sidelines, Henry was whistling the show tune "People."

"Stop that, Henry," Rhea said, turning in his direction. "Who is she, anyway?"

"My new mother? Don't know, except that she's our age. I could have asked for further details but it would have given Uncle Wally far too much pleasure."

"Your father didn't tell you?"

"Why should he? I told you, that's part of Wallace's job. Don't look so appalled, Rhea. We'd all have a Darlington if we could afford it."

Rhea sighed and unfastened her seat belt.

Henry did likewise. Again, Rhea noticed the trembling of his hands.

Who were these people? A holy terror of an artist whose indolence had somehow introduced him to death. A brother whose pent-up resentments had transformed him into a veritable timebomb. A number-crunching puppet by the name of Darlington, redolent with self-importance. A septuagenarian mogul and none-too-loving Casanova making whoopee in Venice. A brand-spanking-new Mrs. Rivers.

For the first time, Rhea wondered if she hadn't been a little hasty in coming over. She couldn't very well parachute. She stretched her arms and stood up.

"Matteo's a lousy bartender," she said. "Be right back." She snatched the two empty glasses and headed toward the bar.

Darlington, absorbed in a telephone conversation, looked up and motioned to Matteo, who immediately sprang from his chair and hurried to the center of the plane to intercept her. She waved him off.

Rhea walked behind the bar, disposed of the small glasses, produced the silver tray and two new glasses (milk shake-sized tumblers), a Baccarat ashtray, a bottle of Dewar's and a bucket of ice. She returned, uncomfortably aware of Henry's eyes fixed on the movement of her hips, set the tray on the coffee table in front of them and poured two drinks, handing one to Henry.

"No thanks," he said, holding up a shaky palm. "I'd better stick with soft drinks."

"Nonsense. Here, take it."

"No, really, I can't."

Rhea remained standing with the proffered drink, staring at him as if she'd never heard of such a thing. "Henry, you're a mass of raw nerves. We can sit here for the next seven hours and drive each other crazy or we can get drunk. Be sensible. Make it easy on yourself."

"You don't understand," he sighed. He produced his banged-up briefcase, plopped it on his lap and opened it for Rhea's inspection. Beneath a manila folder were ten plastic bottles tightly wedged together: five were white and five were cloudy aqua.

"Ulcers," he explained.

"Lord," Rhea said with a frown. She was never one for excess baggage. "Are all those bottles necessary? Couldn't you just take a pill?"

"Yeah, well, there's a pill called Tagamet, but I get a rash and headaches when I take it. So, I'm stuck with the old remedies. It's a bit like playing backyard chemist: the white bottles, Amphojel, constipate and the turquoise bottles, Mylanta, loosen everything up. It's a matter of give and take."

Rhea's face suddenly lit up.

"Wall Street Here We Come!" she exclaimed.

"What?"

"One of Jodie's last pieces is double-framed in spoons and Mylanta bottles. It's a painting of two boys who . . ." She thrust one of the tumblers into Henry's hand and sat down. "Henry, listen to me. Was there ever a time in your childhood when something happened to Jodie . . . when you had to carry him in your arms?"

"In my arms?" Slowly, Henry placed his glass on the coffee table. He opened one of the bottles of Mylanta and took a swig. He closed the briefcase and put it to the side, his hands shaking.

"You know what I'm talking about, don't you?"

He took another swig of the milky medicine before answering. His voice was throaty and low: "Jodie painted that? When? When did he paint that?"

"Recently. It's in my loft."

"How recently?"

"It's one of his last pieces. Finished it about a month ago."

Henry nodded.

"I'd all but forgotten. . . . It happened behind the big house in Tulsa back when . . . well, back before Tulsa got so built up. I dared Jodie to walk on the roof of our tree house. He took the dare and fell a good fifteen feet. The fall knocked him out, he was bleeding like a stuck pig and I thought he was dead. I scrambled down out of the tree, picked him up and carried him to the house. God, I was scared. The longest walk I ever had was with Jodie in my arms. Scared for Jodie . . . but also scared for myself. What would my mother do when she saw us? Now that I think about it . . . it was my mother's distorted expression that I feared most." With a gruff gesture, Henry wiped at one eye. "Jodie painted that? And framed it in Mylanta bottles? The slimy son-of-a . . ."

Henry's anger startled Rhea. "Calm down," she said. "I'm sorry I brought it up."

"Sheer spite . . ."

"What spite? I don't know what you're talking about, Henry. You don't understand the feeling behind the painting. You'd have to see it first. There's something plaintive, almost sentimental about it."

Henry laughed a little too loudly: "You say he finished this piece a month ago?"

"Yes."

"Yes, well, while my brother was being so sentimental, he was also sticking it to my girlfriend, wasn't he?"

Angrily, Henry snatched the tumbler from the table and took a huge drink.

His face turned bright red.

"Achh!" he exclaimed, setting down the drink. "Damn it, I told you I had ulcers!"

Rhea looked perplexed and fascinated at the same time. "Then don't drink it! Lord, is the pain that immediate?"

"Instantaneous," Henry winced, clutching at his stomach. He grabbed the Mylanta and took a large gulp. Then another. Then yet another. After a minute or two, his face began to relax.

"Better now?"

"Much."

She pulled a pack of Lucky Strikes from her purse and offered him one. He declined, pointing to his stomach. She lighted a cigarette and inhaled deeply. "Henry . . . a while ago, I toasted to the capture of Jodie's murderer. You said, 'not likely.' "

"Did I?"

"Why would you say that?"

"Jodie never made life easy for people, did he? Why should his death be any different?"

"What did Darlington tell you about the murder?"

"Just what I told you over the phone this morning. His body was found outside La Fenice. The autopsy hadn't been performed yet, but they were guessing that the death happened sometime in the middle of the night."

"Who was the last person to see him?"

"Don't know."

"Who discovered his body?"

"Don't know."

"Didn't you ask? Weren't you curious?"

"Let's just say I didn't care to get the details from Uncle Wally. It would have given him too much pleasure. Besides, I was more concerned about the disappearance of Lisa. Why did she leave the day of his murder? I suppose that her disappearance makes her a suspect, doesn't it? But that's absurd. She couldn't have strangled Jodie. She's not strong enough."

"That still doesn't exempt her from some sort of involvement. Why are you so quick to defend her? I don't know Lisa, of course, but I have to say that, given the circumstances, you seem blindly loyal to her. You keep blaming Jodie for their relationship but it takes two people to . . . How old is Lisa?"

"Thirty-one."

"Old enough to take some responsibility. I mean, if she were a nineteen-year-old, fresh off the farm, I could understand but—"

"I don't want to talk about this."

"You'll have to at some point."

New beads of perspiration formed on Henry's brow. He took another drink of scotch and immediately chased it with Mylanta. He closed his eyes, waiting for the onslaught of pain from his enemy stomach.

Nothing happened. Just a warming sensation that shot through his entire body. He shuddered. He smacked his lips. He leaned back in his space-age seat.

"Well?" she asked.

"It feels . . . great," he said finally. "Damn near orgasmic. Mylanta and scotch. To think—all these years and I never thought of putting the two together."

"It's the first thing I would have thought of . . . here," Rhea said, grabbing the Mylanta from Henry's hand. "Let me try that." She took a drink of scotch, sniffed the turquoise bottle, then sampled its contents. "Hum. Not bad. Scotch and peppermint . . . better than nothing." Rhea kicked off her shoes. She helped herself to another Dewar's Mylanta.

Henry followed suit. Again, she waited for his reaction and, again, his smile widened.

"I'll pay for this tomorrow, of course," he said.

It was dark now, no ocean in sight. If Rhea craned her neck, she could just make out a faint line of orange along the western horizon.

In the following hours, Henry's mood softened. Some color returned to his cheeks. From time to time his head would slowly swing to the side like a plane banking into the clouds. Rhea would have liked to have posed more questions to him—about his family and, particularly, about Verle Rivers—but she couldn't bring herself to interrupt this brief interlude of relative calm. She stuck to small talk.

Wallace Darlington continued to sequester himself at the communications board, occasionally making important-looking phone calls, a spectacle which did not escape Henry's increasingly bemused and voluble disdain.

"Do you suppose he's really talking to anyone? Or is he just trying to act busy so he won't have to deal with me?"

"I couldn't blame him for that," Rhea said and smiled. "You're a basket case. He does look to be having a good time, though, doesn't he? . . . playing with your father's satellite."

"People can own satellites?" Henry's diction was becoming a little slurred. "God, that's depressing. Give me a kiss, Rhea. Cheer me up."

"You better slow down on that stuff. Maybe you should have something to eat."

"There's food?"

"Cold suppers from Le Cirque."

Henry groaned and took another drink.

Four hours into the flight, Wallace Darlington came back to check on them.

"How are we doing?" he asked with his rent-a-smile, taking visual note of the sizable dent made in the scotch bottle. "You're not drinking, are you, Henry?"

"Of course not," Rhea quickly intervened. "We're doing splendidly, Mr. Darlington, thank you."

With some effort, Henry straightened up in his chair. Rhea didn't like the belligerent twinkle in his eye.

"There's something you could answer for me, Wallace," he said.

"I would be happy to try."

"Where was Dad when Jodie died?"

"Your father?" Darlington's lips tightened. "In his suite at the Gritti with Mrs. Rivers. Naturally," he added. "I believe I told you, Henry, the murder occurred in the middle of the night."

"Oh, yes. You did," Henry smiled. "And where were *you* in the middle of the night?"

Darlington's answer was dry, void of all emotion: "In the Gritti. I had just returned from Geneva on business. Your father warned me that you might try to pin the murder on him . . . or on me. I'm afraid I must disappoint you on both counts. Any other questions?"

Darlington stared at his taunter for a moment, shook his head, then, with even steps, returned to his seat at the communications board.

"That was stupid, Henry," she said. "You should stop drinking."

"Robotic fuck," Henry mumbled. "Thank God you're here. Hostile environment to be winging it alone, wouldn't you say?"

"To be quite honest, Darlington may be condescending but the hostility seems to be coming from your corner. You don't really suppose your father had anything to do with Jodie's murder!"

"It's possible."

"Why?"

"Because Dad is the moving spirit in all things, that's why."

"Oh, come on. Give me a specific motive."

"Maybe Jodie got in the way. He always did." Henry sighed. "What's the point in trying to explain? Once you meet Dad, he'll win you over to his side."

"Side? What are you babbling about? You're drunk. Christ, does it have to be an either-or allegiance between you and your father?"

"Dad is very persuasive. He has a knack for possessing things, people, situations. And, unlike him, I can't afford to ship beautiful women to the Gritti Palace."

"Let's get something straight," she said, putting down her drink. "Number one, I'm not beautiful and, number two, I'm not so cheaply bought—in fact, I'm not bought."

"Okay, sorry—"

"Sorry's not good enough. Don't underestimate me. You and I have a certain affinity based on what Jodie did to us. You want Lisa back. I want my brooch back. You're a spurned brother. I'm a spurned art dealer. But beyond that, I'm a neutral entity on this trip, Okay? Besides, if your father gets pushy with me, my credit at the Gritti is just fine, thank you . . . as was my father's credit before me, as was my grandfather's credit before him . . . long before Verle Rivers of Tulsa, Oklahoma, even *thought* about signing the Gritti register!"

"I feel better already . . . I think."

Rhea paused before going on. In a softer voice she said, "Don't be so quick to understand, Henry. I'll help in anyway I can to find out who killed Jodie. Beyond that, fuck you, fuck Jodie and your father."

She exhaled heavily, reached over and kissed him on the cheek. "You need a shave. Either have something to eat or get some sleep. You're going to need all the energy you can get, once we get to Venice."

He looked at her dreamily. "You want to rest your head on my shoulder?"

"No room," she answered and laughed, in spite of herself. "There's a chip the size of a small safe already there!"

She got up and slid a leather ottoman under his feet. She arranged a thick, soft blanket around him, tucking it around his chest.

"Maybe we'd be more comfortable in the bedroom," Henry suggested.

"You're comfortable enough as it is."

He tried to suppress a yawn without success.

"Good-night, Henry."

She switched off the overhead lamp.

The jet's humming enveloped him with a lulling sense of security. Within minutes, Henry Rivers was sound asleep. Rhea's eyes became heavy too. But she kept a silent vigil on the activity in the fore of the plane: two men—one young, one trying to look young—poring over paperwork in a pool of greenish silver light.

At one point, Wallace removed his glasses and turned around. He squinted, but it was unlikely that he could discern his guests in the darkness, a darkness that suddenly struck Rhea as protective. Giving up, Darlington adjusted his glasses and returned to his papers.

Henry snored softly. A big overgrown teddy bear trying to be tough, Rhea thought. Why had he insinuated that Verle and Wallace had something to do with Jodie's murder? She really was shocked at the idea. It was preposterous. Henry was drunk, she tried to reassure herself. He was just trying to get a rise out of Darlington. On the other hand, the closer she got to Venice, the less plausible the whole situation became. Where did Jodie fit into all of this luxury? The more she thought about it, the more she regarded his murder as out of place, a superfluous event, an event turned inside out.

Verle killed his own son? Far more likely that his sons would have killed Verle! Verle was the man with power, with money, with a brutal disdain for his own flesh and blood . . . a man worth killing. . . .

But Jodie?

*Maybe he got in the way,* Henry had suggested. But how could Jodie get in the way? He wasn't equipped to get in the way. He couldn't have gotten close enough to get in the way. It was obvious, without meeting him, that Verle Rivers was a fortress not to be violated by mere relatives. What they knew of him was what he allowed them to know . . . through the pretentious channeling of Wallace Darlington.

*Your father warned me that you might try to pin the murder on him.* . . . In the darkness, among the turquoise bottles, Rhea rubbed her eyes, deeply perplexed. Why had Darlington planted that little piece of information? Why would Verle suspect that Henry would point the finger at him? It didn't seem plausible. Had Wallace just made that up? This wasn't a time for cat-and-mouse bullshit.

Or was it?

Just as the aircraft began to nose its way into a gaudy European sunrise, Rhea closed her eyes.

She was anything but sleepy.

# 4

Henry and Rhea were playing strip tennis. Each time you won a game, your opponent had to take something off. Eventually, they both won.

Naked, he jumped the net and enveloped her. They sank to the clay court, their sweaty bodies attracting grit like magnets. He looked into Rhea's dark, Brazilian eyes and they suddenly became Lisa's. Her smell became Lisa's. Her voice became Lisa's. Confusion sliced his dream away from him.

He opened his eyes in acute pain: razor blades in his stomach.

Rhea smiled at him.

"Be back in a minute," he said.

Trembling, he managed to right his seat, get up, secure his briefcase with both hands, and escape to the rest room, his blanket trailing behind him.

He turned on the lights and closed the door. The sudden brightness lurched at him. The gray marble counters, the burled wood paneling, the elegant sconces of frosted glass, the pearl-colored bidet—all the sparkling accoutrements mocked him, but none more than the mirrors that ricocheted and multiplied his wretchedness: a virus in the lap of luxury.

He fumbled through his briefcase. Moaning, shaking violently, he popped off the top of a plastic vial of codeine—for emergencies only—and swallowed two white tablets. Henry collapsed on the toilet. He concentrated on *not* vomiting. People said vomiting helped. He never understood that. It never helped him. He always felt worse, afterward. Eyes tightly clenched, sweat glistening at his temples, arms forming a girdle around his waist, he tried to bully his ulcers into submission . . . sort of like overruling hiccups by holding your breath, only more harrowing and a damn sight less effective.

Fifteen minutes passed before the codeine kicked in. First, there were isolated tinglings in his limbs. Then a vague numbness seeped into the center of his body which dulled, if not actually eradicated, the pain in his stomach.

Another fifteen minutes elapsed.

He managed to regain a more or less regular pattern of breathing. He began to be bothered by other parts of his body—always a good sign. In any case, he no longer felt like he was going to die.

He grappled for his kit bag, got up, shuffled over to the opulent basin, washed his face and brushed his teeth. Only then did he dare to really focus on his ravaged image.

"Oh!" he said aloud.

For a moment, his brother passed through him, then disappeared behind the mirrors. He froze, waiting for the sensation to prove itself false. Instead, somewhere, within the vibrations of the jet, he heard Jodie's voice taunting him: *All those years you bad-mouthed me for using dope. What do you think codeine is?*

"Painkiller," Henry answered the mirror. "My medicine was prescribed by my doctor. . . ."

*Just because your pusher has a sheepskin on the wall and drives a BMW . . . just because mine rode the subway . . . what's the difference, Hank? They're both suppliers. Drugs are drugs no matter who gives them to you. Women are interchangeable too, aren't they? I caught the ending of your dream.*

"Did you? Fuck off."

Henry didn't believe in supernatural visitations. Absurd: to be telling what you *didn't* believe in to fuck off.

He pushed back his hair with both hands. His eyes darted around the room for something to supplant his attention. To the side, mounted into the wall, was an elaborate clock that indicated, by twelve cities, current times throughout the world.

| Milano | 8:48 AM |
| New York | 2:48 AM |
| Los Angeles | 11:48 PM |

He pinched the knob on his watch and forwarded the hands to Italian time. He swallowed another codeine tablet and faced the mirror: "That's right, you asshole. I'm taking another one."

He pulled down on the gold-plated door handle and exited.

Adjacent to the bathroom was the door that opened into the bedroom. Without knowing why, almost against his will, Henry found himself opening the door.

Inside, it was pitch-black. Groping with his hand, he found a switch on the wall and turned on the lights—charcoal moire silk on the walls, black lacquer cabinetwork and a central bed on a scale suitable for orgies.

Jodie materialized in the bed, in pajamas, ensconced in a sculpture of pillows, waving and smiling at him.

Henry backed out and closed the door.

In the main cabin, the shades had been drawn up. Light streamed in through the windows.

Rhea was helping herself to croissants and coffee.

Toward the nose of the plane, Matteo looked up and caught Henry's attention with a proffered coffee pot. Henry shook his head and quickly took his seat.

"Safe," he said, trembling.

"You Okay?" Rhea asked, brushing off a crumb from her lap.

"Sure."

"We were beginning to wonder. You were in there a long time. No aftereffects from the booze? You look terrible."

"Probably not enough rest. How long was I asleep?"

"Long time. Exhausted?"

"I don't know. Yes, no . . . weird sensation . . . like being frozen in a forward motion."

"It's called riding on a jet," she said, knitting her eyebrows. "Are you still drunk?"

"Damned if I know," he answered truthfully, thinking of his hallucinatory confrontation in the aft end. "Maybe when we get to the hotel, if I'm lucky, I can get some real sleep before . . ."

"You could lie down in the bedroom."

"No thanks." His stomach did a flip-flop and, by sheer force of will, he erased the image of Jodie among the pillows.

*Somebody, give my bro a break.*

"Good lord," he laughed out loud.

"What is it?"

"Nothing . . . I hope. Do you play tennis?"

"Used to. Still do, occasionally. Why?"

"Never mind."

An hour later, they were on the ground. Rhea, Henry, Darlington and Matteo passed through customs and were immediately confronted by a triumvirate of Italian police: a wall of splendid uniforms and resolute faces. Henry didn't understand a word they were saying but he recognized his name clearly enough and quickly understood, from Rhea's arguing in Italian, that he was at the heart of their officious presence.

"Well, Henry," Rhea said, finally turning to him. "We won't be going to the hotel straight away. Scrap the nap idea. They want you at *Questura*. Now."

"What for?"

"They want to talk to you about Lisa."

"Who's they?"

"The chief of police."

"The chief of . . . how does he know I'm here?"

He looked at Rhea, then at Wallace Darlington who stared back at them from the sidelines.

"That's right," Darlington admitted. "I phoned ahead. Time is of the essence." He turned to Rhea: "There's no reason for you to be dragged into this. Ms. Buerklin, if you'll be so good to come with us, we have a private boat waiting. The police will bring Mr. Rivers to the Gritti, later."

"I will be so good to accompany Mr. Rivers," Rhea responded. And then to the *Ispettore*, the officer who seemed to be in charge, she explained that she was in Venice as Henry's personal translator.

Darlington took two steps forward as if to say something. He seemed piqued but Rhea stared him down. He turned his back on the whole distasteful group and ordered Matteo to collect the luggage.

The police ushered Henry and Rhea through a glass door that separated customs from the main terminal. They turned to the left— tourists watching them with interest—and exited through a second glass door which gave to the outside. A hundred feet away was the dock where motorboats of all descriptions rocked back and forth against their moorings. The police stood by while he and Rhea were helped into a *volente*, a boat with POLICIA painted on its side.

Henry was struck by the sharp, fresh smell of the Adriatic. Mixed with and leavened by the tingling of the codeine, it was as if an inner layer of grime had been ripped away from his lungs. He looked up, breathed deeply. The September sun burned through the remains of a morning haze.

The silent jostling of the police, the roar of an overhead jet, the lapping of water and, along the horizon, the buzzing of water taxis zigzagging in intersecting patterns—all of it converged and funneled into his woozy consciousness with a velocity that left him dizzy and invigorated at the same time.

Once aboard, the police gestured for the two Americans to find seats in the lower cabin. Rhea objected and blocked Henry's descent. She tore into an Italian oration that rendered the police slack-jawed. Then they broke into laughter. A burly man fired up the engine, shaking his head with gruff amusement. The boat was pushed away from the dock.

"What was that all about?" Henry asked. "What's wrong with sitting inside? What did you tell them, anyway?"

"Nothing serious. Just a little Italian foreplay. I told them that penetrating Venice in an enclosure is like getting fucked with a rubber—"

"You wha—?"

"Which is totally unsatisfactory if you intend, as we intend, to become impregnated by the local charms. One meets the waters head on. Don't look so shell-shocked. They won't bother us again until we get to Venice . . . in about twenty minutes. Relax while you can, Henry, and enjoy the . . ."

"The fuck?"

"It sounds crude when you say it but . . . yes, I'm partial to the image," she admitted, then turned her attention to the horizon. "It's that way," she said, cupping her forehead with one hand and pointing with the other.

The boat picked up speed. For the next ten minutes, Rhea stood spellbound, waiting, watching for Venice to emerge from the haze. Henry, too, was mesmerized. He watched the wind shove the gray silk of Rhea's blouse against her breasts . . . a glovelike clutch with only an occasional flutter of material.

"Quit staring at me!" she yelled over the roar of the engine.

"Quit talking about fucking!" he countered.

The police were laughing again.

She moved closer to him. "My reference to copulation isn't as gratuitous as you think. I was trying to make a point and our Italian friends, here, understood immediately. The Venetians have been fucking the sea for centuries. At the height of the Empire, the doge would go out annually on a Cecil B. deMille barge and toss a gold ring into the lagoon. A symbolic, voyeuristic deflowering . . . or wedding, if you're of a Catholic persuasion. The water is Venice's mistress."

"Erotic arrangement," Henry said.

The northern perimeters of Venice came into focus.

"Water is restless," she answered, as if agreeing with him.

What did she mean? He couldn't think clearly . . . maybe he shouldn't have taken so much codeine. Was she equating restlessness with eroticism?

Rhea called his attention to the left side of the boat. A smaller island was coming into view.

"San Michele," she announced. "Venice's cemetery."

It was a squarish, aristocratic-looking island somewhat overgrown at the near, eastern corner, with a scattering of modest tombs. But behind this, marble mausoleums, big as houses, rose among forbidding, operatic-looking cypress trees.

"Grand notion of death," Henry commented. "Very theatrical. Is it still active?" Henry paused and laughed. "I guess you don't call cemeteries 'active,' do you? I meant to ask, are there still lots available?"

"I think so. San Michele *is* active. It's a tourist attraction. Lots of important people buried there. Ezra Pound, Diaghilev, Stravinsky—"

"Maybe we should have Jodie buried there. He always wanted to rub shoulders with the big guys. Now he'll get his chance. Reflected glory."

Rhea turned toward him. "You've hated him for a long time, haven't you? You hated him, you hate Darlington, you hate your father . . . *is* there anyone you like?"

"Yeah, I like my secretary and I like my guppies." *And I like you,* he wanted to add, but fell silent.

Rhea looked amazed. "You have guppies? You're an aquarium freak? Then you should love this town. It's kind of like an aquarium . . . for humanoids."

"Good way to describe my father."

"Like father, like son."

He turned his back on the cemetery and walked to the right side of the boat, the Venice side, in the hopes that the encroaching details of the city might provide him with some suitable, banterlike response to her remark. He couldn't come up with anything but Jodie's smile.

They were well into the north lagoon now. The boat slowed down . . . almost rudely, Henry thought. The "fuck," if that's what the boat ride had been, was cut short, without his consent. He couldn't say why, but he felt abandoned.

Crude stakes rose out of the water along the quay. Empty boats were tethered to them. They bobbed helplessly and Henry felt a wave of empathy for them.

They passed by a macabre church called the *Misericordia*. Rhea adored it. Henry thought it was hideous. On its facade, two grim cherubs hovered, shot through with anxiety. Henry could have sworn they were suffering from peptic ulcers.

For the second time, the boat abruptly decreased speed, this time, to a crawl.

"Beautiful, isn't it?" she said.

Henry nodded his head doubtfully. "Yeah. Great place for a honeymoon . . . if you're in your seventies and have a penchant for wasting sons."

"Come on, Henry. You just like the way it sounds coming out of your mouth. You don't really suspect your father. . . ."

"I don't discount him," he answered.

"Give me a reason."

"He didn't become rich by being a nice guy. Nothing gets in his way. He's consumed by his work, by the world he has created for himself. Distractions don't make him a happy man. And Jodie could be insistent. He was always going too far with people. What was he doing here, if not to irritate Dad? If Jodie got it into his head to bully Dad . . ."

"For what reason?"

"I don't know."

"Then why do you say that?"

"Because that was Jodie's style when he wanted someone's attention. In a way, Dad and Jodie were very much alike. It's always been all or nothing with them."

"Jodie was his son."

"He's killed us enough times in the past."

Rhea paused for a moment. "That's a totally disoriented abstraction," she said.

"That's what Dad does best: he makes you feel at home and then he disorients you."

"You envy him."

"Always."

"And you're far from objective."

Henry laughed. "It's not that simple. Look, I'm no detective. I'm a businessman. A casting director. I place actors in theatrical roles. On a daily basis I'm sent scripts."

"So what?"

"So . . . my job is to find the best person, the most believable actor to bring that script to life. Why shouldn't I use my business expertise, my only expertise when it comes down to it, in determining the identity of my brother's murderer?"

"No reason at all, Henry. But that doesn't explain why you want to cast your father as the murderer."

"Who said I wanted to? As far as I'm concerned, everyone is a suspect. I mean, line 'em up. Who hated Jodie the most? It's fucking try out time. Let's hold an open audition. 'Thanks for coming in. We'll get back to you.' "

"Not everyone may care to try out."

"That happens in my business too. For example, I've taken actors who specialize in musical comedy, put them in a dramatic role, and their careers suddenly take off. They don't think they can do a part which, in fact, they were born to play."

"And you think Verle Rivers was born to be a murderer?"

"Let me finish what I was trying to explain. There's something else about the casting business—a perversity, if you will. Sometimes a part comes along which requires the exact *opposite* of what you might imagine. It's called *casting* against the role. Let me give you an example. Say I'm hired to cast a murder-mystery movie. I know who the murderer is because I've read the script. So do I say, 'Okay, the murdered must look like a murderer. He's got to have evil close-set eyes and thin cruel lips and a pockmarked complexion.' Do I say that? Yes, I say that if I want the audience to suspect who the murderer is at the beginning of the first reel. But that's not very savvy casting, is it? It's a lot more suspenseful if the murderer is likable . . . cute, for example, with a baby face . . . or any physical trait that makes the audience trust him, initially."

"And is your father initially likable?"

"Some people seem to think so. *He* seems to think so."

"I see," Rhea said, frowning. "And how would you cast me, if you were casting against the role."

"Oh, you'd make an Oscar-winning nun."

"A Mother Superior?"

"No, *against* the role. I would cast you as an underling whose sole aim in life was total submission."

"Funny."

The *volente* turned right, into a narrow canal. On both sides, ossified palazzos rose high enough to eclipse the sun. They approached a small, single spanned, stone bridge. It was high arched but one of the policemen ordered Henry and Rhea to duck. Timely advice: had they not complied, they would have been decapitated.

As the boat emerged from the other side, Rhea intoned the word "audition." Then she shook her head. "But this isn't a theatrical contract. This is a real death we are talking about. Which is another way of saying real life, I suppose."

"What the fuck does that mean?" Henry snapped. "What's *your* real life . . . the New York art world? How real is that? And how real was it to you when your partner was murdered? And how real is all this?" Henry added, gesturing toward the alley of sea-ravaged buildings tilting above the narrow canal. "This is just a dead city that gives the impression of being alive because of all the tourists. How real would it be without them? How real is Wallace Darlington's face or a multimillion dollar private jet or a—"

"Okay, Okay, I get your point—"

"No, you don't, Rhea. Let me share something with you: this morning, when I was in the bathroom, I was talking to my brother. And the reason I was talking to my brother was because he was talking to me. Now you tell me if that's real or not."

"You saw him?"

"As clearly as I'm seeing you."

Rhea looked away for a moment. Very quietly she said, "There have been times when I've felt like Emil, my partner, was looking over my shoulder or putting words in my mouth. A lot of people experience that when someone close to them dies."

"Yeah? Well, I'm not a ghost-oriented kind of guy, you know? And anyway, if Jodie actually did visit me this morning, he sure as hell didn't have much on his mind. I mean, take Hamlet's father. He was murdered, right? When his ghost visits Hamlet, it's strictly business: 'Let's spill some blood, son. Your uncle killed me and I'm more than just a little pissed off.' Revenge time at the family castle. That makes sense to me. But what does my brother do? He sneers at me. He wants to ridicule me, just like he always did."

"What are you barking at me for?" Rhea asked. She tamped a Lucky Strike on the back of her hand.

"You shouldn't smoke."

Rhea rolled her eyes. "Try to do something about that hangover, would you? It's getting a little tedious."

"I'm not hung over!" he answered triumphantly. "As a matter of fact, I'm high as a kite, having a great time on codeine."

"Hum. I'd hate to see you when you're depressed."

"That's another thing," Henry grumbled. "I look like shit. Where do you get off looking so good after an all-night binge?"

"Practice, Henry," she answered, exhaling smoke in his face.

The boat turned right again, then left. The engine was at a near idle now as they purred beneath another bridge, immediately after which, the boat glided to the side and stopped. Above them on the sidewalk, there were policemen in abundance, smoking in doorways and, for the most part, ignoring them.

Henry and Rhea were helped up the steps and escorted into a building with ancient marble floors. They ascended a broad staircase to the second floor, were deposited on a huge sofa, long as a barge, and abandoned. The room was mammoth. The doors, if placed on the floor, were the size of Henry's bedroom back in New York. High above him loomed a dusty Venetian chandelier, as big and gray and pendulous as an elephant.

"What is this place?" he asked. "I feel like a dwarf."

"An old palazzo," Rhea said and shrugged. "Five hundred years old, or more. Most likely built by a Greek merchant. This part of town is the old Greek Quarter. The Greek Orthodox Church is right around the corner."

"Thanks for the tour."

"What?"

"That wasn't a sightseer's question, Rhea."

"Oh. Well . . . this is a waiting room, asshole, and we are waiting in it. Over there, to the right, behind that door is the office of the

Minister of Something-or-Another." She lighted a cigarette. "If they keep us waiting too long I'll burst in and do some major name-dropping. Not because I'm particularly sympathetic with you, this morning—it happens that I've got to pee like a racehorse, which is no casual simile."

Rhea proceed to explain how, at an early age, a horse had fallen on her in a jumping accident and, as a consequence, half of her bladder had been removed.

A secretary in heels came echoing down the marble hall. Rhea jumped up, waylaid her and was directed to a rest room. "Be right back," she called over her shoulder.

Henry's dread of being left alone was mixed with an uneasy tingling . . . his codeine tablets . . . had he brought them with him? His stomach was acting up again. He patted the pockets of his sport jacket to assure himself that he had remembered to bring . . .

He felt something stiff and square in his left pocket. He extracted a paper folded twice. He unfolded it. It was the "side" for a casting session of *Long Day's Journey into Night,* a project he'd been working on. The monologue he held in his hand was for the part of Edmund, the younger brother. It was a sad, drunken, self-pitying speech:

> It was a great mistake, my being born a man. I
> would have been much more successful as a sea gull
> or a fish. As it is, I will always be a stranger who
> never feels at home, who does not really want and
> is not really wanted, who can never belong, who
> must always be a little in love with death!

Lousy applicability. He wadded up the "side" and stuffed it under the cushion.

He opened up the codeine vial and took another pill.

"I saw that," Rhea's voice echoed as she rounded the corner.

At the same moment, the minister's door burst open and two men came out. The minister was old and fidgety; he glared at them when he wasn't looking at his watch. An aide approached and the minister excused himself with open relief.

In contrast, the other man was in his mid-thirties, dead-still and astonishingly handsome. When he did move, to shake Henry's hand, it was with the grace and economy of a natural athlete. His name was Dr. Giovanni Lago, *Commissario Capo*, chief of police, the man in charge of Jodie's case. In an instant, Henry could tell he was in the presence of a man who waited for his moment, then acted with swiftness. He was arrogant but was he vain? He was impeccably dressed in a dark suit. His features were finely chiseled without being feminine and his eyes were a fierce blue. And yet there was nothing foppish or narcissistic about him—not like the silly, handsome actors Henry was obliged to hire. When Dr. Lago looked at you, he wasn't saying, "Look at me." He *was* looking at you, or perhaps, through you.

He spoke no English, so Rhea quickly stepped in as translator. If she were struck by Lago's good looks, she didn't let on.

"The situation is this," she told Henry. "We're in the wrong building."

"What do you mean?" Henry exploded. "I've been in a plane all night, they won't let me go to the hotel, my brother's been murdered, and I'm in the wrong building? I don't believe it! What the hell's going on around here?"

"There's a new development. I'm not sure what. We're in Italy, now, Henry. Just relax."

"I know where we are."

"Just settle down, would you? We haven't waited that long. Dr. Lago is going to take us to his office right now. It's only two palazzos away." She reached over and gave him a peck on the cheek.

Henry froze for a moment. In a softer voice he said, "It must be bad, if you're kissing me. What aren't you telling me?"

"I'm not sure," she answered and frowned. "He hasn't said what's happened. Let's just go with him, Okay?"

Henry grumbled, grabbed his briefcase and followed Rhea and Dr. Lago back down the grand staircase—back into the Venetian daylight, down the sidewalk, into another building, up another, less ostentatious flight of stairs and, finally, into a small plain office. There was an old desk, behind which Lago seated himself. With a slight movement of his hand, he invited his guests to have a seat. There were filing cabinets that ate up the remaining floor space. The only items of a personal nature were, on the desk, a blue-green ashtray in the form of a coiled cobra and, on the wall, a simply framed photograph of Lago: dark goggles, white jumpsuit, his palms resting on the hood of a red race car.

Dr. Lago pulled out a pack of Marlboros and lighted a cigarette. He spoke to Rhea, but his dark blue eyes remained on Henry. *"Soffre di tensione nervosa. Quali farmaco ha preso?"*

She answered in Italian, then turned toward Henry. "He wanted to know what you're on. I told him codeine . . . for your ulcers. It is prescribed, isn't it? Good. That makes things easier. Dr. Lago also wants to know if you carry a snapshot of Lisa."

"Not a snapshot exactly. . . ."

Henry produced his wallet. Shuffled within a stack of business cards, he found a flimsy magazine ad, folded four times. He handed it to Lago. Very carefully, Lago unfolded it. It was of Lisa in an Argentinean coffee advertisement: her hair piled on top of her head, her dark cheek resting in one hand, a contemplative cup of coffee in the other.

While Lago studied the photograph of Lisa, Henry surreptitiously studied the mounted photograph of Lago. It suddenly struck Henry that Lago had the soul of a mechanic: a man who was born for precision and speed, who demanded maintenance, excelled in challenge and, as a result, encountered any track, any unfamiliar curve with cool equilibrium.

Lago, leaning back in his chair and shaking his head slowly, said something to Rhea. Henry could just make out the words: *"Bella . . . tragico . . . sfortuna. . . ."*

Rhea gasped.

"What's he saying?" Henry demanded. "Is it about Lisa?"

"What?" Rhea looked confused. "Just hold on a minute, Henry."

Rhea jumped into a rapid exchange with Lago. He shook his head and argued with an imperturbable style that matched his steadfast gaze, which remained on Henry.

There was a moment of silence.

"Well?" Henry demanded.

"Lisa's been found."

"Yes? Where is she?"

Rhea looked down at her lap.

"What's happened? Rhea, what's going on?"

"Lisa's dead. Her body was found on Murano . . . a nearby island where the glass foundries are. Two gun wounds. One in the stomach, one in the chest. Oh, God, Henry, I'm so sorry."

Henry's eyes clouded over. He clutched his stomach. Through the blur, he thought he saw Dr. Lago's face transform into Jodie's.

Without warning—to himself or to the people around him—Henry lurched forward and threw up on the desk. The cobra ashtray was covered in bile.

# 5

Giovanni Lago was, perhaps, a kind man . . . or in any case, he was conservative in his display of unkindness. He stood up and called for help, his blazing blue eyes never leaving Henry. Police underlings popped out of the woodwork and within minutes his desk was mopped up, dried, disinfected and back to normal.

It was Lago who gently but firmly pulled Henry up from his chair and walked him to the window that overlooked the canal in front of Police Headquarters. He waved off Rhea's attempt to help.

Henry tried to focus on the pedestrians walking on both sides of the small canal, going about their daily business. But what he really saw was the flamboyance of vomit against Lago's deep conservatism—a conservatism displayed even in his clothes: his immaculate, dark suit and blue silk tie, his expensively plain black shoes. . . .

Lago extracted a crisp handkerchief from his coat pocket and, with extraordinary care, wiped Henry's mouth and chin.

The simple gesture brought Henry to silent tears. When was the last time someone had wiped his mouth? Thirty years or more; certainly before his mother had died, and never by a man. It was the economy of the gesture that Henry appreciated—that appeased his wounded dignity and helped him to retrieve some semblance of composure.

It was scary: the eruption and alienation of his shame. Shame for throwing up? No. Shame for learning that he had lost Lisa to the lecherous arms of his own brother? No. Shame for thinking that he could hang on to a beautiful model ten years younger than he? Getting closer! (Apparently, he was no better than his father on that count.) Shame for realizing that, in death, his love for Lisa had already died? That he had just been hanging on to something that no longer existed? Yes.

"The Lisa?" Lago asked in broken English. "You love?"

Why was this comforting to Henry? Because his interrogator couldn't speak English? In no other context, with no other man, would Henry have ever done what he was about to do: It was at this window, with an Italian race-car-driving chief of police at his side, with Rhea in the background acting as translator, that Henry emptied himself of his brief history with Lisa . . . how they had met, nearly two years ago . . . how their mutual attraction had been immediate and intense . . . how she moved in with him and, for a year and a half, how life was ordered around their lives, *because* of their shared existence. And then . . . the little flickering of restlessness in her face that occasionally appeared and gradually evolved into a pervasive absence—even when they were in bed together. Everything she did registered impatience, a cruel self-alienation from the very relationship which she had helped to create.

"I've been shooting myself in the foot all my life," Henry concluded. "Lisa was part of that. No more, no less." He turned toward to Rhea. "Tell Dr. Lago I'm sorry about the mess."

Lago shrugged his shoulders with a reply that made Rhea smile. "Dr. Lago says love *is* a mess. Don't worry about it. Hold on, he's telling me something." Rhea frowned. "He says that Lisa's passport was Bahamian. If you have an address for her there, where her family can be reached, he would like it."

"Her parents are in Nassau. My address book is in my suitcase. When I go the hotel, I'll get the address for him."

"Bahamian . . ." Rhea repeated with a knitted brow. She asked for the photograph of Lisa. Dr. Lago passed it to her.

"You didn't tell me she was black."

Henry's eyes narrowed: "I didn't think it was important."

"It's not. It's just that . . . God, she was beautiful. No wonder she had you in love. Was she smart?"

"She was . . . romantic. Apart from that, I'd say she was smart. Her success as a model was hard-earned. When she started in the business, there wasn't much of a market for black models. She helped to create that market."

"Ambitious, smart, beautiful . . ." Rhea mused, "a triple threat. Dr. Lago would like a list of the agencies she worked for in Europe. Did she ever work in Milano?"

"Yes."

"Was she involved in drugs?"

"No. Never."

Another conversation ensued in Italian. Lago leaned forward in his chair as he explained something to Rhea.

"Henry. Lisa had two suitcases. They were picked up by the police at the Paris train station where they hold unclaimed baggage."

"What were they doing on the Paris train?"

"She got on the train here. Obviously, she got off again, but her luggage went on without her. Anyway, inside one of the bags was a kilo of high-grade hashish. Any idea what she was doing with it? The amount would indicate that she was in the drug business."

"I don't believe it. Someone planted it. Maybe my brother? She would have never done that." Henry paused. "Then again, I'm beginning to wonder if I knew her at all. It's almost as if we were talking about a complete stranger."

"Did Jodie ever carry a gun?"

"Of course he didn't. You knew Jodie. That wasn't his style. Why would Lago want to know? . . . oh. He thinks Jodie might have killed her. No way. This whole line of questioning is getting way out there. I mean, I see the obvious implication: that Jodie and Lisa were involved with drugs. But if that's true, why were they taken out separately? And why in different ways? Why was Jodie strangled? Drug people shoot each other, don't they? Why would Lisa get off the train?

Rhea, why didn't Lago tell me about Lisa when we were over in the other building? . . . Why did he wait to—"

"Element of surprise, I would imagine. He probably wanted to see your reaction, to see if you could be caught off guard." Rhea laughed, pointing to the newly mopped desk. "He got more than he bargained for."

Lago scribbled down something, paper clipped it to Lisa's magazine-stock photograph and called toward the open door. An *agente* appeared. Lago held out the photograph and murmured instructions. The *agenti* took the picture and left.

"Feeling a little bit better?"

"Yes, I guess I am."

He did feel better . . . or at least, shored up. He surprised himself. Was it Lago's equanimity or Rhea's general irreverence that produced this new-found subvention? He returned to his seat and asked for an account of Jodie's and Lisa's movements, the night before she, supposedly, had left for Paris.

It had not been difficult to verify their movements, Lago said. Venice has seen everything . . . but a tall American white man with a ravishing black woman stand out, even in a Venetian crowd.

On the fourth of September, Jodie Rivers and Lisa Morris had dined, at 8:00 P.M. at Ristorante Antico Martini. They had wanted to eat at Harry's Bar, but the concierge at the Gritti had explained that Harry's was closed on Mondays. Instead, he secured them a reservation at Martini's.

Martini's long blue awning spilled out onto the *Campo S. Fantin,* a small, irregular-shaped piazza that was also the square occupied by the opera house, La Fenice.

The couple had two bottles of expensive champagne, a large meal, paid the bill in cash, including a generous tip in American dollars and left around 10:00. According to the waiter who served them, there was some sign of personal conflict. No overheard arguments but no real conversation between them, either. He described their meal as "joyless." At first, the waiter assumed that they had been married too long but, noticing the absence of wedding rings, concluded that they were merely lovers in the standoff phase of a quarrel.

At 10:20 the couple hired a private water taxi to take them to the

Lido, the island that, during the warmer months, housed the city's casino. Once moored at the Excelsior Hotel, the driver directed them to the casino, a five minute walk.

Several employees at the casino remembered them, no earlier than 11:00. One blackjack dealer, in particular, remembered Lisa. She bet heavily, and mostly lost, at his table for nearly an hour. Jodie stood behind her. He appeared rather drunk and impatient with her losing streak.

Another water taxi took them back to Venice around 1:00 A.M. They were dropped off at the pier in front of St. Mark's Square, which was, at that time of night, virtually empty.

The night porter at the Gritti confirmed that they returned to the hotel around 1:30.

The next afternoon, Lisa left the Gritti on a hotel motorboat. One odd thing: The boat took her to the train station two hours before the train was scheduled to depart. A porter helped her with her bags and carried them onto the night train bound for Paris. That was the last time anyone saw her, and it was presumed that she left with the train.

In any case, that same evening, Jodie, now alone, retraced his movements of the night before. He dined at Martini's, just opposite La Fenice. He hired a boat to the casino. He lost over five hundred dollars at the same table where Lisa had played the night before. He returned to Venice around 1:00. The only difference in the pattern was that he did not return to the Gritti. He was never seen again . . . alive.

At 5:35 A.M., *La Squadra Mobile,* the police unit on its routine nightly patrol through the back canals, found Jodie's body, supine on the steps of the back entrance to La Fenice. His wallet was missing but his passport was in his back pocket. There were two small flattened nuggets of hashish pressed inside it. His neck was heavily bruised, and the coroner later verified that the cause of death was strangulation. No choking device, other than the murderer's hands, had been employed. And no fingerprints. Death most likely occurred around 4:00 A.M. There had been a struggle. His wrists and arms were bruised as was his left shin, which had probably been kicked. His groin had been kneed . . . the struggle had been considerable.

There was one curious detail: In Jodie's right hand, tightly clutched, was a piece of metal five inches long: smooth and rounded at one end like a butter knife, only thicker; the other end was rougher and had been sawed off from . . . from what?

Lago paused to light a Marlboro.

*"Ferro,"* he repeated.

Rhea shook her head.

*"Rostro,"* he said.

"What's *rostro?"* Henry asked Rhea.

"I'm . . . not sure," she said. "I'm confused. He said a piece of sawn-off . . . but now he's talking about *ferro,* which means iron or sword. And *rostro* . . . I don't know. It may be Venetian dialect." She turned to Lago: *"Per favore, 'rostro': che cosa significa quello?"*

"Ah!" he said. He pulled out a clean sheet of paper from a drawer, unscrewed the cap to his fountain pen and drew, with precise, assured strokes, an illustration of something that looked, upside down, like a jester's cap. He looked at it for a moment, added a small arrow and handed it to Rhea.

She turned it right side up and looked impressed. "Good draftsmanship. Our chief of police is an artist. Here, Henry, take a look at this. Do you know what it is?"

"Yes, I think so. It's the decoration on the prow of a gondola. That's called a *rostro?"*

"Yes. Lago says that Jodie had one of the prongs of a *rostro* in his hand. Sawed off by a hacksaw or something. What do you suppose Jodie was doing with . . ."

"Ask Lago how he can be sure the metal in Jodie's hand was from a *rostro*?"

"He says that there's a Gondoliers' Cooperative, a union, like a yellow taxicab union made up of around two hundred members. Everybody knows everything about each other's boats. The vandalization, a missing prong, was reported days before Jodie's body was found."

"You mean, Jodie had vandalized a boat?"

"That's the implication. And I must say, it's not unlike him . . . especially if he saw some use for it . . . for one of his paintings."

"Christ. Maybe the gondolier caught him and killed him?"

Lago shook his head.

"Maybe someone's lying." Henry suggested. "Maybe it was a gondolier who killed him and left him at La Fenice. His wallet was missing. Maybe he was flashing around a lot of money. It would be just like him to flaunt money. A gondola. The only way to get to those steps is by boat, right?"

Lago smiled for the first time and shook his head.

"He says a gondola was an impossibility."

"How can he be so sure?"

"Because, at four o'clock A.M., it was high tide."

"So?"

"At high tide, there are only two places in the entire city where a gondola can't pass. One is near La Fenice. At high tide, a gondola would have never been able to pass beneath the little bridges all around La Fenice. It's like a fortress against gondolas. It had to have been a smaller boat that took Jodie to his death."

"Okay." Henry sighed. "So what about Lisa? What was she doing on the island of Murano?"

Rhea conferred with Lago for a moment, then turned back to Henry. "That's the big question," she answered and sighed. "Venice is a maze. It is, nonetheless, an extremely difficult place to just get rid of a body. People live on top of one another, here. Everyone knows everyone else's business. It's like a small town, really . . . only incredibly dense.

"The one thing that they do know, at this point, is that Lisa wasn't killed where her body was found. The murder occurred somewhere else. The autopsy hasn't been performed yet but she's been dead for quite a while . . . at least as long as Jodie's been dead."

"What about my father? Is his alibi solid? And what about Darlington and Matteo and whoever else is part of his entourage?"

"That's been verified. The night concierge swears Verle Rivers, his wife, Darlington, Matteo, the bodyguards—all of them were in the hotel all night."

Henry's eyes narrowed.

He picked up his briefcase and opened it up. He took a long swig of Mylanta. He reached over and helped himself to one of Dr. Lago's Marlboros.

"Henry, you're smoking."

He defiantly inhaled, coughed a little, then inhaled again.

"And how has my father taken all of this?"

"Not well. He's been on heavy sedatives, which may explain why he didn't contact you personally. He hasn't left the hotel since the body was discovered." Rhea's face darkened. "Henry, there's another reason why Dr. Lago had you brought here directly from the airport. There's not going to be any good time to tell you this."

"What?"

"Well, there's a . . . technicality that can't be put off any longer. There's been no positive identification of either body."

"Why not?"

"Italian law requires a member of the family, if possible, to make a positive identification."

"What about my father?"

"I told you. He's been heavily sedated and incapable of—"

"Oh." Henry stubbed out his cigarette. "Oh no, no you don't. What about my new stepmother?"

"No good. She just met your brother and, well, Lago had been told that you were on your way."

"So that's why I was put on a private jet."

"Henry—"

"I'm here as a stand-in for Dad? I've been set up, haven't I? The son-of-a-bitch."

"There's also Lisa's body. . . ."

"Now?"

"What?"

"Does Lago want me to identify the bodies now?"

"Yes."

Henry's heart quickened. "At the morgue?"

Rhea nodded.

He stood up. "All right, let's go."

"You're sure?"

"Do I have a choice?"

"Not really."

"Then why are you asking me if I'm sure? Let's get it over with."

Rhea nodded to Lago and he stood up.

They walked down the stairs in silence and emerged into an early afternoon streaming in sunlight.

"Do we take a boat?"

"No, it's within walking distance. The civic hospital is only about five minutes from here."

"All of us?"

Besides Rhea and Dr. Lago, the three *ispettori* who had interceded them at the airport had joined them. The prospect of marching to his brother's corpse in the midst of a fucking cortege was almost more than he could handle.

From police headquarters, they turned left and, almost immediately, turned left again down a long, narrow *calle*, with unadorned houses towering on both sides. A squat housewife, burdened with two net bags full of groceries, had to stand back in a doorway to let the group pass.

They turned right, then left and crossed two small canals spanned by stone arched bridges . . . up, over and down . . . up, over and down. Another left turn, then a right, and finally a *calle* that opened onto a large *campo* bathed in sunlight. In the center, there was an equestrian statue on a high pedestal. The arrogant determination on the rider's face looked just like Verle Rivers speculating on the stock market or planning a hostile takeover. To the right was a huge Gothic brick church and, adjoining it at a right angle, was the hospital.

Henry stopped in his tracks. "That's a hospital?"

It was indeed a formidable facade, *trompe l'oeil* in effect and laden with sumptuous grotesqueries, lions and men doing weird things to one another—later, Rhea would explain that the large reliefs were of Saint Mark healing and baptizing Saint Annianus.

"It's a very famous building," Rhea defended the structure. "Originally, it was the *Scuola Grande di San Marco,* the Fifteenth Century fraternity of the Venetian artisans. Inside, each group had their own private nightclubs . . . outrageous parties, I've been told."

"Is that right?" Henry said as they neared the stairs leading to the grand portal. He grabbed her arm. "I swear to God, Rhea . . . if you share with me one more historical point of interest, there's going to be an additional murder in Venice."

"Sorry."

"I can't take your happy shit any longer."

"I said I was sorry."

"Or this group! Nothing personal but . . . I mean, do we all have to go in? If it's them inside, I'll say '*Si.*' If it's not, I'll say 'No.' Right?"

Rhea conferred with Dr. Lago. Lago shrugged, motioned to an *ispettore* to accompany Henry inside. Henry handed Rhea his briefcase. She gave a little wave of good-bye and Henry rolled his eyes.

"I speak English," the *ispettore* confided to him, once they were inside.

"Great," Henry said.

It took a moment for his eyes to adjust to the sudden darkness. They were within a vast hall, multipillared, with gargantuan wooden beams high above. At the end of this they turned right which gave onto a large courtyard confined by several stories of open galleries. As they passed, he looked up—the ancient nightclubs?

They went through so many doors—inside and outside again—and made so many turns that Henry began to wonder if this cop weren't taking an unnecessarily long route just to fuck with his head a little. In any case, he never would have found his way out on his own. Finally, they came to a door with a sign that read *OBITORIO: VIETATO L'INGRESSO*

"Morgue: no entrance," the *ispettore* translated. He smiled and opened the door.

They entered a long, broad hallway. The odor of new construction, of freshly poured concrete, filled Henry's nostrils. There was the echoing of hammers and workmen nearby.

"Wait here." The *ispettore* walked down the hall calling for someone. No answer—just a brief silence and then the resumption of hammering. He returned to Henry, shaking his head. "Maybe go to lunch . . . but they knew we are come!"

"We're in Italy now," Henry offered, borrowing Rhea's line.

The *ispettore* muttered something in Italian. "Come," he said, taking Henry by the arm and ushering him into a room marked SALA ANATOMICA

"You wait here. I go find."

Henry didn't need a translator to know where he was. It was the autopsy room, a large square room with eighteen foot ceilings. The floor was of a modern composite marble tile. The smell of new paint and disinfectant filled the room. Along the walls—four on one side, four on the other—were low-lying granite slabs, slightly concave on the top to cradle, he supposed, corpses awaiting autopsies. In the center of the room was an aluminum worktable, nine feet long, with a drain in the center (right about where a dead man's heart would be); there was a sink at one end with faucet and hose and another drain. There were four bare light bulbs suspended above the gruesome contraption.

Trancelike, he backed away from it and walked over to the right corner: here was another worktable with a human brain in a heavy glass canister and a large shallow bowl of talc. Above this hung rubber gloves, and above these were high windows that rose to the ceiling.

He massaged the bridge of his nose. The stillness of the room made him acutely aware of how tired he was . . . or hypnotized from all the changes he had been put through in the last few hours.

*Hank?*

He ignored the voice. Against the far wall, there were large green plastic garbage cans, neatly lined up in a row. Henry walked over and lifted one of the lids. Some sort of human organ was floating in formaldehyde. He dropped the lid and walked to the other side of the room. On this wall was an enormous chart. After he studied it for a moment, he realized it was calibrated so that doctors could write down the weights of human organs.

Henry walked over to the granite slab upon which his brother reclined—his legs crossed, his hands comfortably behind his head.

*It's rather nice here, don't you think? The hard coolness of the stone . . . soothing . . . good for the back . . . gazing up at these high windows and thinking of absolutely nothing. You ought to try it, Henry. Come on. Lie down.*

"No thanks. I might never get up again. Is that why you're here? To take me with you?"

*What makes you think I want you with me?*

"And where's Lisa? Why can't I see her?"

*What's the matter? Scared? Afraid what the cop might think if he walked in and saw you supine? I double-dog dare you.*

"Did Dad have you two killed? Just tell me that. Is he behind all this?"

"Mister, you okay?" asked the *ispettore,* now standing in the doorway.

Henry spun around and faked a yawn. "Sure, I'm fine. I was just reading aloud the chart over there."

"Yes?"

"Did you find the bodies?"

"Everything new at morgue," said the *ispettore.* (Was he apologizing or bragging?) "Everything tipsy-topsy. Come. I find fridges. We look."

Henry was led down several corridors where workmen were covering the new walls with cream-colored tiles.

At the end of one hall were three aluminum refrigerators the size of small darkrooms.

The *ispettore* rubbed his hands together, then opened the door to the first one. He flipped a switch that turned on an inside light. It was a double-decker body cooler. Empty. At the back, twin fans whirled in silence. The *ispettore* closed the door.

They moved over to the second cooler. The *ispettore* flipped the switch: inside was a bright yellow corpse, it's head pointing toward Henry. The shelf pulled out easily for a better look.

Henry grabbed hold of the *ispettore's* arm and gasped.

"Your brother?"

"No, no, no," Henry said, swallowing hard, "but . . . why is he yellow?"

The *ispettore* mimed drinking out of a bottle: "Liver all gone," he said.

Henry nodded.

They moved to the final cooler. The *ispettore* flipped the switch and opened the door. This time there were two corpses: the one on top was a fat woman, the one on the bottom was a man. The *ispettore* slid out the bottom corpse.

The body was gray. The face. It was odd: death made Jodie look so much like his mother. . . .

Henry bent over the ashen face.

"No wisecracks, Jodie?"

He kissed the forehead. It was ice-cold on his lips.

"Good-bye, Jodie."

He straightened up and turned toward the *ispettore*. He cleared his voice.

"*Sì,*" he said.

Somewhere, in the empty concrete shell of the building, a table saw ripped through lumber. The blade's high-pitched whine made Henry shudder.

Around the corner came two men in white, pushing a long metal table on canisters. There was a body on the table, covered with a sheet.

The *ispettore* rushed toward it. He spoke with the orderlies briefly, then motioned for Henry to approach. They pulled back the sheet. Her face was swollen, purple. He looked away almost immediately. He felt nothing but revulsion.

"*Sì,*" he said, backing away. "I would like to leave now."

The saw wailed through the corridors.

Henry was dry-eyed.

# 6

The night before, while Rhea and Henry were flying to Venice, John Tennyson had busied himself with a different mission.

The view from Ornella Marsh Saltzman's seven-room apartment was spectacular at twilight. It looked down over the canopy of the inner city forest. Beyond this, Central Park West rose like an edificial eclipse perforated with thousands of lighted windows. In the darkening cityscape, John Tennyson could just make out the dome of the Hayden Planetarium.

Given what Rhea had told Tennyson about Ornella, he wasn't surprised by the grandeur of the view—the Fifth Avenue address, the condescending doorman, the paneled elevator which opened directly into Ornella's neo-Adams foyer, the attractive maid waiting to meet him who ushered him into the living room and brought him a drink while Mrs. Saltzman concluded a meeting in the library—all of these niceties prepared him for the inevitable vista. But he was fairly amazed that Ornella Saltzman would be so eager to share the vista with him. Earlier in the day, when he had phoned her, she had insisted on the earliest possible interview: that very day, and at her place.

She didn't keep him waiting long. Her approach was cordial but businesslike, and she came straight to the point.

"My husband won't be back until tomorrow. That gives me very little time to be open with you. I'm also running late for a dinner engagement. I hope that—whatever embarrassing questions you might put to me—you would do so at once. And I have some other information that might be of help. I *want* to be helpful, Mr. Tennyson, but not in an official capacity. The only reason I'm willing to talk to you is because you are Rhea Buerklin's friend. She assures me that you can be discreet."

"As long as discretion doesn't compromise the truth," Tennyson clarified.

"That's reasonable enough," she said. "And I assume that your only role in this case is as a friend of Rhea's."

"Yes."

"Good. By the way," she added with a smile, "this is not the first time you and I have met. I was at Al Kheel's opening, the week after Rhea's partner was killed."

"I'm sorry, I don't remember."

"No reason why you should. You had your hands full with a different slew of suspects. I was of no interest to you then."

"How long had you known Jodie?"

"If you mean in the biblical sense, about a year, off and on. Nothing terribly intense. Our relationship was strictly recreational. I've been a patron of his work about twice that long. You may smoke if you wish."

"Thank you."

Tennyson extracted a pack of Marlboros. To his surprise, she offered to light his cigarette for him. He leaned forward. Was Ornella flirting with him? He couldn't be sure. Her fastidiously tailored dress was anything but aggressive and her full-bodied figure bordered on the matronly. Tennyson guessed her age to be around fifty. She was handsome but certainly not the sort of woman he would have imagined Jodie to be involved with. As if reading his mind, Ornella said:

"Shall we get the sex part out of the way? Jodie's infatuation with me was of the gigolo variety. I bought his work, introduced him to people who also bought his work and, in exchange, he favored me with his attentions. I never had any illusions as to what he felt for me.

I was a stepping stone of sorts. And why not? He was ambitious enough to appreciate my ability to chair major dinners. But we did have our moments of genuine fun. I shall miss him."

"You weren't in love?" Tennyson asked.

"That wouldn't have been farsighted of me."

"You say that you're interested in discretion," Tennyson commented. "Your husband doesn't know."

"That's correct. I should like to keep it that way."

"Then . . . why Jodie Rivers?"

"What?"

"You say you want discretion. I was around Jodie enough to know he could be very vocal about his lady friends."

"Did he ever speak of me?"

"No, but . . . I'm puzzled why you would choose to get involved with a man like Jodie. Weren't you taking a risk?"

"It's true," Ornella answered and laughed. "Jodie could be positively incendiary with gossip and, at the best of times, his behavior was inappropriate. But Jodie wasn't stupid. He had a good thing going with me. It was to his advantage to hold his tongue. I took certain precautions. I made sure our public meetings were confined to art-oriented events . . . events in which his professional ego became promotable. At those times, he would all but forget about me, which was just the way I wanted it. Almost without exception, our . . . other meetings were conducted on Martha's Vineyard. The only person—other than Jodie—who could have exposed our liaison was Rhea Buerklin. And you know as well as I that she's too busy, too content with her own life, to involve herself with gossip."

"But why Jodie?" Tennyson pressed. "Was the attraction his art?"

"Blue chip investment, his art." Ornella shook her head. "The attraction was physical. I've never seen such beautiful hands on a man. When they took note of you, it was with the urgency of a blind man. He was, you know: a blind man in everything but his work."

"Your trips to Martha's Vineyard: your husband never caught wind of them?"

"On the contrary. He was aware of every single one of them. Jodie was hired by my husband to paint a fresco in our dining room up there. Mr. Saltzman is so often away. It was only natural that I would be interested in accompanying Jodie . . . to supervise his progress. And when the dining room was completed, he began work on my powder room. That's what he was painting when, a few weeks ago, he stole the Redon."

"You're sure it was Jodie?"

"Absolutely. Jodie was always removing it from the wall so that he could admire it in better light. He was entranced by Redon . . . so soft . . . everything Jodie's work wasn't. And then there was the fact that—"

"Excuse me," Tennyson interrupted. "I want to get something clear. Why would he steal it . . . if it would be so obvious that he was the thief?"

Ornella put her hands in her lap. "He no longer gave a damn."

"And he knew that you weren't in a position to turn him in," Tennyson suggested.

"It would have been more trouble than it was worth. I've been through several divorces, Mr. Tennyson, and always to my advantage. Knowing the legal system is a woman's best armor. The legal system boils down to a matter of timing. I know when to hold on, when to let go. This was a time for the latter."

"Because you didn't want your husband to find out. How would he have reacted—your husband—had he found out about you and Jodie?"

Ornella laughed. "He wouldn't kill Jodie, if that's what you mean! In any case, my husband has been in London these last two weeks. I'm afraid he has a watertight alibi."

"I see. Jodie went on a binge of stealing. You say that he no longer gave a damn. Do you know of any reason why he would undergo this change?"

"I've been thinking about this . . . ever since Rhea phoned me with the news. Yes. I think I can pinpoint the change in Jodie . . . that's why I so wanted to speak to you today. Something I haven't told anyone . . . it has to do with his childhood."

"I'm listening."

"As you probably know, Jodie grew up in Tulsa, son of a prosperous oil man who was mostly absent from the household. His mother died when he was barely a teenager. His brother was five years older . . . they were not close. Not much of a family life, if you see what I mean.

"There was, however, a domestic retainer, with whom Jodie felt quite close. A Cherokee Indian, actually. A man by the name of Jimmie Cloudfoot or Cloudface or something to do with clouds. . . . I can't remember. In any case, this Indian, now an old man, died about two months ago. His niece contacted Jodie with the news that Jimmie had bequeathed him two large cardboard boxes filled with Jodie's youthful drawings . . . drawings which he had completely forgotten about, which he had discarded as a kid and which his mother had faithfully saved. When she died, Jimmie kept them.

"I know about all of this because Jodie solicited me for the airline ticket. He seemed genuinely upset about the old man's death. He was determined to attend the funeral and pick up, personally, the drawings."

"And you purchased the ticket for him."

"Yes."

"Did you see the drawings when he returned?"

"Only one. I wanted to see all of them but Jodie insisted that the time wasn't right." Ornella stood up, walked over to a low-lying coffee table at the far end of the room and returned with a large manila envelope. "Here," she said, "I had the original photocopied so that you could take this with you. There's no reason for you to open it now. You'll find it illuminating but it will require a bit of studying on your part and, as I indicated, I'm rather pressed for time this evening. Let me just say that, although it is a marvelous rendering for a ten-year-old, it is nevertheless a child's rendering. It's interest is primarily historic, not aesthetic."

Tennyson put the envelope to the side. "Why do you attach such importance to it?" he asked.

"I don't. Not the drawing, per se. But stapled to the back is a handwritten short story, penned by Jodie's mother—a story inspired by Jodie's drawing. According to Jodie, there were twenty-seven of these little stories attached to drawings, varying in length, from six to ten pages each. Jodie was enraptured by the stories. More than enraptured, really. Possessed, I'd say."

"And what's the story about?"

"Ah," Ornella hesitated, then gave a little laugh. "It's not easy to summarize. Not heavy on plot. It's an odd hybrid of autobiography and fantasy with . . . rather demented moralistic overtones. You'll see for yourself when you read it. The point is this: He had enormous plans for his mother's stories. As soon as he got his upcoming show with Rhea out of the way, Jodie planned to create a huge series of collages. Her stories were to be pasted together to form a background over which he would superimpose his own work. 'A seething collaboration,' was how he characterized the project to me."

For a moment, Ornella's gaze became far away, focused somewhere above the New York skyline. She sighed and turned back toward Tennyson.

"I've see many incarnations of Jodie Rivers. He was always something of a chameleon. But his last one, after he returned from Oklahoma, was by far the most intense, the darkest. The stories not only fanned his imagination but fanned his rage as well. Did Rhea tell you he plucked out his eyelashes?"

"Yes. She attributed it to self-promotion."

"Partly. Everything he did was self-promoting. But the *idea* came from the story I just gave you. He told me he wanted 'to see, without obstruction, how vile human nature could become.' Jodie's exact words." She looked Tennyson straight in the eye. "He was talking about how vile *his* nature could become. He was preparing himself— and perhaps me—for multiple betrayals. He was about to go out of his way to hurt the people closest to him and he knew it. That's what the thefts were all about—to cut people off. He placed no importance on material possessions."

"Perhaps not," Tennyson said with a shrug. "Nevertheless, the items he chose to steal were of tremendous monetary value . . . at least," he hastened to add, "from where I'm sitting, they were valuable. And, I think, from where Jodie was sitting as well. Rhea is convinced he was cut off by his father."

"Yes, he was."

"Maybe he needed the money. A drug debt, let's say . . . or a gambling debt."

Ornella shook her head. "Jodie never gambled on anything but his own well-being. And he was not heavily into drugs. He smoked marijuana. Period. He was always putting down other artists who had squandered their talents on narcotics. Besides, if and when he needed money, he could always come to me. I'd already advanced him ten thousand dollars for the collage project. Indeed, that's the only reason why I was allowed to see this particular story . . . so that I could be excited, baited by the project."

Tennyson looked out through the French doors. It was quite dark now.

"Why didn't Rhea mention them?" he mumbled.

"I beg your pardon?"

"The drawings and his mother's short stories. Why didn't Rhea mention them to me? It doesn't make sense that she wouldn't have suspected their influence over him."

Ornella sighed. "Here comes the difficult part. Rhea didn't suspect because she didn't know of their existence. She didn't know of their existence because Jodie didn't want her to know. In fact, he made me promise that I wouldn't tell her about the drawings, the stories or his trip to Tulsa."

"But why? Rhea represented his work. I would have thought that she would have been the first person to be told."

Ornella shifted uncomfortably in her chair: "I should have told her, I know. I don't feel good about keeping this from her. The truth is . . . after his upcoming show, Jodie was planning to leave Rhea's gallery."

"Why?"

"I think . . . there is not a good reason. It was part of his new incarnation: arbitrary amputations with the past. I think he was dead set on hurting himself in any way he could. In retrospect, I'm certain that Jodie had become a seriously ill man."

"What were you going to do, Mrs. Saltzman? Were you going to become his representative, behind Rhea's back? Were you going to mount the show for him?"

"Goodness, no. But I did like the idea of becoming his sole patron . . . at least for a while. Naturally, by supporting the project, I would have first choice of any of the pieces."

Tennyson changed the subject: "Did he mention to you that his father was in Italy?"

"No."

"Do you know Verle Rivers?"

"Everyone knows of him. I've never met him. My husband and he have mutual business associates. By all accounts, he's a rich vulgarian. A very rich one. The type the Knickerbocker Club used to keep out but doesn't anymore."

"Did Jodie ever mention his father's will?"

"I brought it up once. I asked him point blank, 'What will you get when your father dies?' He said: nothing, as far as he knew. Jodie could have been lying about that. Jodie lied whenever he got a chance. Still, I got the impression that he had ambivalent feelings about an inheritance."

"How do you mean?"

"Living hand-to-mouth suited Jodie. It kept his art hungry looking . . . on the edge. It helped to give his work focus. It kept his hatred of money vitally alive. He once told me, in an entirely different context that, should he ever come into money, he would quit painting."

"Why?"

"He said that money leaves a stronger impression than talent. He said that being a rich painter was a contradiction in terms. You can own the paint factory, he said, and you can own the act of painting, but you can't own both at the same time."

"What about Jodie's brother, Henry Rivers? Did you ever meet him?"

"No. They were barely on speaking terms. Jodie found him rather pathetic, I think."

"What about Lisa Morris? Did you know her or know about her?"

"No. But it doesn't surprise me. Sexually, Jodie was hyperactive. A hobosexual, if you see what I mean. And if this Lisa is one of John's girls, I'm sure she's ravishing."

"Who's John?"

"John Casablancas. The owner of Elite modeling agency."

"We found out this morning that Lisa went to Italy with Jodie. She left Venice, the day he was killed. As of this morning, they still hadn't found her."

Ornella shrugged. "That is nothing to me . . . unless she is somehow responsible for his death . . . which I doubt. She couldn't have been an important enough fixture in his life. I'm convinced that, with the exception of his mother, women were supremely peripheral."

"And that didn't bother you?"

"Bother?" Ornella answered his question with questions: "Why should I complain? Friends are easy to come by, aren't they? I didn't need Jodie as a friend, did I?"

"I've never found friends that easy to come by."

"No? Then I can only assume that you and I have traveled remarkably different paths." A frown came over Ornella's brow. "I suppose you'll be talking to Rhea."

"Yes."

"You'll tell her about the secret I was keeping from her . . . about Jodie planning to leave her gallery?"

"It might be important."

"It puts me in a rather bad light. . . . We've been friends for such a long time. . . . I should have been more forthcoming with her."

"Frankly, I doubt that she would be too surprised."

"Yes." Ornella looked relieved. "She's so sensible, isn't she? That's why Rhea never spends much time trying to solidify her position in society. New York has become such a free-for-all. Her expectations are nonexistent. Of course, indifference is easy if you've always had pots and pots of old, old money."

Ornella's maid entered the doorway.

"Pardon me, Mrs. Saltzman, but Mr. Fulton has returned your call. Would you like to take it in here?"

"Oh, dear. Yes, thank you, Susan." Ornella looked at her watch and nodded. "I'm afraid I'll have to . . ." She stood up and extended her hand. "I can't thank you enough for coming tonight and I hope that I've helped in some way. Again I must warn you: I'm not so sure how willing I will be to collaborate from this point on. As I said, my husband returns tomorrow and—"

"I understand." Tennyson stood up. "I'll have Rhea contact you if I think of anything else."

"That would be very kind of you."

"There is one more thing. Do you have any idea where Jodie kept the other drawings and stories?"

"I assume he kept them in his loft, in TriBeCa."

"You wouldn't happen to have a key."

"No, I'm afraid not. Oh! I was going to tell you something about the story but you interrupted me: Jodie's mother wrote of a lavender rose."

"Lavender rose?"

"The Redon pastel that Jodie stole . . . it's a still life of a vase of flowers. Dispersed within the arrangement are three lavender flowers. Any fool can see that they are peonies but Jodie insisted that they were lavender roses. It may be a minor detail, but I want you to understand how everything that Jodie experienced was beginning to filter through his mother's stories. Well . . . you'll see for yourself. Now, if you will excuse me . . . I really must take that call. Susan will show you out. Good-bye and thank you again."

As he was leaving, Tennyson heard Ornella pick up the phone and say:

"Bob, the most dreadful thing has happened. You remember Jodie Rivers, don't you? It seems he's been murdered. Yes, in Venice. Isn't it a pity? And what's worse, my powder room is only half-finished. What can I do with a half-finished powder room?"

# 7

It was early afternoon by the time Rhea and Henry left the morgue. A police boat transported them to the Gritti Palace. Henry, silent and oblivious to his surroundings, went immediately to his room for a much needed nap.

Rhea found her way to the back of the hotel where overseas calls could be placed in the privacy of a paneled booth. It was 8:00 A.M. in New York. Tennyson would probably still be at his apartment.

"Good, I caught you. Morning, John. Got a bulletin flash: Lisa Morris's body was discovered this morning . . . on the island of Murano. Two bullet wounds. . . ."

She proceeded to relate what she had learned through Dr. Lago, including the fact that Interpol had recovered Lisa's drug-filled suitcase from a Paris train station.

"And there are eye witnesses," Tennyson asked, "that swear that she got on the train?"

"Yes. But no one has come forward about seeing her getting off the train."

"How did Henry react, when he found out about Lisa's murder?"

"He threw up all over the chief of police's desk. Pretty ingenious way to cover up his guilt, don't you think?"

"And what do the police think?"

"They're proceeding as if these were drug-related murders. Maybe they're right. Henry, on the other hand, keeps insinuating that his father has something to do with the murders."

"Why?"

"Who knows? The poor guy's unhinged. I got him drunk on the flight over here and I guess I shouldn't have. He's taking codeine for his stomach ulcers and . . . well, his behavior is becoming more and more erratic. Wide mood swings. As for his accusation: on every level, he distrusts his father. Big ongoing grudge. That's about as clearly as I can explain it at this point."

"What's the father like?"

"Haven't met him yet. I just checked in a minute ago. There was a note waiting for me at the concierge's desk. I was supposed to ring up Verle the minute I got here but I wanted to catch you before you left for work. Verle may be in worse shape than Henry. According to Dr. Lago, he's been heavily sedated ever since he was told of Jodie's death. He's taking it pretty hard, I guess . . . which Henry doesn't buy for a second."

"Sounds like you've got your hands full. Where's here?"

"What?"

"Where are you staying?"

"Oh . . . we're all being put up at the Gritti Palace."

"Palace? I thought you said you were in a hotel."

"It used to be a palace. One of the doges, Andre Gritti, owned it. But that was centuries ago. Nowadays, it's part of the Ciga chain, owned by the Aga Khan actually."

"You don't say. You sound familiar with the place."

"It's where my father always stayed . . . and don't get ironic on me, John. There's only two places one stays in Venice. The Gritti or the Danieli. It's not that much of a coincidence."

"I suppose your palace has a fax?"

"Why?"

Tennyson gave a quick recount of Jodie's youthful drawing and the accompanying story written by his mother. "Ornella seems to think the story is crucial in understanding Jodie's movements these last few months."

"You don't sound convinced."

"I don't discount it. To tell you the truth, I've read the goddamn thing a dozen times now," he said. "I had to use a dictionary and I'm still not sure what it's about . . . though it does mention a lavender rose which, Ornella insists, refers to her Redon pastel. There's also something mentioned that might relate to you."

"What?"

"No . . . I think I'll let you read it for yourself. It's like talking about *not* believing in astrology. If you talk about it, even in the negative sense, it somehow implies that you place importance in it. I might be more convinced if I could read the other stories. Jodie told Ornella that there were nearly thirty of them. Apparently, Jodie's plan was to create a whole new series of paintings based on and incorporating her stories. And there's one more thing. . . ."

Tennyson cleared his throat, then explained how Jodie was planning to leave Rhea's gallery.

Rhea took in this news before saying: "Figures. I wonder how long Ornella had been sitting on this little tidbit! She must have been having a field day." Rhea sighed. "So how did you and Ornella get along? Did she try to get into your pants or did she present you with her famous cut-and-dried routine?"

"I don't know. We got along all right. She was condescending but candid and to the point. I can see how someone might be attracted to her."

"Oh, you can, can you?"

"She was cold, though. Dealt with Jodie's death as if they were barely acquainted. No sentiment at all. You may laugh but . . . I think she wanted to impress me with her practicality."

Rhea did laugh. "She was making a pass. No slut like a Fifth Avenue slut. Practicality! That was her way of signaling that she's available without any strings attached. I'm surprised you didn't catch on."

"Maybe I did." Tennyson changed the subject: "So what else have you learned?"

"I've learned that I'm getting too old to run around without sleep. I'm exhausted. And Dr. Lago has invited me to dinner tonight."

"Great." Tennyson checked himself. "That's fast work."

"Italians don't waste time . . . not with women."

"I wasn't talking about Italians," Tennyson grumbled. "I was talking about you."

"While Henry was identifying the bodies, Dr. Lago and I waited for him outside the hospital. It was a relief to be around an adult for a change. After spending the last twenty-four hours with Henry, I was beginning to feel like a nursemaid. Besides, I'm the only one in the Rivers entourage who speaks decent Italian. I've already earned my keep as a translator and no one appreciates it more than Lago. He seems quite bright. I'm sure you would like him."

"I already hate him. Where's he taking you, to his place?"

"No. To the restaurant where Jodie dined the last two nights of his life. It's on a campo—a little square—where there's also a church and, catty-corner to the restaurant, La Fenice, the opera house where Jodie's body was found."

"Romantic."

"Lago is a looker. A race car nut. He wears the sexiest cuff links. Lapis lazuli wafers in frames of black wire that match his eyes—"

"Enough already! Jesus."

"You should be relieved that Lago likes me. Yesterday, you griped that I was putting myself in danger by coming over here. Well, now I have the local law in my corner. What's wrong with that?"

"Nothing . . . so long as the local law is clean."

"Clean? Now the Venetian police are suspects?"

"You've never heard of dirty cops, Rhea? Listen, I've got to go. Give me the number of the hotel fax and I'll get Lipski to send this stuff to you. He's at the precinct. There's a copy in my desk that he can fax you right away. . . ."

Rhea didn't wait long at the cashier's office. As Tennyson promised, the documents came through almost immediately. Rather than go up to her room quite yet, Rhea decided to study the papers on the open terrace of the Gritti. If she took a nap now, she would never get up. Better to take in the view of the Grand Canal, armed with an espresso . . . and a glass of white wine of course.

As she passed by the busy concierge's desk, she almost ran into Wallace Darlington.

"Did you talk to Mr. Rivers?" he asked.

"If you mean Verle, no. Not yet. To tell you the truth, Wallace, I'm a little talked out. I was going to relax a bit, on the terrace, before. . . ."

"I understand, Ms. Buerklin. I'm on my way to his rooms right now. Perhaps I might tell him that he could join you?"

"You mean . . . he would want to come down here? That's fine with me only . . . I was told that he had sort of isolated himself since Jodie's death and that—"

"I'm sure he'll be down," Wallace said with a knowing smile. He gave a crisp little nod and then, turning left, headed for the elevator.

Rhea turned right, walked through the small empty bar, opened a French door and proceeded out onto the deep veranda.

The open expanse was protected from the mid-afternoon sun by enormous striped awnings—a glamorous tent for the cognoscenti. There were well-dressed people, mostly elderly European couples, seated at the small tables covered in peach linen. Rhea chose a table farthest from the water. A young man took her order almost immediately.

She crossed her legs, rubbed her calves and gave a tremendous sigh of relief. A briny breeze wafted its way across the terrace.

How she loved this view! Boats of all descriptions—with a black predominance of gondolas—churned through the Grand Canal and left the choppy surface spangled by the sun's reflection. Across the way was Peggy Guggenheim's white palazzo and, down to the left, jutting out onto the lagoon, rose the multiple domes of the Santa Maria della Salute, erected in celebration of the end of the plague.

That's what it was like to seat oneself on the terrace of the Gritti Palace: to survive the end of a plague. And though she would never tell this to anyone, it had always been in the back of her mind to retire here, to spend her twilight years—if her money and liver held out— guzzling booze at this very table.

Her order came: one espresso, one white wine and one cucumber sandwich. She took a bite . . . yes! . . . How that simple flavor came back to her! Why could she never make them like this at home? Mingling with the taste were memories of Papa. For a moment, she could almost believe that her father had momentarily darted into the bar to fetch his brand of cigarettes, "Prince," a Danish brand that the bartender always kept available for him. . . .

She took a sip of coffee, then wine. Thus fortified, she turned her attention to the Gritti folder which contained the papers that Tennyson had faxed her. Inside the folder was a line drawing in pencil, executed on school notebook paper with three holes spaced evenly down the left-hand margin.

Jodie's drawing was of an exterior scene. On the top of a broad grassy knoll stood a large brick, many-gabled, three-story house. Dominating the foreground was a grand piano. Instead of having legs, the piano was held up by three identical Indians in feathered head-dresses and loin cloths. A woman stood at the keyboard, staring directly at the viewer. In the cloudless sky, a squadron of World War II aircraft dropped bombs over the house. What impressed her most was that, although the rendering was childlike and clumsily cluttered, the brash finesse of Jodie's adult style was already evident.

She took another sip of coffee.

She put the drawing to the side and stared at the handwritten story. The calligraphy was erratic: at times perfectly erect—at other times swinging wildly to the left, then wildly to the right—as if the words had been periodically assailed by violent gusts of wind.

She finished her wine, ordered another and read the story:

*MURDER HIM*
or
*BIRTH IS A CONTRACTUAL AGREEMENT*
by
Lorna Rivers

Lorna Rivers, authoress of "The Punctilious Glance," "Petals and Hatchets," "The Hapless Hapax Legomenon," and other forgotten stories, reclined upon a shaggy blanket of wild labiates. She thought violent thoughts under the sun. Heliotropic stars twinkled and burned on the inside of her closed eyelids. Lorna liked herself at that moment: Vengeance on a freshly bruised bed of mint.

In the distance, she heard the voices of her two sons. She uprighted herself and looked up to the crest of the lawn spilling down from the house. Though she couldn't hear what they were saying, she envied the way they took command of the descent in lean, youthful strides. Elegant in their casual chatter. The younger was blond. The older, swept back with dark brown hair.

"An arboreal afternoon, Mother," they said in unison. Sunlight ricocheted off their irreproachable teeth.

"So," Henry said, "is this what one calls a negotiation?"

"Talk to us of diseases and desires, Mother," Jodie said.

"Very well, then," she said. Her voice was throaty but well-enunciated. "I want you to kill your father."

The boys glanced at one another. Then they smiled at her, waiting. Beautiful but stupid, she thought. She got to her knees. She caught the gleam in their eyes. She stretched out her sagging arms and pulled them to her ample breasts. The muscles in their necks smelled of honey and lead. She felt very powerful at that moment. If she wanted to, she could snap off their arms. Gnaw on them like chicken legs.

"How?" Jodie asked. "How do you kill a father?"

"Oh, never mind how," she answered. "Our combined desire would be enough. We don't actually have to put a hole in him. Just agreeing upon the act would be delicious enough."

But Henry wouldn't agree to the plan.

Arranged in a collapsed circle of heavy breathing, they watched the sun slide across a glass sky until herbaceous shadows grew among the apple trees.

They dusted off their knees and trudged up the hill for supper.

A toast:

"To the forever absent father."

The tinkle of pellucid crystal. Teeth clenched around warm mouthfuls of wine. Lips stretching into smooth wet smiles. On the plates before them, thick juicy slices of circumlocution. For the boys there were also side dishes of raspberries, chestnuts, oranges yellow as butter, and alfalfa sprouts with the bitter nutty aftertaste of sperm. Lorna Rivers munched on her knife.

"But what if," Henry cautioned, "your fantasy took on it's own existence?"

"There is a certain species of rose indigenous to hyperborean regions. Its color is lavender. Look closely. That flower grows, like a smile, behind my ear. When such roses bloom, you don't ask questions. You simply pluck them."

"But this is your fantasy, not ours," Henry objected.

"All the more reason to steal it," Jodie said with a grin.

Lorna turned to her younger child: "I knew you would understand," she said. "You drew this fantasy long before I wrote it."

She snapped her finger and suddenly, magically, they were transported back to the garden (or "backyard," as Verle called it). It was daytime again. All three were gathered around a solid glass grand piano. The legs of the piano were ice sculptures of Jimmie Cloudfoot.

The boys applauded.

She bowed slightly, then lifted her fingers. Her fingernails were made of ivory. An arrogant brooch was pinned through her lips so that she could not smile.

Her ivory nails reached out for the ivory keyboard. She played a contrapuntal tune by Couperin. World War II bombers eclipsed the sun and the entire garden began to swirl around them in stained glass sensuality. She threw back her head, lips jammed together by the diamond brooch. She watched the garden travel in a brocade of upside down textural whirls. She felt her clothes melt away from her. Other glass pianos began to appear: two three four five—eight ten twelve—the trundling garden became filled with pianos plucking themselves. The volume spiraled and completely overpowered the screaming bombers above.

The brooch unfastened itself and flew into the hands of Jodie. He looked up at the sky. "Father's back," he said. "Shall we try to catch the bombs or avoid them?"

"The bombs are of no importance!" she yelled over the din of music. "It's the hovering of the aircraft that's lethal! Don't you see, my youngest? (Henry will never understand, poor fool.) You're safe as long as you stick to a first-person narrative. It's that third-person version, that outbred real life nonsense of your father's, that must be daily diminished, frustrated, nullified and ultimately conquered. Shut him out and stick to your dreams, my darling! Suck on your paintbrush. Go for real sustenance. Take his life and make it your own!"

The vibrations of the music shook the ground with stunning tremolos. Like the pianos, her body became translucent. She was strung up on a musical staff racing toward the planes: the five parallel lines cut into her like taut wire. The black notes riddled her body and clung to her wounds like shrapnel.

As she gained altitude, Lorna Rivers gazed down upon her hideous home that gave itself plenty of room, smack-dab in the center of a hideous would-be city.

She was ecstatic with her own invisibility.

# 8

What to make of Lorna's story?

A legacy of madness? Had Lorna really had such a lingering influence over her younger son? Had her story (or stories) induced his irrational behavior? *When such roses bloom, you don't ask questions. You simply pluck them.* Had a lavender rose cued the theft of Ornella's Redon? Had a brooch impaled through Lorna's lips prompted Jodie to steal Rhea's jewelry?

Rhea tried to think back. . . .

In the several years she had known Jodie, he had mentioned his mother only once: a cold, statistical reference that she had died when he was ten, giving Rhea no indication that Lorna hung over him like an unappeased spirit—a vengeance never laid to rest.

What people didn't talk about . . . what people didn't know *how* to talk about . . .

Rhea's mother had died while giving birth to her. Had she ever mentioned her mother to Jodie? Had Rhea ever confessed to him that much of her life had been colored by her mother's death? Of course not.

The power of communication was overrated or, at least, underdeveloped—in the end, it hardly mattered which—the ear always tricked, colored, and garbled information. And the tongue had a way of reducing life-changing events to encapsulated, fraudulent-sounding traps of self-pity. The vacuum remained. Silence, in spite of life's chit-chat, predominated.

A water taxi idled up to the moorings of the Gritti Palace terrace. A British movie idol and his entourage disembarked while a hotel employee, dressed in dust-emerald livery, held the boat steady. The Room Division Manager appeared from nowhere and welcomed him. The actor's luggage (expensive but overly new, Rhea thought), accumulated behind him. He surveyed the terrace to make sure all eyes were on him, then advanced to the interior of the hotel.

Did people ever really know when they were and weren't acting? Were people equipped to make that distinction? Had Jodie been mad or had he just wanted to appear that way for his onlookers' benefit?

And, either way, who had been Jodie's *final* audience?

A hundred annoying thoughts crowded around her, vying for her attention. As if to stave them off, Rhea ordered a bottle of mineral water and another cucumber sandwich, this time more for sustenance than culinary gratification.

She reread Lorna Rivers's story.

Like the British actor's baggage, the circumstances congregating around Jodie's murder seemed excessive—quite literally, an overkill.

Lisa's murder, for instance, and her suitcase full of dope . . . where did that fit in? Who or what had changed Lisa's mind—why had she deboarded the train bound for Paris? Why, at the time of his death, had Jodie been clutching the prong of a gondola *rostro*? And if Lisa and Jodie were involved with a smuggling operation, why were they dispatched separately—he, on the steps of La Fenice and she, on the island of Murano? Why, if the murders were connected, were the victims killed by different methods?

Or should Rhea simply take this excess baggage and shove it into the water? The hard evidence pointed toward drugs. Jodie and Lisa— ever the opportunists—were moving drugs for someone. They tried to double-cross that someone. That someone had them taken out. Simple. Obvious. So why couldn't she follow this logical line of pursuit?

A shadow fell across Rhea's table and she looked up. An older man of daunting stature stared down at her.

"Howdy, Rhea," he said, offering his hand. "I'm Verle." He tucked his chin so that his brow became prominent. His thick white hair—almost maestro length—made him resemble an overgrown Beethoven in a business suit—a suit, she noted, of a cut and cloth less expensive than Wallace Darlington's. Was he suppressing a smile? It was impossible to tell. His eyes were concealed by opaque sunglasses with thick black rims.

She stood up and shook his hand. His firm grip bordered on the exhibitionistic. "Hello, Mr. Rivers—"

"Verle. Call me Verle." His voice was deep and you could have cut his corn-pone accent with a butter knife.

"Please, Verle," she said, "Won't you sit down?"

"Thanks." He complied by taking the seat next to her rather than the chair opposite. "Is someone with you?" he asked, gesturing toward the wineglass, the plate and the espresso cup that populated the table.

"No," she answered, sitting down and lowering the folder of faxed material to the other side of her chair. "This has been my first chance to fuel up since I arrived. Would you like something to drink?"

"Whatever you're havin'."

The waiter cleared the table and brought them a carafe of cool white wine.

"Tasty stuff," he said, smacking his lips.

"I'm sorry . . . terribly sorry about Jodie," she said.

"Yeah. Well, we're all sorry." Verle's brow furrowed. "It was disgraceful to die like that, wasn't it."

Disgraceful? Rhea didn't know how to reply. Was it sorrow or disgust that elicited such a comment? She tried to deflect the subject.

"What are the funeral arrangements?"

"The body's gonna be cremated tomorrow. After that, I don't know what to do . . . what Jodie would have wanted . . . where he wanted to be . . . I don't know. Maybe you got some idea?"

"Henry suggested he might like being buried here."

"Never thought of that. Well . . . when you're dead, you're dead. Guess it don't make much difference where you're dumped. Damned sight easier than shippin' him back to the States. Does that sound calloused?"

"Well, it doesn't sound particularly sentimental."

"Just 'cause I'm in my seventies, people think I want to live among an old man's memories. They're wrong. Never have, never will. As far as I'm concerned, my whole life is ahead of me."

"Your new wife . . ." Rhea suggested.

"That's right. My new wife. And, anyway, I never had much use for graveyard ceremonies . . . that sort of stuff." He took another sip of wine, then asked: "Did you love Jodie?"

"L-love?" Rhea sputtered, completely caught off guard. "Well . . . no. No, I didn't. But I loved his work."

"No sweet-patooties under the easel?"

Rhea grimaced.

"Don't mean to embarrass you, Rhea, but I don't like to waste time. Ain't no percentage in it. Besides, with a beautiful woman like you I would have thought—"

"Jodie and I had a business relationship. Nothing else."

"His loss. You may be the only woman who didn't shuck for him, God rest his soul."

Verle drained his glass. Rhea quickly refilled it.

"Thanks. Who the hell was he?"

Rhea shrugged. "He was your son."

"Henry's painted a dark picture of me, hasn't he? That's to be expected. *Anyone* who's been around Henry for more than thirty minutes gets an earful of how negligent I've been." Verle hesitated. He stared out at the water. For a moment, he seemed to be embarrassed with himself. "Who was he?" he repeated, this time as if he had other things on his mind.

"I knew him as an artist. A fine painter who was getting better with every painting."

"He was also deeply screwed up," Verle said with a sigh. "Well, it's a screwed up world. I've spent my whole life makin' money, Rhea. I know that that ain't a popular notion these days. I know how this younger generation of runt-yuppie-businessmen like to honk their horns about quality time spent with their families. That's punk grunt,

Rhea. Window dressing, pure and simple. Any man seriously trying to make a buck out there knows there ain't no time for playin' wet nurse. I'm not trying to excuse myself but that's the way it was and that's the way it is."

"According to Henry, you set new standards for not being a wet nurse," Rhea commented.

Verle took a sip of wine.

"You want to engage in personalities?" he asked, his voice full of irony. "You're a businesswoman. You don't have any children, do you?"

"No."

"Plannin' on any?"

"No. I have no choice, Verle. I can't breed. Twenty years ago a horse fell on me—crushed my pelvis. Half my bladder was removed. And for good measure, the surgeon threw in a hysterectomy, no extra charge."

"You could always adopt."

"You *want* me to have children?" Rhea set down her wine. "Or do you just want to establish that I'm in no position to judge? Let me be frank. I do judge."

"I can see that."

"If I had children, they would be my priority. Maybe that's why I never wanted to adopt: I'm selfish and I've never been ready to make that commitment. I'd probably make a thorough mess of motherhood. But I do know this, if I were placed in that position, I'd do my best. You, on the other hand, have never tried. At least, that's my impression."

"The impression Henry gave you."

"I don't need Henry's opinion in order to know that you get out of a relationship what you put into it."

Verle started to speak but Rhea held her ground. "Look. In spite of what Henry has told me about you—all of it bad—I am determined to try to understand. You're a remarkable person. Everyone knows that."

"Yep. And, as long as we don't get into moral issues, there's no reason why we can't get along, is there?"

For the first time, Verle flashed his superb set of white teeth. The resemblance to Jodie's smile was as uncanny as it was unsettling. Underneath the table, she felt his leg brush up against hers. She moved her leg away slightly and asked:

"Why did you fly me over here?"

"Hell," Verle rejoined with laughter. "Why did you accept?"

Rhea was determined to make him answer first.

As if guessing this, Verle said, "Jodie told me you were cantankerous."

She downed her drink and poured herself the last of the wine. She lighted a cigarette before asking: "Do I have a show in October or do I not?"

Verle patted her hand. "I like a woman who can plow and drink at the same time."

Rhea's hand revolved to the top position and patted his hand in kind. "A man thirty years my senior and a newlywed, to boot. Let's cut the bullshit, Verle. Jodie stole a brooch from me—"

"He did?"

"For starters, yes, he did . . . bristling with diamonds and sapphires . . . no casual theft. He was also planning on changing galleries without telling me. Then he came over here and cut a deal with you which—I've got a bad feeling—was not a pretty thing either. He was trying to screw me every way he could. Why don't you just give me the gory details? I've prepared myself for the worst."

Verle withdrew his hand and turned more toward Rhea, his sunglasses reflecting the stripes in the awning overhead.

"Okay. Jodie was fixated with the idea of havin' a sell-out show *before* next month," he began. "Here was the sneak: if I'd buy all the pieces under various false names, you would never know the difference and a pre-sell-out show would be an enormous boost to his career. You would automatically hike the prices of his work and within a couple of years' time, I could feed the paintings to Sotheby's and auction everything off at a goodly profit."

Rhea jerked her head: "Wait a minute. A scheme like that doesn't stiff me. Even if I didn't know what was going on, I would still get my fifty percent, right?"

"Right."

"But Darlington led me to believe that—"

"Let me finish. You think I was interested in Jodie's deal?" He added with a laugh: "Of course, if a man slaps me a deck of cards—even an upstart like Jodie—you can damn well bet I'm just mean enough and bored enough and rich enough to stay at the table and play. No, what I told him was this: I said I wasn't in the market for art . . . least ways, not *his* art. Besides, I said, there was no assurance that a sell-out would automatically upgrade his career. Am I right or am I right? You need candy ass reviews and all the auxiliary hype that goes with it. I don't know jack-shit about art, Rhea, but I do know how it's bein' peddled in New York these days. I asked Jodie if he could guarantee me good reviews, or, for that matter *any* reviews, which, of course, he couldn't. I asked him if he could guarantee higher prices at Sotheby's. Again, he couldn't. The worth of art depends entirely upon the public's desire at any given moment. Not my kind of merchandise. I prefer something with tangible value."

He took another drink. Already physically imposing, Verle's presence became even more expansive. It was as if someone had waved a wand and Verle had magically become twenty years younger. He sat up a little straighter. His hand movements became more animated. Was it the rapid consumption of wine or the boilerplate talk of hostile deal-making that so invigorated and transformed him? His handsome, deeply tanned profile, framed by white hair and backlighted by the glittering water of the lagoon, was undeniably mesmerizing. It was all she could do to keep from snatching his sunglasses away from his face. She resented any obstruction to this powerful, craggy countenance.

"I'm a reasonable man," he continued in a self-mocking baritone voice. "And Jodie was my son. I told him, I might be willin' to give him a leg up—given the family connection—but just a temporary one. More wine?"

There was a brief hiatus while the waiter returned with a fresh carafe. "Service is first rate around here, ain't it?" Verle said, grinning, taking the initiative this time to fill their glasses. "Tell me, Rhea," he continued. "How much would all of Jodie's pieces be worth?"

"For the new show? He was promising me twelve to fourteen

pieces, ranging from fifteen to thirty thousand each, depending upon the sizes of the canvases. The whole show, if it were a sell-out, would straddle or overrun the two-hundred-thousand dollar mark—minus my fee, of course. Jodie would have taken home around a hundred grand."

"Um-hum. And what were the odds, without my help, of him having a sell-out?"

"Hard to predict. Ever since Black Monday, things have been iffy. And Jodie was in an especially tricky price bracket. The big guns—the artists whose work goes for six figures or more—seem to continue to appreciate. But the lesser stars, like Jodie . . . well, it's been a slower go. He did have a small core of faithful patrons. I could be fairly certain of selling half his work. Anything over that would be an improvement of my estimation. Gravy, as you say down south."

"So, without my help, he could have counted on fifty thousand dollars?"

"Yes, I'd say so. More or less."

"And when would he actually get his money?"

"Between thirty and sixty days of the actual sells."

"Fifty thousand dollars," Verle repeated, shaking his head. "Not many melons for two years' work."

"It's more than most artists earn."

"We ain't talkin' about most artists. We're talkin' about my son. Jodie wanted money and fast . . . that much was obvious. Why the hell couldn't he wait until October? By the way, he was resentful of *your* cut."

Rhea shrugged. "Artists always are."

"He called you a fuckin' parasite—pardon my French."

Rhea's face registered no emotion. "I've never expected my artists to love me. Art dealers give painters their credibility. Without our backing, they can't presume to put *any* price on their work."

"Yeah, well," Verle's smile grew. "He also had a problem with that: he thought you underpriced his work."

"Artists always do. Look, Verle, could we dispense with the gloved thrusts? What was this 'leg up' you were going to give him?"

"What? Oh, yeah. I took a fallback position. I told him I wouldn't give two cents for his pictures but, since he was my son and I was celebratin' my honeymoon and all . . . you know, he caught me in a generous mood . . . I told him I'd give him thirty-thousand."

Rhea took a sip of wine, totally unconvinced. "You don't give away money."

Verle reacted as if he'd been cut to the quick. He put his hand to his heart. "I didn't say give away. I told him I would *loan* him thirty thousand, using his art as collateral. If he could pay me back by October first, fine. If not, the paintings would automatically become mine."

Rhea paused for a moment while taking this in. "I see. You had papers drawn up to that effect?"

"Drawn up, signed and witnessed . . . which is more than you do at your gallery, ain't it? You still use the old handshake as a contractual agreement." Verle clucked his tongue. "That's not sound business, Rhea."

"A handshake has worked for me ninety-five percent of the time. In my business, you've got to operate, to a certain extent, on mutual trust."

"Maybe you ought to find a new business."

"You knew that Jodie wouldn't or couldn't pay you back by October first. In effect you were buying two-hundred thousand dollars worth of merchandise for a fraction of its worth. Then what were you going to do, leave me stranded without a show?"

"Oh, I'm sure you and I could have struck a deal."

"What sort of deal?"

Again, his knee brushed against hers. Again, she moved away.

"I told you, I didn't want the goddamn stuff. I would have been glad to unload the collection for, say, one-hundred-twenty-five-thousand."

Rhea glared at Verle but tried to keep the anger out of her voice. "One-twenty-five . . . and is that what you are proposing to me now? Do you expect me to buy what is essentially already mine . . . and half of which is already in my possession?"

"Nope," he smiled. "I may be a poor excuse for a father but nobody can ever say that I made money off my family. You want the goddamn paintings . . . you can have them." He extracted from his coat pocket an original contract with Jodie's signature at the bottom. He handed it to her. "Here, take it. Rip it up. I don't care what you do with it. We'll just pretend it never happened."

Rhea stared at the contract without touching it. "Is this the way you dispense with your own guilt? And what if Jodie *hadn't* died? October comes, he can't repay you . . . then what? Were you going to tear up the contract?"

"Sort of. I was gonna send you a copy, you were gonna go ape-shit for a few days, and we were all gonna kiss and make up after you reimbursed me for the loan."

With open disgust, Rhea pushed the contract back to Verle's side of the table. "And you actually gave him the money?"

"Just fifteen thousand of it so that he could be flush while he was here. The rest was gonna be wired to Jodie by my Geneva bank, once he returned to New York."

"Where's the fifteen thousand now?"

"Twelve hundred was recovered from the safety deposit box he was usin' here at the hotel. The rest, I reckon, was either squandered on that model, or the blackjack table, or . . ." Verle's voice became quieter. "Or stolen by the murderer. His wallet was missing."

"Yes, I know. Do the police know about it? The loan, I mean."

"Why should they? It was between me and my son. The management quietly handed over the safety deposit key . . . no fuss, no bother." Verle flashed his winning smile. "And you should be damn glad they did."

"Oh? Why's that?"

"Ain't tellin'," Verle responded and smiled. "Not yet."

Rhea sighed. "Was this the first time Jodie ever asked you for cash?"

Verle snickered. "Are you kiddin'? The little twerp was always hittin' me up."

"Had you ever given him any money?"

"Sometimes. When I thought his schemes made sense. That loft of his, for instance, down in TriBeCa. I bought that for him way back in nineteen seventy-six. Four thousand square feet for one hundred-ninety thousand. It was a good deal. Two years ago it was worth six hundred thousand . . . though now, with the real estate glut, it's probably gone down some—"

"Are you telling me that Jodie owned that place?"

"You didn't know?"

Rhea's expression clouded over: "I paid his rent—quote, un-quote—on a half dozen occasions."

Verle slapped his knee with a hearty laugh. "He was screwin' you every way he could . . . well, just about every way—"

"Does Henry know you bought him the loft?"

"Not unless Jodie told him . . . which I doubt."

"Why?"

"If you snoop around and find cookies in the cookie jar, do you go tell your brother or do you save them for yourself? Jodie may not have been too money-smart but, even a six-year-old can be cunning."

"Henry told me that he never got any money from you."

"That's right."

"Why would you give Jodie money and not Henry?"

"Because Henry never asked for any."

"In all these years he's never—"

"Never. There's somethin' you'd better understand about my oldest son: The very existence of Verle Rivers is a humiliation to him. He's like his mother, God rest her soul, proud as they come. Well, pride is old-fashioned these day. And I always thought that blind pride was about the spookiest thing a man could indulge in. Henry would rather starve to death than to ask me for anything."

"Maybe he doesn't need your money," Rhea suggested.

"I shouldn't put him down. He's eked by in the casting business . . . not that the stakes are that high to begin with . . . but, for a cottage industry, he's held his own. Above water, anyway. He survived last year's writer's strike which put a lot of casting agents out of business. Still, it put an end to office improvements. He had to lay off a secretary."

"You seem to be fairly familiar with his operation."

"Information's blue chip, you know that, Rhea. As Wallace likes to say, 'it effectively inters the opposition.' "

"Is Henry the opposition?"

"Only in *his* mind. Let me give you an example. For a few years, now, Henry's wanted a fax machine. Hell, he *needs* a fax machine. All day long, he mails head-shots of actors to directors on the west coast. That's his job. In the end, a fax would save him lots of money. And it's not as if he don't have the capital. He's got sixty-five thousand dollars in a money mart. Henry's stingy, that's his problem. Short of a Japanese invasion—which, of course, has already happened—he won't touch that money. Well, to get on with my story . . . I said to Henry, 'Henry, I buy faxes by the goddamn truckload. Why don't you let me give you one?' You know what he said? 'I wouldn't give you the satisfaction.' Get the idea, Rhea? It's pitiful. Henry's made three trips this year to L.A. He's in the midst of a career crisis. Should he take a Hollywood job with a steady salary and a chance to get into production—which is what he really wants to do—or should he remain in New York. He can't make up his mind and it's damn near killin' him. That ulcer of his is pure masochism. It gripes my ass. . . . Hell, I'm in the communications business! You think I don't have friends out in La-La Land? You think I couldn't help him if he'd let me?"

Rhea stared at Verle as if she saw him in a different light.

"There's something I still don't understand about this deal you made with Jodie." she said. "If you wanted to help out your son so much, why draw up a contract . . . why loan the money . . . why not just give it to him? You knew Jodie wouldn't pay you back."

"I told you: Jodie approached me as one businessman to another. I was playin' with his deck of cards even if it wasn't a full deck. The whole thing was ludicrous. As for the contract . . . it was Jodie who insisted on the contract, not me, which I thought was loopy as hell."

"Had he ever asked for a contract before?"

"*Hell* no. Jodie wouldn't know a contract if he tripped over one. But he wanted it in writing . . . signed the goddamn thing without even readin' it. I could have been buyin' back his loft and he never would have known it. Contract! Somethin' had happened to him. He didn't want handouts anymore. I gave him shit about it. I accused him of bein' around Henry too much."

Verle suddenly shoved back his chair and stood up. Once again she was reminded of his imposing height and his penchant for staying one step ahead of the action. It was impossible to anticipate what he was going to do or say next.

"Will you excuse me for a minute? Gotta go fetch somethin' that you might find of interest. I'll be right back, I promise."

With a sly, quick nod of his head, he turned and disappeared inside the hotel.

Rhea looked about her, confused, tired and out of touch with herself. Everything seemed displaced. Even the man sitting at the next table—dark, muscular and reading a Portuguese newspaper—seemed ill-suited to the terrace of the Gritti Palace. The man made her feel uncomfortable. It struck her that his interest in his paper was feigned. Why?

And then she realized: Earlier, she had noticed this man watching them or, more precisely, watching Verle—not to the point of being rude but, nevertheless, he displayed considerable interest in Verle. Now that Verle was gone, the man was totally absorbed by journalism.

What about Verle? Had he "won her over" as Henry had forecast? No, but there was something hearty and ingratiating about his openness. True, he had an ego the size of an ocean. He manipulated matters to his personal advantage but, at the same time, he could be self-effacing and very charming. Unlike Darlington, he was void of pretension and stuffy regimentation; everything about him smacked of the entrepreneurial, the loose, the free-wheeling. She liked that a lot. And, of course, there was Verle's smile . . . that Jodie-Rivers-hotdog grin that gave him a boyish quality and that belied his wrinkles and thick white hair. Here was a man who had spent his entire life confronting, overpowering, and finally, easing away from his adversaries with a reckless grin.

A man Rhea could like?

A man a son could love?

Had she been taken in?

One thing was certain: Jodie and Henry paled by comparison. Jodie had shared his father's recklessness. He had certainly burst through life's doors without invitation but, unlike his father, he had lacked self-assurance; his motivation had been colored by envy and hatred. Verle was too busy being successful to be plagued with hatred. And Henry? Continually locked out by his own stubborn vanity and wounded sensibilities—"old-fashioned," Verle called it—he shuffled and fussed about with an outstretched calling card no one in this family cared to read.

Verle returned. He sat down with a sigh, smiled at her, and placed a small object in the cup of her hand. Even before looking down, she new what it was. By touch alone she remembered its exact weight and clumpy configuration. She said nothing.

"Well, it's yours, ain't it?" he chuckled. "You said diamonds and sapphires, didn't you?"

"Yes."

"I was wonderin' where the hell Jodie got it. I'm no authority on gems but Babs assured me it was the real thing."

"Who's Babs?"

"The new wife. She said Jodie couldn't have afforded the platinum in that there brooch, let alone the rocks. It's a hefty thing."

"I . . . I don't know how to thank you."

"Well, I do!" He said with an easy grin. "I think a smooch is in order, don't you?"

He jutted his jaw in her direction. She leaned sideways and kissed him on the cheek. Just as she did, she caught the man at the next table quickly averting his eyes.

"Well, go ahead, put it on," Verle insisted with a nudge.

"I . . . I don't normally wear jewelry . . . especially during the daytime."

Verle laughed. "What the hell is normal about today? Can you tell me that, Rhea? Normal." Verle groaned in a descending tonal pattern. It was as if his baritone voice had collapsed under the weight of the idea of normality. "I've lost a son who I never had to begin with . . . and another son who would love to see me belly-up . . . ain't nothin' normal around here. Go on. Put it on for me."

"Well . . . just for a minute."

"That's right. Humor an old man. We'll call it my reward. I love to see spangles on a woman."

"You're anything but old, Verle."

"You got that right."

Rhea turned over the brooch and fumbled with the slender pin. In a lower voice, she said, "Don't look around but the man at the next table keeps staring at you."

Verle snapped his neck around. "You're botherin' the lady!" he growled. He turned back to Rhea: "Don't pay any attention to Osmar."

"You know him?"

"He's my bodyguard . . . or one of my bodyguards. Got a parcel of them, these days. Everybody gets them mixed up. They both look alike. Big and dark and ugly as sin. Names are alike too. Osmar and Omar. Osmar, there, is Brazilian and Omar's a goddamn Arab. The way you can tell them apart is that Osmar has them big hairy eyebrows and Omar has a string of worry beads he kind of flips around in his hands. Drives me crazy."

"Why do you need bodyguards?"

"Embarrassin', ain't it? These days, everybody's got beef taggin' along behind them. . . . it's a goddamn power fad, is what it is . . . dime a dozen. Not mine: They earn their keep, I can guarantee you that. Waiter! Could we have some more wine, please?"

Verle grabbed the brooch from Rhea and said, "Here, darlin', let me have the honors." His large fingers deftly worked the clasp and with a light, expert movement, fastened it to her blouse just above her left breast.

"There!" he said. He sat back to better admire it—the brooch or her breast, she could not tell. "Beautiful, beautiful, beautiful. And Jodie never did put the makes on you? Lordy. He *must* have been out of his mind."

Just then, Nico Passante, the general manager of the hotel came up to Rhea's side of the table. She quickly took off the brooch. She started to rise but he insisted that she keep her seat. He leaned over and kissed her on both cheeks. They talked for a moment in Italian. He nodded to Verle, said something to a hovering waiter and then went back inside.

"Well, now!" Verle exclaimed, openly impressed. "What was that all about?"

"He asked me about some old friends of the family, that's all."

"Friends of the family," Verle repeated.

Instead of the ordered carafe, a bucket of champagne was delivered to their table.

"What is this?" Verle demanded.

"Compliments of Signore Passante," the waiter answered.

Verle shook his head with a smile. "You love this shit, don't you?"

"Champagne?" Rhea asked.

"No, not champagne. I'm talkin' about playin' kissy-face with the general manager. Here I am: I've got the presidential suite and I'm payin' for four other rooms too . . . must be spendin' a king's ransom at this place. . . . hell, I could probably buy this place if I wanted to . . . and the G.M. wants to ask *you* about your family. Your dad was from an old blue-blooded German family, ain't that right?"

"You've done your homework. No big secret."

"A limo brat."

"Right. And what was your father?"

"My father was a goddamn mule trader."

"Bragging or complaining?"

"I ain't ashamed, if that's what you mean. My dad worked hard all his life. I've never denied who my people were or where they came from."

"Probably because it's the most expedient thing to do," Rhea suggested.

Verle laughed. "We may come from different universes but you and I think alike, you know that?"

"I hope not." Rhea answered with a suppressed smile. "Why do you think Jodie needed the money this time?"

"Since all these drugs have been discovered, I guess he could have been in trouble with somebody . . . maybe needed to pay someone off. . . ."

"You don't sound like you believe that."

"I don't. My gut impression is different. He didn't need money. If he needed money, why the hell didn't he hock that jewelry of yours? Nope, I think the little shit was tryin' to impress me. All that pre-show sellout business—his insistence on a contract—I think he was tryin' to say to me, 'Dad, I'm a big important businessman. I've got a commodity that's worth talkin' about.' That's what I think. Pretty pathetic, if I'm right."

"Pretty vain, if you're wrong."

"Vanity has nothin' to do with it. Let's be realistic, Rhea. What could he have done to impress me? I don't think he knew *what* he was doin'. Pluckin' out his eyelashes . . . he had a burr up his ass about somethin' . . . *that's* for sure. He didn't make sense half the time. It gave me the creeps, I can tell you. The older he got, the more he reminded me of his mother."

Rhea looked up. "Why?"

"Never mind. Too complicated."

The sun was no longer directly over the Gritti terrace. It had traveled some distance to the right, up the Grand Canal. They hadn't been there all that long but Rhea felt comfortable with this man, as though she might have known Verle all her life.

"Why did you ask me to Venice, Verle?"

"I thought it would be obvious by now. I want to get to the bottom of this. I want to know who killed my son."

"I'm no detective."

"No, not a professional one. But you've been interviewing me like one."

"Have I?"

"A little bit."

Rhea shook her head in disgust. "It's a flaw of mine. I get this uncontrollable desire to . . . to rout when I'm confronted with mystery."

"I'm no fan of mystery either. Anyway, I've got a wagonload of detectives headed this way. This mornin', I hired a firm out of Washington. Bunch of ex-CIA boys."

"Then why do you need me?"

"Sometimes nonprofessionals can be more useful. You understood his life as an artist, didn't you? Everything's related. I've got to cover the bases the best way I know how. And I knew Henry would be close-mouthed. I'm just tryin' to understand—"

"Then . . . why be so vague? You've got a plan for me, don't you? You're stalling, Verle."

Verle shrugged. "When you put on that brooch and then snatched it off when the G.M. came by, it tugged at me. I'm a little rusty when it comes to expressin' my feelin's but, I don't want Jodie's career to be like that goddamn brooch . . . exhibited one minute, buried the next."

"Exhibited," she repeated carefully.

Verle reached for her hand once again, this time without the flirtatious pawing.

"I want you to give him one hell of a last show. You make sure they remember Jodie Rivers. Do an advertising blitz. Hype the shit out of it, Rhea. Make it take hold. Use his murder as a salient point, if you have to. I don't care. Just do whatever you have to do to get people down to that show."

"The timing's not right, Verle. The art magazines that advertise next month's shows are already on the stands."

"Then postpone his show! Put it on when you can do it right. I'll make it worth your while."

Unwittingly, Verle Rivers had struck a very deep chord in Rhea's impetuous nature. She was a compulsive conceptualizer, which often translated itself into unusual presentations of art. A different show for Jodie: Her unreadiness to think about it right now nevertheless opened a floodgate of disparate torrents suddenly manifesting themselves and eddying all about her. And as the possibilities braided around her, one image in particular became the dominate current: In compliance with Jodie's last inspiration, Rhea could mount a show that incorporated Lorna's stories.

"What are you thinkin'?" Verle asked impatiently.

"I don't know. You've taken me by surprise. I have an idea, but it would be contingent upon so many things."

"What things? I told you, don't worry about the money."

"It's not that."

"I'm listenin', darlin' ."

Rhea took a deep breath. "We'd have to find the stories first."

"What stories?"

Rhea chose to ignore the question. "What I've got in mind might not be so pleasant to you. A can of worms, Verle. It has to do with your first wife, Lorna."

"Lorna?" Verle's tone changed slightly. He moved back in his chair. "What do you know about Lorna?"

"I'm not sure. She had a grand piano, didn't she?"

"How did you? . . ."

"Maybe I shouldn't do this," she said with a sigh. "Maybe this isn't the right time. Maybe there never will be a right time. . . ." Rhea reached down and brought up the folder. "Here, take a look at this."

He opened the folder. His brow rose into heavy creases. "Lorna's handwriting," he mumbled. "Where did you get this?"

"Just read it. I'll explain afterward."

For the first time, Verle removed his sunglasses. Rhea was shocked at the condition of his eyes. Encased in dark circles, they were horribly bloodshot. His pupils were glazed and unnaturally dilated.

"Where did you get this?" he demanded again.

"Just read it, Verle."

He brought out a plastic vial of tablets and took one.

He extracted a pair of reading glasses from his inner coat pocket and slowly put them on. His arms telescoped backward and forward until the paper had been adjusted to the correct distance. The story trembled in his grip. He squinted his eyes. His lips moved silently.

Verle Rivers may have been resolute to remain young, but he read the printed page like a conquered old man.

# 9

The telephone awakened him.

For a moment, he didn't know who he was, where he was or what day it could possibly be. He rubbed his eyes and sat up a little. The room was quite dark but the heavy brocade curtains, drawn across the windows, didn't quite meet. A knife-slit of light penetrated the room and settled on the pile of clothes he had worn on the plane. He checked his watch.

Time: 4:30 P.M., local time.

Place: Gritti Palace.

Person: Henry Rivers, recently back from the morgue.

Had the police brought him to the hotel? He had a fuzzy recollection of a boat ride . . . of Rhea massaging his back while pointing out the Piazetta next to the Doge's Palace. . . .

The phone continued to ring. He fumbled for and picked up the receiver.

"Yes?"

"Henry, that you? It's Dad! You gonna sleep through the whole goddamn day? Siesta's over. Rhea Buerklin and I are down here on the terrace havin' drinks . . . gettin' snockered. She's some woman, ain't she? Whatcha say you get your lazy ass down here and join us? Rhea says she needs a chaperon."

"Rhea Buerklin doesn't need anybody. Where's your new wife?"

"Out there somewheres buyin' out the town, I'd imagine. Are you comin' or not?"

"Give me thirty minutes."

"Hold on! You ain't fixin' to go back to sleep, are ya?"

"Thirty minutes," Henry repeated and hung up.

He pressed a button next to the bedside table. The overhead chandelier came to life. Undulating tubes and scores of crystal droplets fractured the light and cast mottled patterns down over the silk-covered walls. Jodie was sitting in the chandelier, smiling and waving to him.

Henry pretended not to notice.

He picked up the phone and placed a call to New York.

Even before she said "hello," Henry knew that Joella, his assistant in his casting operation, was on the other end: He could hear the jangling of her charm bracelets, which drove him to distraction and which he had banned from all auditions. Now, with an ocean between them, the noise somehow reassured him.

"How is it?" she asked.

"Opulent nightmare," he answered, staring at his brother who still dangled from the ceiling. "Lisa's been murdered as well. . . ."

After he filled her in on the details, he added, "There may be a detective getting in touch with you."

"John Tennyson? He already has. In fact, he's coming to the office a little before noon. What does he want, Henry?"

"Don't worry about it. He's on our side and it's not official. He's a friend of Rhea Buerklin's. Be as helpful as you can. He's just trying to retrace Jodie's movements before he came here and killed Dad."

"Killed your father? What are you talking about?"

"What? I didn't say that. There must be a bad connection."

"Is it your wife, Henry?" Joella asked, using her euphemism for his ulcer. "Is she acting up again?"

"She's been pretty naughty. Any word from Paramount?"

"Not yet. The office is like a miniature ghost town. Henry? What's so funny?"

"Believe me, nothing."

After he hung up, he got out of bed, padded over to the curtains, drew them back, then swung open the tall windows to let in some fresh air. His third-floor room—not at the front of the hotel but, rather, at the eastern end of the building—allowed him a partial view of the Grand Canal. It was a stupefying vista for someone who usually awoke to the dull, rectangular shadows of Twenty-first Street. The azure sky was brushed with clouds the color of tea roses. Below his window, motorboats churned the dark water into quicksilver. Across the sprawling basin, the baroque facade and enormous white dome of Santa Maria della Salute glowed in the late afternoon sunfall like a ripe warm melon. Glorious.

Why was he trying so hard not to be impressed? Because the view mocked him? Because he understood how thoroughly he didn't belong here? *You ain't fixin'* . . . It wasn't the view. It wasn't the exuberantly hushed details of his room. It wasn't the leering presence of his mirage brother.

It was the sound of his father's drawl . . . *you ain't fixin'* . . . still gurgling through his mind like an unwanted stimulant, like an old-fashioned coffee pot percolating against his drowsiness and against his will. After all these years, Verle Rivers's voice still bullied and conjoled.

The more Henry brooded about his forced visit to the morgue, the more humiliated and angry he grew. It seemed he had spent his entire life being abandoned by his father and, what was worse, he had never learned to fortify himself against the inevitable insult.

How could he ever gain control?

As if sheer muscle tone might help, he dropped to the floor, naked, and executed fifty push-ups. He rolled over on his back and forced out sixty lateral crunches. Vigorous folly.

He got up and trudged to the bathroom. He walked over to and examined a racklike contraption that kept his towels warm. He took a cold shower trying hard not to be impressed by the bathroom's amenities. He dried off, shaved, brushed his teeth and then, returning to the bedroom, consulted the meager choice of apparel packed in his frowsy nylon suitcase with the broken zipper. He put on a black T-shirt and a rumpled brown suit, stuffed a bottle of Mylanta in his coat pocket, swallowed two tablets of codeine, grabbed the key to his room and, hair still damp, left his room.

He was greeted by a long hallway where an army of gilded arms pierced up and through the walls holding, in their gilded fists, the corridor lighting of the Gritti Palace. He followed this to its end, turned right and headed toward the elevator.

The elevator was tiny but beautifully paneled. He pushed a button and it silently made its descent. The genteel susuration mocked the rattletrap elevator at his office, which now flashed through his mind.

The elevator stopped on the ground floor. He took a deep breath and pushed opened the hinged door.

He passed the busy concierge's desk, entered and passed through the bar and—taking a deep breath—walked out onto the terrace. It was quite crowded now. For a moment he didn't recognize anyone. *Good, they've already left.* He was just about to turn around when a deep resonant voice called out his name. He turned toward a corner table.

Verle Rivers stood up.

He had aged since Henry had seen him last. His thick gray hair had gone completely white and he was wearing it longer these days. But had he really aged? He still stood tall, shamelessly fascinated with himself. His superb white teeth and dark tan still fascinated. He still had that odd habit of rolling his shoulders when someone approached him (as if he were readying himself for a boxing match), and he still shook hands with a vicelike grip.

"Sit down, sit down, Henry! Rhea calls the Gritti terrace the most serene place on earth. Says she'd like to retire here, if I let her."

"What do you have to say about it?" Henry growled, massaging his right hand and taking the seat opposite them. How long had they been drinking? Their woozy mood intensified his aggravation.

"You missed the first part of the conversation," Rhea explained, stubbing out a cigarette. "Verle's bragging about buying this place."

"You bought the Gritti?"

"No, no," Verle laughed. "Like everything else worth ownin', you gotta buy a conglomerate to get the one thing you really want. But, by God, I might some day. Wouldn't mind signin' my name to this old pile of rocks. There's somethin' about this hotel . . . gives me a hard-on just thinkin' about it."

"Me too," Rhea said, putting her drink to her lips.

Both men's eyes landed on her.

"In theory," she amended.

Henry sighed and looked the other way.

"Oh-oh," Verle said, nudging Rhea with his elbow. "Someone got up on the wrong side of the bed."

"Not at all," Henry said, still hoping against hope that he could extinguish their levity. "I'm delighted to see two timid people some-how managing to overcome their inherent . . ." He turned toward Rhea: "I told you that you two would become chums."

"Not as chummy as Verle would like," Rhea rejoined in a sobering tone. "He keeps brushing his knee against mine."

"Do I?" Verle asked innocently.

"Yes, you do."

"Well, I'm a big man. Got big knees, that's all. Need a lot of room." He looked out over the water. "And there's a lot of room in this town if you got the money. All these palazzos, just rottin' away, waitin' for somebody to come along and do somethin' with 'em. Yes sir, my kind of town. 'City of Merchants' they call it."

"Shylock's hometown," Henry inserted.

"That's right," Verle grinned. "And he was one hell of a successful merchant, wasn't he?"

"No, he wasn't a merchant," Henry grumbled. "He was a usurer—not that you would make the distinction. And in the end, he lost his ass."

Verle knitted his brow. "He did?"

"That's right. Lost all his money and, for extra added punishment, he had to become a Christian."

"No kiddin'?" Verle exclaimed. "That's tough. Well, what the hell did Shakespeare know about makin' money? He should have stuck to poetry. The point is—"

"The point is," Henry interrupted his father, just managing to refrain from banging both of his clenched hands on the top of the table, "that we're all having a wonderful time. That's what's important. We're here to enjoy ourselves."

There was a moment of silence.

Verle set down his drink. "No, we're not here to enjoy ourselves, you glum little asshole. You're brother saw to that." The cowpoke inflection disappeared from his voice. "But we are here to continue. Do you have any objection to that?"

"No," Henry said with a smile, "it's just that some of us have an easier go at it than others. Some of us don't visit the morgue before cocktails."

Verle looked at the tablecloth. "Life's the only agenda we've got . . . even if it don't mean a goddamn thing. Death, on the other hand . . . I'll be a corpse soon enough without havin' to look at corpses. Just can't do it. 'Druther be pecked to death by a duck. If I'd gone over there, they'd a-had to stick me in there with Jodie . . . either that, or cart me out in a wheelbarrow."

Henry remained unimpressed: "Three nights ago, an agent by the name of Leo Stayne said I used my diamond-in-the-rough accent to my own advantage. I didn't mind the accusation at all. But now that I see the prototype in action, it makes me want to throw up."

"Yep," Verle nodded, repressing a smile. "I heard you were pretty good at throwin' up. What'll you have to drink, son?" With a barely perceptible nod of his head, Verle caught one of the waiters' attention. "Rhea, are we stickin' with the champagne?"

"If Henry has no objection," she answered.

"No objection."

"More champagne," Verle ordered.

Henry stopped the waiter: "And could you bring me a small empty glass? A shot glass if you have one."

"Make that two shot glasses," Rhea quickly added.

"Make it three," Verle chimed in, never to be left out of anything.

The waiter nodded and disappeared into the bar.

"Now . . . what's with the jiggers?" Verle asked, suspiciously eyeing the turquoise container which Henry had just pulled out of his pocket. "What you got in that plastic canteen?"

"Mylanta."

"Your lanta?" Verle asked in a lower voice. "It's not illegal, is it?"

"Perfectly legal," Rhea assured him. "Sort of like a health food drink. Good for the stomach. It's the latest thing."

"Is that right? Well, as long as it ain't illegal. . . ."

Henry rolled his eyes.

"No harm in askin'," Verle defended himself. "When the cops came here to search Jodie's room, they found hashish. How should I know what you boys take? What do you think, Henry? Was he dealin' drugs?"

"If he was," Henry answered, "he wasn't making any money out of it. Jodie couldn't count to ten, let alone conduct a business . . . too deep into the future for him."

"That sounds about right." In an abstract manner, Verle bit his lip, then asked Henry: "What about the Ethiopian?"

"What Ethiopian?"

"Lisa Morris. The Queen of the Nile you boys were passin' back and forth like a football."

"She was Bahamian, she wasn't a pusher and we weren't passing her back and forth."

"I don't know what you'd call it then."

"Jodie wasn't in love with her. I was."

"Is that a fact? Well, she was all over him and the police found all that dope in her suitcase. How do you explain that?"

Before Henry could respond, Verle continued:

"Lisa was a nervy broad . . . wouldn't give Babs the time of day. I didn't like her much. She was a looker, I'll say that much for her. You boys have good taste. Some of these black gals make your eyeballs fall out. Of course, in my day, the whites and the blacks . . ." Verle turned toward Rhea. "Don't get me wrong. I ain't no bigot. My father was a quarter Choctaw. Hell, I'm a half-breed myself . . . or an eighth-breed, anyway. I don't give a merry goddamn what color gets the eggbeater beatin'. All I'm sayin' is that it wasn't done thirty years ago."

Verle took a drink of champagne and chased it with Mylanta. "Not bad. Kinda covers up the taste of the liquor, which is okay by me.

Never did believe people who said they drank for the taste. People drink to forget."

"What are you trying to forget, Dad? That Jodie wouldn't *let* you forget? Is that why you had him killed?"

For a moment, there was absolute silence. Osmar carefully folded his paper. Rhea went on red alert, half expecting Verle to lurch across the table and deck his older son. Instead, he fiddled with his tie for a moment, then looked up with a quizzical expression:

"No, dipshit, I had him killed so that I could be closer to you. You're such wonderful company that I wanted you all for myself." He laughed for Rhea's benefit. "It's great when father and son can get together and be assholes to one another like grown men are supposed to be. Pour me some more of that lanta, son."

"Pour it yourself."

"Take in your sails, would you, Henry?" Rhea interrupted, no longer able to check herself. "You're being an ass."

"I understand that!" Henry snarled. So fucking tiresome. He had no means to fight Verle. It was like a lousy play in which one fabulous cameo role dominated the otherwise lackluster cast. Even Jodie's and Lisa's melodramatic murders hadn't managed to upstage Verle's allure: outwardly chirpy, crass and capable of saying anything; inwardly disdainful, smoothly indifferent and never entirely present. It was so stupid and pointless—to turn his back on someone who was already facing the other direction—and yet, that was what he inevitably did, thereby perpetuating his lumpish role in the wings of Verle's stage triumphs.

He picked up the Mylanta and refilled the three shot glasses.

Verle checked his watch. "My goodness. Look at the time. Babs should be back by now. Henry, you gonna join us for dinner?"

"I . . . I don't know. What are the plans?"

"Me and Babs and you and Rhea. A double date," Verle said and smiled. "Babs is champin' at the bit to meet you all. We got reservations at Harry's Bar for eight-thirty and—"

"I'm afraid that's impossible," Rhea said quickly. "I've made other plans."

"Well, cancel them," Verle scowled.

"It may not be to your advantage that I do. Dr. Lago has invited me to dinner."

"Well, I'll be! Lago's got better sense than I thought." Verle smiled broadly in Henry's direction. "Beat us to the punch, didn't he, Henry?"

Henry said nothing but glared at Rhea as if he'd been betrayed.

"Dr. Lago," Verle said as if thinking out loud. "Don't know what to think of that guy. A little too pretty, if you ask me. And the minute he started shootin' questions at me yesterday, I could tell his initial concern was for the Gritti."

"You mean, to protect it?" Rhea asked.

"No, not to protect it. It's what the Gritti implies: People who stay here are heavily connected . . . often politically. Heads of State and all that shit stay here. No, his initial concern was to establish any political implications. Once he ruled that out, it just became another homicide to him. A foreigner's death, a rich kid's son . . . and now Lisa . . . maybe mixed up with drugs or maybe just a robbery that turned into a murder . . . which just don't ring true to me. If you're gonna rob someone, especially a big galoot like Jodie, wouldn't you pack a gun?" Verle set down his drink. "I don't think your Dr. Lago's gonna be much help to us, Rhea. But it'll be damned interestin' to see how he performs when the moon comes out, won't it, Henry?"

Verle stood up. "Well, if you change your mind about dinner, you know where to find us."

"You're not leaving!" Henry protested. "I just got here."

"Shouldn't sleep through the whole goddamn day." Verle bent over and kissed Rhea on the cheek. He turned to Osmar, who was now standing. "When we get upstairs go fetch Wallace. I need to find out . . ."

Verle and Osmar disappeared inside the hotel.

"Who was that guy?"

"A bodyguard."

"You see how he treats me, Rhea?"

"Oh, for Christ's sake. You were practically begging for it. The minute you came out here you did everything you could to piss him off. What did you expect?"

A pall of uneasy silence fell over the table.

The setting of the sun was imminent. A waiter walked over to the opposite corner of the terrace, where a long metal pole with a crook in it rested against the stone facade. He angled it away from the wall and, with quick revolutions, rolled back the striped awnings. In spite of Henry's agitation, he had to admit that it was a marvelous stage effect: Like any well-designed set, the retreat of one part of the scenery transformed the entire terrace. Earlier, the water had predominated. Now, though the water continued to lap noisily against the pilings, it was the darkening sky, streaked with purples and golds, that became the focal point.

"Don't go out with Lago tonight," he pleaded. "I don't know if I can stand being alone."

"You don't have to," she replied. "Have dinner with Babs and your father. He'll be nice to you if you're nice to him. Your father's not looking for war, Henry."

"Only because I don't have an army. Where's the challenge? Be with me tonight."

Rhea paused to weigh the offer. She stole a glance at the folder resting against the leg of her chair. It had been her intention to show him Lorna's story in the hopes that he could shed light on its importance. Now, in Henry's present state of wretchedness, she had second thoughts. Fanning the fire would be counterproductive, if not openly cruel. The least she could do was to wait for a better opportunity, which was the extent, she now realized, of her compassion. There were limits. Spending the evening nursing Henry's wounded spirit when, instead, she could be picking Lago's mind went against every efficacious bone in her body. She didn't know how long she could remain in Venice. A couple of days at most. It was an injustice to Jodie not to make the most of every moment. . . .

"I can see that you need a woman, Henry, but I'm not the right sort. It would be stupid to blow off Lago. Surely you can see that."

Henry's face fell.

"Look," she finally suggested, "if I get back in time, I'll have a nightcap with you. How's that?"

"The operative word here is 'if,' isn't it," Henry replied. "You don't give a damn."

Rhea sighed.

"Before we go, I think you'd better take a look at this."

She handed him Lorna's story.

Instantly recognizing his mother's handwriting, Henry shot Rhea a look of pure hatred.

# 10

Tennyson parked his car in an open lot on Nineteenth Street between Fifth and Sixth Avenues. The neighborhood was a study in demographic transition. Originally, the surrounding buildings, solid but uninspiring, had been used for light manufacturing. In the last decade, ever since professional photographers had moved in, a certain glamour had insinuated itself into the district. Sharing the sidewalk with workmen (loading their semis with textile-related goods) were actors and models laden with heavy knapsacks on their way to auditions and ponytailed businessmen on their way to sleek restaurants.

He entered a twelve-story building on the uptown side of the street. Inside the derelict Art Deco foyer milled a group of handsome youths awaiting the elevator. Except for one young man in khaki slacks they were uniformly clad in shorts, which seemed incongruous to Tennyson. It was a cool September day and you could almost feel fall in the air.

"What are you guys here for?" the kid in pants asked in a sarcastic voice. "*South Pacific?*"

"Industrial commercial," one of the youths grumbled. "Burlington socks."

"I've worked for Burlington. Good exposure."

"Not this time. According to my agent, there's no face work. They'll be shooting from the waist down."

The elevator doors opened and the actor-packed compartment begrudgingly made room for Tennyson.

They all piled off at the top floor, which had been turned into a conglomerate of casting offices, audition spaces and electronic studios. The actors, after bunching around a blackboard that indicated session rooms assigned for the day, disappeared around the corner to the right. Tennyson consulted a glassed-in receptionist, then took the corridor to the left. He passed several casting offices and stopped when he reached the end of the hall. There was a sign on a door that said, simply, "RIVERS," and below that, a sign that read ALL ACTORS PLEASE INQUIRE AT FRONT DESK.

From inside, he could hear the squeaky punch commotion of a stapler at work. He knocked. There was a moment of silence. He was about to knock again when a woman's voice told him to come in.

It was a small but sunny office. Shoved into the four corners of the room were desks—all empty. On the carpeted floor sat, cross-legged, a redheaded woman in her early thirties sorting out a dozen or more piles of paper.

"Are you Mr. Tennyson?" she asked, not bothering to look up.

"Yes. You must be Joella."

"That's right. Have a seat. I've got to finish collating these 'sides' that just arrived . . . two days late! The auditions are scheduled for Monday and the actors will be banging down the door this afternoon. I won't be but a minute."

"You don't have any help?"

Joella looked up a little defensively. Her green eyes were aggressively made-up, but not unkind. "When things are really busy, we bring in a temporary or two. For the most part, it's just Henry and me."

Tennyson couldn't guess how many bracelets she had on but he wondered if the noise they made didn't help to provide this woman with a little company. Everything about the room implied inactivity. Two of the desks were obviously not in use. The four phones were silent. The large hand drawn calendar of September, pinned to the wall, was only half-filled with appointments; pink virgules were meticulously slashed through the days as they transpired. The piles of head shots and assorted books were a little too neatly stacked.

"Mr. Tennyson, I don't know if I can be of much help," she said. "I hadn't seen much of Jodie recently and, when I did, I didn't like what I saw. I'm not the most objective person to be talking to."

"But you knew him."

"Too well."

"Anything might help. How long have you been working for Henry?"

"Six—no—seven years."

"Would you say that you know him well?"

"Very well."

"Were you here in the office, the last time Henry saw Jodie?"

"Yes. It was two weeks ago, today."

"Was it unusual for Jodie to come here?"

"For the last year, yes."

"Why's that?"

"I assumed you knew. Henry and Jodie had a big falling out over Lisa Morris."

Tennyson looked puzzled. "Yes, but I thought that occurred only a few months ago."

"Oh, no. That happened last year. Of course, to hear Henry talk about it, it was only yesterday and you'd think they had been lovers for decades. Actually, Lisa lived with him for only a few months. Then, when Henry found out that she was seeing Jodie . . . God . . . Henry deserved better. Much better."

"You didn't like Lisa?"

"Henry either couldn't or wouldn't see it. All he saw was the Lisa Morris in those big layouts in Vogue . . . all dreamy and feminine."

"What did you see?"

"Queen Kong. She treated Henry like dirt. Ordered him around. And on the few occasions she came here, she barely recognized my presence and it was only to ask for a cup of coffee or some other menial task. I know you're not supposed to say bad things about dead people but Lisa was a major league bitch."

"Any theories as to why she hitched up with Henry?"

"I can tell you exactly why. She'd turned thirty . . . been in the modeling business for ten years . . . knew that that couldn't go on forever. She had to spend more and more time out of the country to get work. She was trying to break into acting. I think you can figure out the rest."

"Did Henry cast her in anything?"

"No. She had no experience, no training . . . and . . . to have gotten her a role would have been paramount to admitting to himself that that was all she wanted him for."

"Did you discuss this with Henry?"

"Are you kidding? Nobody could say anything against her. Henry, of course, blamed Jodie for the break-up but, if you want my opinion, I don't think Lisa needed any help from Jodie. I don't think Lisa Morris ever thought of anyone but Lisa Morris."

"She wasn't in love with Jodie?"

Joella cast a sour look. "Jodie and Lisa were a perfect match."

"What do you mean?"

"They were both incapable of having a bona fide relationship. She was in love with the mirror and Jodie was in love with every woman who ever looked good in a mirror."

"You're an attractive woman. Did Jodie ever come on to you?"

"I just said he came on to every woman. The Holy Mother wouldn't have been safe in his presence. Not that he meant anything by it. It was more out of habit than anything else. As for his interest in me, I'm sure he displayed it just to antagonize Henry."

Tennyson paused. Why would Henry care if Jodie flirted with Joella, unless there was something between Joella and Henry?

"Forgive me if I seem personal but—"

"I know what you're going to ask," Joella interrupted. "There's never been anything between us but hard work. I'm loyal to him and I adore him. He's taught me everything I know about this business. But I have my own man, Mr. Tennyson, and we've been very happily unmarried for a number of years now."

Joella got up off the floor with an armful of collated "sides." She plopped them down on her desk, took a seat and swiveled her chair in Tennyson's direction.

"I will say this: I'd do anything to make Henry's life simpler. I've never seen anyone try so hard to create an honorable life for himself and under such adverse conditions. People don't understand that about Henry. When they see his best instincts, they think he's a spook."

"Honorable instincts," Tennyson repeated.

"Yes, honorable. It's an odd word to be applying to anyone these days, isn't it? Deep down, Henry's a romantic. That's his problem. He once described it as a family affliction . . . that it was the Rivers's lot in life. Verle turns his romanticism into money. Jodie turns— turned—his into art. Henry turns his into ulcers."

"You mentioned adverse conditions. Were you talking about ulcers or Lisa or? . . ."

"Who I really had in mind was Jodie. He took open pleasure in messing around with Henry's mind. He belittled him and his square life-style any chance he got. He put down Henry's business, called it 'The Couch Unused' . . . referred to Henry's ulcer as 'the only wife he would ever have,' that sort of thing . . . always needling him for no reason. Until Henry put an end to it, Jodie would barge in here any time he damn well liked. He never called beforehand. It didn't matter if we had important clients here or a casting session going on. . . ."

"Until, two weeks ago, when he came to the office unannounced."

"That's right. I could have slapped him into next week, when he walked through that door."

"What was he like that day? Anything different about him?"

"He'd plucked his eyelashes—God know's why—but apart from that, he was the same old asshole Jodie."

"Drugged up? Was he high?"

"Could have been. It was hard to tell with Jodie."

"If this office was off limits, Jodie must have had some pretext for coming."

"Um-hum. A mean-natured one. Jodie had just heard that their father had remarried. He dropped by to share the happy news with Henry. He suggested that they fly over and meet the bride. It was so ugly. You could see it in Jodie's face: how much he was hoping to get a reaction out of Henry."

"Why?"

"Jodie thrived on that kind of bullshit."

"Did he succeed in getting a reaction out of his brother?"

"Who knows? I don't think anything his father does really surprises or shocks Henry, but you never know. Besides, we were very busy that day casting a show for a regional theater. The producer, a real pain in the ass, had come into town with his ridiculously arrogant director—the out-of-towners are always the most problematic—and we had our hands full. You know, placating the rural egos."

"How did Jodie manage to steal Henry's American Express card? Doesn't Henry keep it in his wallet?"

"Yes. Yes, but, unfortunately, he sometimes keeps his wallet in his gym bag. Henry belongs to a health club down the street and he goes there in the mornings before coming to work and . . . We were running back and forth between the office and the session room down the opposite corridor. It was the wrong time for confrontations. We were trying to ignore Jodie. The last time I saw him, he was right where you're sitting, using the telephone. The next time I came back into the office, he was gone."

"When did Henry discover the theft?"

"Lunchtime . . . when he needed money to go to the deli. He immediately called American Express but, by that time, Jodie had had a good hour and a half jump on us. The news was worse than we expected. Three thousand dollars in cash, the full amount of his line of credit. It had just been withdrawn from the American Express Service Center on Park Avenue."

"Three thousand dollars. Did Henry consider that a lot of money?"

Joella smiled grimly. "Fatter times came back to haunt us. Two years before, when business had been roaring, we were connected with a London musical that was being brought to New York. Henry had to make two trips to England. In a rare moment of optimism, he arranged for his credit line to be extended."

"But how did Jodie manage to hit on American Express? Didn't they demand positive identification?"

Joella nodded her head. "He also stole Henry's driver's license. The brothers looked enough alike—at least, the photos looked enough alike—to fool the Am-Ex officer. There were back up precautions as well. The officer asked Jodie for the maiden name of his mother. No problem there."

"But what about the signature? Didn't they check—"

"Mr. Tennyson, Jodie Rivers was an artist. Not a bad attribute, if you're into forgery."

The telephone rang. Joella immediately yanked off her right dangling earring and—expertly reaching back, without looking—picked up the receiver.

"Hi, Leo. No, Henry's going to be gone for a few days. If you're calling about Braithwait, I read him yesterday and I liked him. He's an old, wild offbeat type but his voice is the right instrument. It was like getting a bassoon to do a violin's part: quite effective. One snag: Braithwait is major stupid, isn't he? I don't think he understood the script and the director said he didn't want anyone intimidated by the material. The only good thing about *that* was that just about *everybody* was intimidated by the material. And Braithwait looks good on tape. Yes, Bernard read for the role but don't worry about Bernard. Bernard's got that weary, cafeteria smile which is *all* wrong. Besides, he's too old for the part. Nothing left but a rack of bones. Looks like he could croak any minute. I taped him but we immediately burned it. He's finished."

Tennyson didn't understand much of the conversation but the rapidity and the decisiveness and the authority with which Joella elevated and deprecated actors made Tennyson believe that she was quite a bit more than a mere secretary in this enterprise. Another line rang and she put Leo on hold:

"Hi, Brenda. Everything looks good except that we're running up on empties for the 'Rubin' role. I think we'd better look through the submissions again and lower our sights. The guys you want aren't going to work for one hundred ninety three bucks per week. Brenda, darling, there's *always* buzz about Off-Broadway shows moving to Broadway—you know that, these guys know that, and they aren't biting. What about some fresh meat? Can you hold? Hello, Leo, I'm going to have to get back to you. Brenda, I'm back. Clean out your ears. You ready? What about Sam Waterston's son? Of course he has no experience but the director is such a starfucker that you *know* he'd love to have Sam Waterston's son. . . ."

The more Tennyson heard, the more he wondered how "honorable intentions" fit in with this hard-talking business. Like Joella's noisy bracelets, the room was suddenly a flurry of hard, metallic animation. It was easy to see how Jodie might have lifted a wallet without being noticed.

Conversely, the instant she hung up, the room once again felt vacated. The telephone was the vapor lock of this business and, for a moment, Joella didn't seem to know what to do with herself or how to retreat to a normal rhythm of conversation.

"Where were we?"

"It must not be easy," Tennyson observed, "to be an actor in this town."

"It's not easy being an actor in any town."

Tennyson changed the subject. "Did you ever meet Henry's father?"

Joella's face darkened. She mulled over the question before answering: "No. Henry doesn't see him that often and, when he does, it's usually uptown somewhere for dinner."

"Verle Rivers never came down here?"

"Not to my knowledge. And I'm sure Henry would have told me."

"Isn't it a little odd for a father not to be curious about his own son's business?"

Joella laughed for the first time. "I seriously doubt that Verle Rivers considers this—or *anything* under seven digits—a business."

Tennyson nodded. "What was the relationship between Jodie and his father?"

"The same as Henry's relationship with his father, I would imagine: putrid . . . putrid and cruel." Joella leaned back with a slightly impudent smile. "You don't like me much, do you?"

"Like you?" Tennyson was nonplussed. Her defensiveness seemed to come from nowhere. "I have no reason to *dis*like you. Why would you think that?"

"You think that casting agents are cruel when it comes to actors. Tell me the truth. That's what you were thinking when I was on the phone, wasn't it?"

Tennyson smiled. " 'Fresh meat' struck me as a little harsh."

"And cops aren't harsh?"

"The people I seek are usually murderers."

"Yeah, but you meet a lot of other people along the way, don't you? Don't tell me you don't pigeonhole people . . . reduce them to a break-down of characteristics . . . cold hard facts. It's all the same, isn't it? A necessary means to an end. Let me tell you something about actors. You can step on an actor, you can spit on an actor, you can even tell him that he's the lowest, least-talented piece of shit on earth, but as long as you're talking to him or about him, as long as you're paying attention, even if that attention is totally negative . . ."

"Do you actually talk to actors that way?"

"There are ways of getting around it. Say a role calls for someone exceedingly ugly. We try never to tell the actors that. We soften it by saying, 'We need someone who is dark and sullen and we thought you were the only one for it.' "

Tennyson shrugged. "Joella, what's your point?"

"You were asking me about Jodie's relationship with his father. There's only one way to be cruel to an actor and that is to *ignore* him."

"So?"

"So that's precisely what Verle Rivers has done to his sons, all his life."

"You've spent some time thinking about this," Tennyson observed.

"I've had no choice. Once you get to know Henry, you realize the extent to which he is consumed by the man. He talks about his father all the time." Joella cast a sour smile. "You want a break-down on Verle Rivers? You've come to the right office."


In the following half hour, Joella related to Tennyson, in amazing details, the steady uphill pattern of Verle Rivers's life.

He grew up in a two-horse Oklahoma village, from peasant stock, with no money and no likely prospects for a better life—except that he'd been born with a kind of irrepressibility. Even in youth, he stood out. Joella had seen a picture of him as a teenager, white teeth predominating, with his lackluster family grouped behind him—as if they were investing all their hopes in his smile—as if they already knew he was the one who would go forward.

"As far as I know," Joella continued, "he never looked back. He studied hard and somehow wrangled a scholarship to Tulsa University. Not exactly Harvard, but an enormous breakthrough for his family. First college graduate. Anyway, he plowed through books and boys with equal ferocity."

"Boys?" Tennyson raised an eyebrow.

"Figure of speech. Verle became the star of the college football team—a handsome young buck with boundless energy—an Adonis–quarterback type who literally bashed his way into the limelight. It seems the Oklahoma oilmen, who subsidized the team, sat up from the sidelines and took notice. They cheered him on and, as the victories accrued, they began to court him. The football field: That's where he made his first real connections in the business world."

"Local aristocracy helps poor boy."

"Well, according to Henry, the local aristocracy, as you call it, couldn't have gone back more than one generation. Oklahoma didn't become a state until 1907 or something like that. Anyway, built for big things, fueled with adulation, using his new-found sponsors in any way he could, Verle went straight from the football fields to the oil fields, where he made a fortune before he was thirty."

"First major goal achieved.

"Next, he imported Lorna, Henry's and Jodie's mother, a banker's daughter from Baltimore. I've seen pictures of her too. Pretty but sullen looking. Not happy . . . definitely not a happy camper."

Tennyson interrupted. "You said 'banker's daughter.' Was that the attraction?"

"I really don't know if she had money of her own, or not. But she came from an old family, which can be better than money."

"How do you mean?"

"Back then, old families were pretty rare in Oklahoma. Practically nonexistent. Henry's always thought that that was the attraction . . . that it was Verle's way of upping the ante with the local stuffed shirts. Verle built her a big fancy house as was befitting her heritage and gave her orders to stake out the Rivers's social territory."

"Did she?"

"No. She hated Tulsa and despised its new wealth. A Yankee exiled to Siberia. Kept to herself. Didn't make friends. Took to firewater. . . .

"Meanwhile, Verle was mostly gone. Absent. Off to the War of Money, conquering new oil fields like an erstwhile Crusader. He did come back often enough to get her pregnant two times. That kept her somewhat occupied."

"Somewhat?"

"Henry grew up with a cook, a nanny, and an Indian butler named Jimmie Cloudfoot, who acted as a surrogate father . . . if not other things."

"What other things?"

"Henry says that, if his mother ever had a confidant, it was the butler. There's even some speculation that they may have been lovers. I think Henry hopes they were."

"Why?"

"He saw his mother as a very lonely and unused person. She became an alcoholic. She died when Henry was fifteen. Fade-out, end of sad life."

"What did Verle do, once she died?"

"Verle continued with his ascension, of course. The boys were left in the care of Cloudfoot."

"Henry despises his father?"

"I don't know. He's certainly obsessed by him . . . fascinated, in spite of himself, with his career. Who wouldn't be? He tries to keep a sense of humor about it. Henry keeps saying, 'when is he going to become Citizen Kaned?' "

"Meaning?"

"You know, like at the end of the movie: Citizen Kane, the Great One, left alone and forgotten, a prisoner in the realm he has created for himself. Doesn't seem likely at this juncture, does it? Verle just keeps getting richer, his friends keep getting more important, he's got a new wife. He's invincible. Always one step ahead of everyone. In the mid-eighties, when the bottom fell out of the oil market, Henry thought Verle finally might have met his match. He was wrong. Verle had already sold all of his oil holdings. By nineteen eighty-four, he was solid into communications, pharmaceuticals, third world investments and Eurodollars."

"Henry keeps you abreast of things, doesn't he?"

"Not just Henry. I read that 'pharmaceuticals' stuff in *Forbes*. What in the world is a Eurodollar? Can you tell me? I've had a dozen people explain that to me and I still don't get it."

Tennyson found his moment. All the other questions had been leading up to this one: "Is Henry the major beneficiary?"

"What?"

"Who gets all the money, when Verle dies?"

Joella seemed to have been caught off guard. For a moment, she cocked her head as if she were playing back everything she had said.

"I don't know," she finally answered.

"You don't know," Tennyson repeated with a frown. He shook his head. "You know everything else. I don't think I've ever met an employee who knew so much about her boss. Are you trying to tell me that, in the seven years you've worked for Henry, he's never talked . . . never even speculated about his father's will?"

"If he did, I don't remember."

Tennyson stood up. "Well, you've been very helpful and I really appreciate it. Hope I haven't taken up too much of your time." Tennyson made for the door, then stopped. He turned back around. "One more question: What was Henry's reaction when he realized that his own brother had stiffed him for three thousand dollars?"

"How would *you* react?" Joella laughed.

Tennyson shrugged. "What did he say?"

"He said exactly what I would have said, given the circumstances. He said, when he got his hands on him, he was going to . . . you know, kill him."

Tennyson nodded his head.

"Well, he didn't really mean anything by it," she insisted.

"Still, in light of what has happened, it's an unfortunate choice of words."

"Oh, come on! The only reason I told you what Henry said was because I knew he really didn't mean it. Do you honestly think I would have repeated—"

"Definitely not," Tennyson interrupted. "It's very clear that you're selective with your information."

# 11

It was dusk. Most of the clientele had already finished their cocktails, signed their checks, and abandoned the terrace, by boat, for restaurants in other parts of the city.

Rhea wanted to speak to the concierge before going up to her room, so Henry said good-bye to her in the lobby.

"Is the concierge just an excuse?" he asked.

"What do you mean?"

"To keep from getting stuck on a tiny elevator with me?"

"That, too," she said, rolling her eyes. "I promise, I'll call you the minute I get back from dinner."

Henry nodded, walked to the elevator and entered, alone, with a shamefaced expression.

He would have liked to blame his new-found humiliation on his father but he couldn't. It was Rhea who had deflated him by her easygoing camaraderie with Verle; by her announcement that she was dining with Dr. Lago—a romantic possibility that made him feel absurdly jealous—and finally, by her surprise presentation of Lorna's text. Hideous read—not so much a story as it was a thinly disguised command from the grave—unwanted, putrefied memories coming back to haunt him! How could he have allowed himself to share them with Rhea? It was no use denying it, in the short time he had known her, he had become inordinately attracted to Rhea. The last thing he wanted from her was pity.

The elevator stopped. He opened the door and walked down the hushed corridor, trying to play back everything he had told Rhea.

". . . and Mom was a drunk by the time I was old enough to make any judgment. Poor soul. She always smelled of cloves. I thought that was what all mothers smelled like until I realized it was to disguise the smell of brandy. She was crazy. . . .

"Crazy . . . in a world of her own that had nothing to do with real life. The few objects in real life that did amuse her were purposefully distorted by her—revamped, disfigured—to comply with her fantasy world. When Dad bought her that Steinway—a beautiful instrument—she hadn't had the piano two weeks before she attached paper clips to the strings. It gave the piano a pinched, tinny sound . . . a cross between a harpsichord and a cheap player piano. Eventually the clips vibrated off and tumbled down into the recesses of the piano. She replaced the fallen with new ones, without ever bothering to extract the old ones so that, within a year's time, the piano not only tinkled, it rattled and clattered with all the excess metal buzzing against the soundboard. It was the distortion that kept her at the keyboard for hours on end—playing the same pieces, over and over again, often as not, in a lower octave so that she could get a better vibration. To this day, I can't listen to Mozart without hearing vibrations in the background. . . .

". . . then there was the Frisco. She loved to take me and Jodie to the outskirts of Tulsa, where the Frisco Railroad headed east toward Missouri. We'd put pennies on the rails and wait for the trains to flatten them. It was a game she played with us. She'd barge into our room, her eyes unnaturally glittering, her hands full of pennies. 'Who wants to smash in the face of Abraham Lincoln?' she'd ask. And we'd pile into her light blue T-Bird and head for the tracks. The look on her face when the train roared by . . . an expression of pure hatred. . . ."

"Hum," Rhea had finally responded. "Lorna doesn't sound so crazy. Sounds more like a performance artist, if you ask me."

What else had he told her? Henry shook his head remorsefully as he withdrew the key from his pocket and opened the door.

His hangdog expression was instantly transformed into one of alertness. He sniffed the air suspiciously. A pungent odor permeated the room. It was the unmistakable stench of Wallace Darlington's cologne. He checked the bathroom, then the bedroom to see if anything was disturbed. His suitcase lay open, still unpacked and much the way he had left it. Everything seemed in order. Still, his stomach flip-flopped. What the fuck had Wallace been doing here?

The telephone rang.

He yanked the receiver off the hook and snapped, "Who is it?"

There was a moment of silence before he heard the jangling of Joella's bracelets, followed by her voice: "It's me. What's wrong?"

"Everything, Joella. What's up?"

"That detective, Mr. Tennyson. I didn't like him at all."

"I told you to be helpful to him."

"Oh, I was! He played me like a bloody violin . . . had me telling him all sorts of things about your family."

"So? That's why he was there . . . to find out about Jodie."

"No it wasn't," she corrected him. "And it wasn't until toward the end that I realized . . . I think he suspects you . . . as the murderer . . . or, at least, the person who hired the murderer. The more he talked, the more I realized he was shaping his questions to incriminate you. If you ask me, he's already cast you."

Henry laughed.

"What's so funny?"

Henry absentmindedly waved to Jodie, who was peeking from behind the curtains. "Believe me, Joella," he replied, "there are worse things than being accused of murder."


The concierge, who had known Rhea since she was a schoolgirl, was very helpful. He pulled the record of telephone calls made from Jodie's and Lisa's room. Included in that list were five calls to Paris

~ 146 ~

ranging from ten to thirty minutes each and all placed to the same exchange. He wrote down the Paris number on his card and handed it to Rhea with an avuncular wink.

"Do the police have this information?" she asked.

"I don't know. Yesterday was my day off. I wasn't here when the police—"

"It doesn't matter. Thanks."

Rhea got on the elevator, pleased with her intuition. Lisa had been seen getting on the train bound for Paris. Even if she didn't have any jobs slated by her French agency, it would have been natural for Lisa to get in touch with her girlfriend beforehand. But there had been five calls of lengthy duration placed over a six-day period.

To Rhea, that busy pattern indicated two possibilities: one was sinister—drug runners finalizing the details of a transfer—and the other was mundane—idle models toiling over the never-ending update of girl talk. Since Henry insisted that Lisa wasn't involved with drugs, Rhea dwelled on the latter possibility. What did models jabber about? Had Lisa been bragging about the accommodations in Venice? Or Jodie's sexual prowess? Or the wealth of Jodie's father?

One way or another, Rhea was convinced that this model in Paris could be a wealth of information—that to know how Lisa's last week had unfolded would be paramount to understanding how Lisa got herself killed.

One problem: how could she get the model to talk? When Henry had called her, back in New York, he had struck out. Of course, that was before anyone knew of Lisa's death and Henry had not mentioned to the model that Jodie was dead.

Another problem: Rhea didn't even know the model's name. All she had was a number in Paris. She could get the name and have it verified by Henry but, again, her intuition interceded. She was fed up with having her sensations filtered through the Rivers entourage, especially Henry. His equilibrium was shattered. He exhibited less and less restraint and, at this point, pumping him for further information seemed like a hazardous, if not cruel, maneuver.

Come to think of it, she probably shouldn't have shown him Lorna's story.

Rhea promised herself that, from here on out, she would be more selective with her meddling.

Like Henry's room, Rhea's was located on the third floor. But hers was on the opposite side of the building—the street side which abruptly ended with the pedestrian entrance to the hotel next to the small gondola station bobbing in the Grand Canal.

She closed the door behind her, switched on a light and crossed over to the French windows. Across the stone way were the apartments owned and rented, on a weekly basis, by the Gritti Palace. Their balconies, now darkened, were laden with flower boxes packed with black geraniums.

God, it was getting late! She was to meet Dr. Lago in forty-five minutes. She had to take a shower. How would she have time to pull it together?

She turned away from the view, hurried over to an ornate desk which was placed at an angle in the far corner of her room. Referring to the concierge's card, she placed a call to Paris.

She got a recording—a woman's voice: "... *et apres le son de le* . . ."—after the sound of the beep—

Rhea took a deep breath and left a message in French: "Hello, You don't know me but it has fallen upon me to phone you with some very bad news. My name is Rhea Buerklin. I own a gallery in New York and represent Jodie Rivers's work. I'm calling from Venice. There's been a tragedy. Jodie Rivers and your friend, Lisa Morris, have been killed in Venice. I know what a shock this must be and I'm terribly sorry to have to break the news to you in this way but it's urgent that I speak with you. I'm staying at the Gritti Palace. My number is 041.79.46.11. Please get in touch with me at the earliest possible moment. It doesn't matter how late. . . ."


Henry called his father.

"What was Wallace doing in my room?" he demanded.

Verle let out a belly laugh. "And a howdy-do to you too!"

"I asked you a question."

"I heard you. What makes you think Wallace was in your room?"

"Not hard to figure out. He left his stink all over the place. What was he doing here?"

Verle laughed again. "He probably wanted to steal all them valuables of yours."

"Are you going to tell me or not?"

"Now, now, now," Verle groaned. "It's no big deal. Wallace was doing it out of courtesy. I was gonna have the porter do it but Wallace offered to bring it instead."

"Bring what?"

"Jodie's suitcase. I thought, since you were his brother, that you might want his things. I didn't know what else to do with the goddamn things. Isn't his suitcase there?"

"I don't see it. Hold on." Henry put down the receiver and opened the closet doors. Since he still hadn't unpacked, the closet was the one place he hadn't felt necessary to check. Inside, on the floor, was a badly dented Haliburton and, on top of it, lay an extra key to his room. He returned to the phone. "Yes, the suitcase is here. And so is the key. How did Wallace get a key?"

"I gave him the key, okay? Listen, I'm glad you called. Babs is feelin' a little puny tonight. Says she'd rather eat in tonight. We're gonna have to cancel our dinner plans, if you don't mind."

"I don't give a flying fuck about dinner!" Henry exploded. "What the hell do you want with a key to my room?"

"I don't *want* a key to your goddamn room. The key happened to be with Jodie's things, that's all. Now you got two keys."

Henry hesitated for a moment. "Why would my key be with Jodie's things?"

"Oh," Verle said, as if he just understood something. "Oh! Didn't anybody tell you? I thought you knew. You're in Jodie's and Lisa's room. It doesn't matter, does it?"

"You stuck me here on purpose, didn't you?"

"Goddamn it, there are only so many rooms in this hotel. You're lucky to have that one."

Henry changed the subject: "Rhea showed me Mom's story."

"Yeah, I figured she would. Your mother didn't have all of her ducks in a row, did she? I've never read such artsy-fartsy crap . . . couldn't make hide nor tail of it."

"I thought the meaning was fairly clear."

"I bet you did. And what did *you* inherit from Jimmie Cloud-foot—a voodoo doll with my name on it?"

"Now who's being paranoid?"

"What?" Verle asked, not understanding. "I didn't say anything about you being paranoid."

"You didn't?"

"Son, what's wrong with you?"

"Nothing. I'm fine. I just didn't know that Jimmie had died until Rhea told me. It caught me off guard, that's all. Why didn't it catch you off guard? Did you know that he had died?"

"Nope. Why should I have known? I haven't talked to him or seen him in years."

"Jodie came over here to kill you, didn't he, Dad?"

Verle paused before answering. "Jesus in a bucket. I've heard a lot of sorry-ass wishful thinkin' in my day, but that just about—"

"Did he or didn't he?"

"Why ask me? It's not the kind of scoop a murderer shares with his victim, is it? Henry, do you want me to fetch you a doctor?"

Rhea ran to the phone, leaving a trail of water behind her. She had just emerged from the shower.

It was Tennyson with an update of his meeting with Joella.

". . . and Henry's been lying about a lot of things, Rhea. He lied about not suspecting that Jodie was going to Venice. Jodie came to the office and told him about Verle's honeymoon. He said he was going and suggested that they both go over together. Henry also lied about the time frame of his romance with Lisa Morris. They only lived together for a few months and that's been over a year ago. But here's the biggest lie of all: Henry is now the main beneficiary in his old man's will."

"How do you know?" Rhea asked, letting her towel drop to the desktop.

"Henry's assistant, Joella, knows everything about the family. And she spent a hell of a lot of energy painting Verle Rivers in the least favorable light. She's very loyal to Henry . . . I wouldn't be surprised if she's had an affair with him or with Jodie or with both . . . anyway, she wants to portray Henry as a paragon of virtue and the old man as an archvillain. So I asked her point-blank, 'Who gets the money when Verle dies?' And she told me that she didn't know."

Rhea picked the towel back up. "I don't understand, John. If she says that she doesn't know, what makes you think——?"

"Because the meat honked. Look: She wanted me to walk out of her office hating Verle Rivers. If Verle Rivers had actually cut Henry out of the will, Joella would have exposed it, explored it for my benefit and exploited it for all it was worth. But she didn't do that. She suddenly shut up and played dumb. And the reason she did that was because she *knew* that Henry was sitting pretty, that it didn't comply with her black portrait of Verle. She wasn't about to extinguish the fire she had so carefully built.

"She's very smart. Henry is Joella's meal ticket—or, more precisely, Verle is Joella's meal ticket. Henry may not be waiting for his father to die, but Joella *is*. It's just a gut instinct but I'll bet you my badge on that one. She's great looking, ambitious and, from what I saw, damn proficient at her job. She could be working for anyone in town but she stays with Henry in a two-bit operation. Why? Because she knows that, down the pike, the money's going to be knee deep. And why would she think that?"

Rhea answered for him. "Because Henry has told her that."

"Um-hum. See my point? Oh, by the way, have you met Verle's wife yet?"

"No, not yet. She hasn't been a priority."

Rhea proceeded to tell Tennyson about Lisa's phone calls to Paris. Tennyson sighed. "Are you safe over there?"

"Perfectly."

"You're sure?"

"I'm getting ready to dine with the chief of police. I don't know how I could seek better protection."

"Oh, so this is just a dinner of politics."

"Lay off, John. It's been a very long time since I had any sleep."

"Oh, so it's a dinner of rest."

After Rhea hung up, she went into a kind of trance; shoving herself into clothes without really choosing them, brushing her teeth without tasting the toothpaste, applying lipstick without really seeing her reflection in the mirror.

The phone rang again and it startled her. She realized that she had lost all sense of time. Hoping that it was the model returning her call, overcome by fatigue, she rushed to the desk and picked up the phone. It was the concierge, informing her that Dr. Lago was waiting for her in the lobby.

"Oh, God," she said. For a moment, she almost decided to cancel their date. "I'm running a little behind time. Tell him that I'll be down in five minutes. Oh! and, while I'm gone, if I should get a call from Paris . . ."

# 12

Rhea hadn't slept since before she left New York. As she descended in the elevator, she cautioned herself. She understood the quirky nature of her libido well enough to know that, on more than one occasion, it had been fatigue-induced. And here she was, going out to dinner, on a beautiful moonlit night, in a town afloat with erotic interference.

And Lago was a heart-stopper; man enough to make any woman take stock of her sexual needs. She was especially attracted to his directness. But it was more than that. Lago was in a position, were he in the mood, to share privileged information. Was that why she had she accepted his dinner invitation? To pump him? Was she developing a fetish for detectives? For a split second, she envisioned John Tennyson turning his back on her in disgust. The question remained: Was she hoping to be seduced or was she the one who intended to do the seducing?

When Rhea entered the lobby—swallowing a yawn and deciding, at the last moment, to secure the top two buttons of her red, sleeveless blouse—she caught Dr. Giovanni Lago speaking to the night concierge. He had on the same dark suit and tie as he had worn earlier in the day. His appearance, though slightly weary from a day's work, was as finely drawn as she had recalled it; his eyes, the same blazing blue, his posture, ever an indication of his alertness. Upon seeing her, Lago abruptly broke off his conversation and greeted her with a prolonged handshake. His grip was firm and tranquilizing.

"You look beautiful," he said in Italian.

"So do you," she responded with a shrug.

"How was your meeting with Signore Rivers?"

"Did the concierge tell you?"

"I have other sources."

"Were you spying on me?"

"It's my job."

Rhea stifled another yawn, and made a mental note to keep her wits about her. They left through the revolving door that gave on to the stone-paved street. They turned right and headed away from the Grand Canal. It was quite dark now. Rhea glanced up and noticed that she had left the lights on in her room.

Then something else caught her eye. On the second floor, directly below her window, she spied Osmar, standing at *his* window, smoking a cigarette and silently returning her gaze. It was the Brazilian's proximity—near enough that he might have flicked his cigarette, then jumped her—that sent her mind racing.

*"Di che cosa si tratta?"* What's wrong? Lago asked.

She looked up again but Osmar had disappeared.

"I'll tell you later," she answered, taking his arm and urging him forward.

At the first intersection rose the baroque facade of the church *Santa Maria Zobenigo.* Lago stopped at a nearby kiosk and picked up a copy of *Il Gazzettino,* the local newspaper. He offered it to Rhea.

On the front page was a picture of Lisa Morris, reproduced from the coffee ad Henry had relinquished to Dr. Lago earlier that day. The headline read THE ROSTRO MURDERS. The article was sensational in tone. It described Lisa as a famous model whose beauty had been extinguished on the island of Murano, home of the Venetian glass foundries—the very island where, centuries before, the mirror had been invented. "Beauty shattered," was the ironic caption under the photograph.

Henry Rivers's arrival was also reported in inflated terms. He was characterized as a Broadway *nababbo,* a man of power and prominence. The description made Rhea sadly shake her head.

But the big news was that a reward had been offered.

"Reward?" Rhea asked, returning the paper to Lago who, in turn, handed it back to the vendor.

"Verle Rivers," Lago answered with a sour inflection. "The father has offered one hundred thousand dollars to anyone with information leading to the capture of the murderer or murderers."

"You . . . you don't sound very pleased."

"Not at the moment, no."

"But that kind of money would be a fortune to most Venetians. Surely, it will bring people forward—"

"It's brought people forward," Lago assured her, as they resumed their walk. "Before the reward, there were no leads. Now, everyone has important information. At this moment, there's a line of informants a block long outside of headquarters. It'll take days to get it all on paper, let alone to pursue the leads. Verle Rivers couldn't have devised a better way to complicate matters."

"You're not suggesting that he's trying to cloud the case?"

"I suggest nothing. But at this point, I see no need to view the case as complicated. The drugs in Lisa Morris's suitcase and on Jodie's person tell a fairly clear tale."

"But the family discredits the idea."

"Families are always the last to accept these things."

"I have my doubts, too, Giovanni."

"Oh? You didn't discount the drugs this afternoon. What's changed your mind—your meeting with Verle?"

"Maybe."

Rhea proceeded to encapsulate the meeting—not forgetting to mention Lorna's story and the strange pall it had cast over Verle and Henry. She concluded by saying, "It may sound overwrought, but I think that so many murderous thoughts have consumed the Rivers family for so many years that someone's death was almost inevitable."

"Lisa Morris wasn't part of the family. How do explain her murder?"

"Maybe the two murders aren't related."

"Do you really believe that?"

Rhea sighed. "I don't know what I believe. All I know is that there's this wheel of hatred and suspicion and distrust within the family. First of all, there was Jodie: He could be charming, but he also had an uncanny ability to alienate people. As for the mother—even though she's dead, she seems quite adept at fanning the flames. Then there's Henry who's paranoid and behaves as if he despises his father and insists that Verle is somehow behind the whole thing. And Verle . . . well, I don't know if he actually suspects Henry of wrongdoing, but he's a genius at toting up the odds . . . it's bound to have crossed his mind, especially if Henry is to be the main beneficiary of his estate."

"If?" Lago asked. "Did you hear something about it?"

"Indications only. No proof." Rhea caught Lago's eyes. "Why don't you—the police—force the issue? You could, couldn't you?"

"If there were reason to. . . ." Lago thought about it for a moment, then changed the subject: "According to my men, Verle seemed jovial on the terrace. He's suppose to be in mourning . . . heavily sedated."

"I think he's all those things. At one point, he popped a pill in a desperate fashion. And toward the end of our meeting, when he took off his sunglasses, his eyes looked like they had been scrubbed with sandpaper. If you ask me, he's in terrible shape."

"What about the new addition to the family? You mentioned everyone but Verle's new bride."

"I haven't met the bride. She was out all day, shopping. But you already know that, don't you? What's she like?"

"A fluffy dessert." Lago laughed. "I wasn't crazy about her. She flirts and pianofortes at the same time."

"What does that mean?"

"Just a local expression. She makes a big show of her devotion to Verle."

"What's wrong with that?"

"Nothing," Lago answered, "except . . . it's been my experience that devotion is a virtue developed over a long period of time. Signora Rivers plays her piano a little too loudly."

"Hum. And you think Verle is being taken for a ride?" Then, playing with the idea, Rhea added: "Do you think she is the main beneficiary?"

Lago looked straight ahead. "I think that Verle Rivers buys only what he can afford. He's the kind of man who surrounds himself with people who owe him everything . . . his wife, his children, his employees—"

"Like Wallace Darlington? *There's* a horrible man."

"A cold fish," Lago agreed. "His only personal allegiance seems to be to Verle. I doubt that he has any private life at all. But that's my point. It's essential for Verle to collect people like Wallace Darlington. They facilitate his omnipotence."

"You've made a study of him," Rhea observed with a wry smile.

"He's an interesting old man . . . of an ancient breed." Lago stopped walking and gave a self-deprecating gesture. "All Venetians are historians and, therefore, to some extent, idiots. What glory we have is based upon our past and, therefore, we are idiots with a past. And our past is based upon the careers of exceptional businessmen. Verle Rivers runs his life in much the same way that our doges ran the Venetian Empire five hundred years ago. Let me give you an example. When the doges built their extravagant palazzos, they did so, partly, to overshadow their neighbors. But they never lost sight of function: Much of all the palazzos' space was designed to be used as warehouse." Again, Lago laughed. "You see what I'm saying? Verle would have made an excellent doge: gaudy but practical. Like any businessman, he loves playacting. And like any great businessman, there are ulterior motives behind nearly everything he builds or contemplates. As for this 'wheel of hatred' you were talking about . . . it's not surprising, is it? A man with his power . . . he's always having to prove his strength to himself and to his entourage . . . and the way he proves it, probably—more often than not—is by bullying and humiliating them."

"Not killing them?" Rhea asked.

"You mean Jodie? Why kill his own son when he has crueler methods at his disposal?"

Again, they resumed their walk. A few blocks before they reached

St. Mark's Square, they turned left into a narrow twisting passageway lined with tourist-related shops. People were out in droves and it was slow going.

"Well," Rhea said, "the idea *is* strained. Verle seems to be doing everything he can to get to the bottom of this. He told me this afternoon that he's hired private detectives to check things out. I think that's why he flew me over—in the hopes that I might shed some light. And now he's offered this reward. Still . . . when we left the Gritti, you asked me if something was wrong. There was something wrong."

"Let me guess. You spied one of Verle's bodyguards watching us from a second-story balcony."

"You saw him too?"

"He was practically on top of us."

"Well, doesn't that disturb you? You see what that implies. The night of Jodie's murder, Verle's entourage had an ironclad alibi, right? They were in the hotel and the night concierge swears that none of them left the hotel. But with a room overlooking the street, what's to prevent the bodyguard—or anyone connected with Verle's entourage—from slipping away from the Gritti unnoticed?"

Lago shook his head, unconvinced. "Hotels are never ironclad alibies. There's numerous ways to leave them unnoticed. Besides, you're contradicting yourself. First, you say that Verle is doing everything he can to solve the murder . . . and then you suggest that he had the means to commit the murder. You must give me a motive. You see my predicament, Rhea? Until someone supplies me with me a better motive, relying on the Guardia-di-Finanza is my best bet."

"Who or what is the Guardia-di-Finanza?"

"It's the crime division that deals with smuggling, drug traffic, etcetera. The port of Venice has always had strong shipping ties with Asia. Enormous amounts of contraband find their way to our waters and there's always the continual influx of foreigners to meet them."

As if to illustrate his point, two dozen boisterous German youths, singing and jostling each other, rounded the corner. Rhea and Lago stepped over to the side of the alley to let them go by.

"You must get sick of us," Rhea mumbled.

"Who?"

"Us. The tourists."

"Sick of tourists?" Lago asked as if he had never thought of the idea. "But why should we? We've been making money off of you for a thousand years. Even during the Crusades, we sold ships and souvenirs to your knights on their way to the Holy Lands. There have always been tourists in Venice, thank God." With a barely perceptible smile, he added: "Tourism gives me the opportunity to meet people like you."

They soon reached the *Campo San Fantin*—a square flanked by a church, a *scuola,* the opera house and, closest to them, *Antico Martini,* the restaurant where Jodie and Lisa had last eaten. As they approached, Lago said: "I asked to be seated at Jodie's table. But if you would prefer another—"

"No, that's perfect," Rhea insisted.

The front half of the restaurant was outdoors and spilled out into the square, its perimeters delineated by black iron balustrades, large potted plants and a dark blue awning.

The maître d'hôtel, standing at the entrance, was expecting them. He solemnly shook hands with Lago, smiled at Rhea, and ushered them to a corner table in the outdoor section. Their table, covered in white linen, was illuminated by a candle-lit hurricane lamp of delicate glass. Two waiters in white shirts and black bow ties immediately approached and made a fuss over Lago's presence. They suggested a local white wine, a soave from Verona and, for their main course, the *saltimbocca*—fillet of veal glued to a slice of ham and a sage leaf with cheese.

"Is that good for you?" Lago asked, taking her hand.

"Is what good for me?" Rhea responded, swallowing hard.

"The veal."

A breeze filtered through the restaurant and an intoxicating sensation, not in anticipation of a culinary experience, skittered up her bare arms. She scrutinized Lago's eyes to see if he was being ironic. They revealed nothing but a steady intelligence—as dry and hard and polished as lapis lazuli cuff links.

"Yes," she finally answered, clearing her voice and drawing away her captured hand by reaching for a cigarette. "It's good for me."

Lago lighted her cigarette and then one for himself.

The wine came. The first sip made Rhea shiver. She emptied her glass very quickly and, just as quickly, Lago refilled it. Rhea surveyed the restaurant. "Why do you suppose Jodie chose this place? It's so romantic."

"What's wrong with that? He was with a beautiful woman," Lago responded, as if that explained everything.

"It's *neatly* romantic. Civilized. I would have thought he would have taken Lisa to some place rowdier, more informal in feeling . . . perhaps with a younger crowd . . . like one of those places close to the Rialto. Did you say that he behaved himself?"

"Yes. He was very quiet. The waiters characterized Jodie and Lisa as having been sullen . . . not enjoying themselves at all. At one point, Jodie even had his back to Lisa, while sketching on a piece of paper. I have the sketch. One of the busboys, when clearing the table, kept it for himself. After Jodie's murder, he brought it to our attention."

Lago extracted a folded paper from his inner coat pocket and handed it to Rhea.

"What do you make of it?"

"Well, it's of a . . . I've forgotten the word in Italian. . . . It's of the mythical bird that rises out of it own ashes. In English, it's call the *phoenix*. I can't imagine why Jodie drew it unless . . ."

"Unless it represented something that Jodie saw or experienced or anticipated that night?"

Rhea didn't answer.

"This afternoon, while you and I were waiting for Henry outside the hospital, you said that Jodie thought in symbols. Do you remember?"

"Yes, but I didn't mean *just* Jodie. I think all artists do that. It's their way of coding the world. In their paintings, they tend to revert to and rework the same symbols over and over again . . . whether it be a material object, or a setting, or a person, or a shape, or even a color."

"But this afternoon, you were referring to a new symbol: the *rostro.*"

"Again, when an artist sees something new, something that pleases or tantalizes his eye, he tends to adopt it as his own. I have no doubt that Jodie intended to incorporate the *rostro* into his work. Especially, if he went to the trouble to saw off one of the prongs."

"By the way," Lago interrupted, "we've found the hacksaw. Jodie's fingerprints were all over it. It was discarded not far from the gondola station where the boat had been vandalized. We've even located the shop where the hacksaw was purchased."

Rhea's brow creased. "You mean, Jodie was carrying around a hacksaw that last night? Surely, if he brought it to the restaurant or took it to the casino—"

"You forget: the boat was vandalized three nights before his murder."

"But he had the *rostro* prong with him when he was killed. He must have been carrying it around in his pocket for some reason. For what? Good luck?"

Again, Lago refilled Rhea's wineglass. She held it up to the light with a skeptical expression. "I don't know, Giovanni. You're the expert, but this just doesn't feel like a drug crime to me. Jodie couldn't plan two seconds into the future, let alone follow through with a predetermined drug transfer. Even this restaurant seems wrong. It's too conservative of a choice . . . the kind of place for which you must make reservations a week in advance."

Lago shook his head. "The Gritti could secure reservations on thirty minutes' notice. You're holding back, Rhea. What is it that you're afraid to suggest?"

Rhea took a long sip before answering: "Jodie's spontaneity . . . and his erotic nature. This town would have seduced him. Jodie had two obsessions in life and both were constantly used as a means to define himself: creating art and having sex. And you're asking me to believe that he was occupied with a business proposition."

Lago started to top off her glass but she held up her palm. "This is my third glass."

"Yes?"

"You're still on your first glass."

Lago avoided her eyes but hand signaled that it didn't matter.

Rhea cocked her head. "I saw that photograph in your office. You race cars."

"Yes. It's a man's sport. I compete when I have the time."

"Um-hum," Rhea mused. "Checking the tires, tinkering with carburetors, maximizing intake . . . your mind is always at the next curve, isn't it? What do you plan to do with me if I get drunk?"

"Would you like to find out?"

"I think you're the kind of man who doesn't have to prove himself through sex. You're the exact opposite of Jodie. That's why I was never attracted to him."

"You flatter me."

"And you flatter *me* while extracting information."

Lago's smile broadened: "I could accuse you of the same thing. In any case, I wonder if it's possible to get you drunk. I've been told that you and Verle drank quite a bit on the terrace. It doesn't seem to have phased you."

"It's a matter of conditioning. And at this point, I'm so exhausted that alcohol works as a kind of fuel to postpone collapse."

"Not an aphrodisiac?"

"Venice is an aphrodisiac. Alcohol is a staple." Rhea leaned forward. "And I'll bet you my last dollar that Jodie felt the same way. Don't you find this case vaguely erotic?"

Lago paused for a moment. "Murder is not erotic."

"Of course not. But the events leading up to a murder can be erotic, can't they? Honestly, I'm not trying to be bizarre. I'm just thinking out loud about Jodie's nature and about symbols and the way the local press is covering the case. Interracial lovers have been murdered. Lisa was gorgeous, and the Rivers family makes glamourous ink, but the press has also picked up on the *rostro* as a kind of symbol. Let me ask you this: Is the *rostro* wrapped up in some sort of erotic symbolism? The ornament is strictly Venetian, right?"

Lago furrowed his brow. "Yes and no," he said. "Some say its origins are Roman. Others say Turkish. Still others say that it was an ornament on ancient Egyptian boats that transported the dead to the Underworld. The most popular theory, of course, is that it's strictly Venetian in origin."

"And what does this theory say the *rostro* symbolizes?"

"Again, you must take your pick. Is it a lily? Is it a Doge's hat? Is it a coxcomb? Is it the Rialto bridge? Is it the sea? Everyone has a different interpretation. Some say that the six forward prongs represent the six different districts of Venice and that the one facing backward symbolizes St. Mark's Square."

"I wonder," Rhea said, shaking her head. "There must have been something about it that he translated into his own, personal experience. But what?" Rhea picked up Jodie's sketch. "And what was the significance of this mythical bird?"

Lago raised his eyebrows. He gestured toward the campo, in the direction of the opera house looming a mere hundred feet from their table. "That building," he said, "is not the original one. Did you know that?"

"No."

"The original was built in seventeen ninety-one and destroyed by the great fire of eighteen thirty-six. Six months later, it was rebuilt in its own ashes."

"*Teatro La Fenice!*" Rhea exclaimed. "Theater of the phoenix! Of course. Jodie wasn't drawing a bird, he was drawing the theater. But what did it mean to him? Surely he couldn't have foreseen his own murder."

"Perhaps it's just an unfortunate coincidence. Or perhaps he was planning to meet someone there, later that night. It would be a quiet place to exchange drugs . . . especially this year. This past year, the interior of La Fenice has been undergoing extensive renovation. For insurance reasons, it's closed to the public until November."

"God, I wonder if Jodie knew that?"

Their dinner arrived but Rhea barely touched her food. She kept thinking about La Fenice. It was such a blind spot that she hadn't known what *fenice* meant. She had known the theater all her life. One of her first memories was of La Fenice. Her father took her to the premier of Stravinsky's *The Rake's Progress*, in 1951.

When she told this to Lago, he laughed: "You must have still been in diapers."

"I was only four and the only thing I really remember is all the beautiful ladies in their jewels . . . and carnations . . . red carnations were everywhere. I've been back since. I attended an opera about ten years ago but there were no carnations."

As if reading her mind, Lago put down his knife and fork. "We can go now, if you like. In fact, we can go inside the theater, if you like."

"But you said it was closed."

Lago feigned a grave expression: "I think the night watchman might let me in." Lago motioned for the waiter to come over and asked for the check. "If, as you say, Jodie worked in symbols . . . perhaps, by taking a closer look . . . and while I have you with me . . . You'll be returning to New York soon. . . ."

Rhea asked for another bottle of the Veronese wine—uncorked—to take with them.

"More fuel?" Lago smiled.

"Maybe I'm trying to get *you* drunk."

They quit the restaurant, hand in hand, and approached the left side of the theater, which was flanked by a canal. From this angle, the back entrance to the opera house, where Jodie's body had been found, was hidden from view. But Lago made a sweeping gesture with his arm to point out the ancient stone apartment buildings that formed a collar around the back side of the canal. In effect, from all directions, apartment windows looked down upon and gave view to the back entrance. If there had been a struggle, it did, indeed, seem unlikely that no one had heard or noticed anything, even late at night; the area's acoustics—rather like an aquatic amphitheater—were such that the encompassing stone walls formed a vast echo chamber.

They backed away from this vista, without further comment, passed by the front of the opera house—a dull, neoclassical facade—and followed a narrow sidewalk that hugged the far side of the building. It twisted around the irregularly angled perimeter until it stopped abruptly in a dead end at the very back. By leaning over the railing and craning her head to the left, Rhea could see the broad back steps where Jodie's body had been found. They were harshly illuminated by a lonely but very bright utility light. There was a lot of dust and debris on the steps, indicating that the back entrance was rarely used. Lago explained that, in addition to Jodie's footprints, there had been another set—footprints of a large man in jogging shoes, to judge by the corrugated pattern of the soles.

Turning away from the water, they retraced their steps a few yards and stopped at the side door of the ticket office.

Lago knocked. A few moments later, the door opened six inches and a tiny old man peered up at them. Upon recognizing the chief of police, the night watchman immediately invited them in. He ushered them past a glass-enclosed room, through a turnstile, and into a poorly lighted room large enough to be of indefinite proportions. With a wink, he motioned for Lago to wait. He disappeared for a moment. When he returned, he announced that the lights to most of the areas of the opera house had now been turned on but—"just in case"—he supplied Dr. Lago with a flashlight. If the night watchman ever looked directly at Rhea, she never noticed it. In any case, he soon retreated and left them to their own exploration.

The air was close and quite warm. Lago shucked off his jacket, revealing his black shoulder holster and gun. He loosened his tie. "We'll have to watch our step," Lago warned. "Too many unions are working on the interior. They leave their equipment everywhere. The director of the theater confided in me yesterday that he doesn't think they will be finished in time for the official reopening in November."

Lago took her hand and led her up a steep dark stairwell. They must have climbed thirty feet before they reached the landing which, Lago explained, was the fly gallery.

Just beyond them soared the vast backstage area. There seemed to be acres and acres of plank flooring, slanting toward the back side of the proscenium, which was closed off from the main auditorium by a gargantuan fire curtain. Seventy feet above them was a gridiron of hallucinogenic complexity, suspended with ropes and cables and scenery and lights. The implied weight of the objects, dangling far above them, made Rhea slightly dizzy. She bumped into a circular saw. A pyramid of sawdust tumbled down the front of her skirt.

Lago watched Rhea dust herself off. He caught her eyes for a moment but said nothing.

Next, yanking off his tie as he did so, he led her through a side door which, to Rhea's surprise, opened directly into one of the proscenium boxes in the second tier of the main auditorium. The temperature inside the box was sweltering; the smell, dank and slightly metallic. Rhea's pulse quickened.

She approached the edge of the balcony and looked out.

It was just as she had remembered it. The auditorium both rose and fell away from her view in dramatic semicircular relief. Directly below her was the orchestra pit, bristling with raw lumber, ladders and assorted carpentry tools. Beyond this, on a slightly raked floor of burnt orange carpet were four hundred or more parquet seats, ranked in long neat rows and of dusty, crimson plush and tarnished gilt. In shiny contrast, were the five-tier balconies, newly gilded—piled upon one another by delicate columns and illuminated by glittering, double-candled sconces—all converging at the back of the theater where, framed in massive swags of velvet, the Royal Box reigned in garish isolation. Rhea looked up: the Baroque ceiling, swirling in newly gilded stucco, gave way to swooping cherubs.

Again, she experienced a moment of dizziness. She felt a rivulet of perspiration escape down the inside of her blouse. The wine bottle was sweating too and had left a dark stain against her skirt. She pulled out the cork, took a long drink and handed it to Lago.

As he took the proffered drink, she watched the contours of his chest stretching against an open shirt. She quickly turned back toward the auditorium.

"So exquisite," Rhea said, biting her lip. "This is the kind of place Jodie would have loved . . . the decadence . . . it's what I was trying to explain to you at the restaurant, Giovanni. Jodie gravitated to places where he was forbidden. Forbidden," she repeated the word. "That's what eroticism is really about, isn't it? That which is forbidden? And this place is so evocative of the Eighteenth Century. You can almost see the courtesans milling about with their fans and beauty marks . . . the flunkies in their powdered wigs. Jodie would have loved this place—especially now that it's violated with scaffolding and modern equipment. It's like a vain old woman caught in the middle of a face-lift. I wonder if he somehow managed to get inside? Do you believe in a woman's intuition?"

"No. I believe in intuition, period."

"Well, my intuition says that Jodie was here. This is the first time, since I've been in Venice, that I really felt Jodie's presence."

Lago set down the bottle and came up next to her. "It would have been difficult. I told you, for insurance reasons, security is tight."

"That wouldn't have stopped Jodie—not if he put his mind to it. With that big boyish smile of his, he could have talked his way into the Vatican Council. And if that didn't work, he would have bribed his way in."

"If he did bribe an employee, the truth will come out soon enough. A hundred-thousand-dollar reward tends to diminish the importance of a job. The first thing in the morning, I'll have my men comb the place . . . see if there's any evidence that Jodie was here. He left a trail of clues wherever he went."

Rhea pushed her hair, damp at the temples, away from her face. Quite involuntarily, the gesture turned into a stretch and finally a yawn. Lago watched her closely. When she lowered her arms, she thanked him for bringing her. He shrugged, looking unmoved or, somehow, unconvinced.

"You're beautiful," he said.

Rhea's breath quickened. "Do you have a woman, Giovanni, or do you just have lots of women?"

Lago's reaction was immediate, as if his tacit understanding of the situation no longer needed to be repressed. He pulled her to him and kissed her, very hard, on the lips. She began to unbutton his shirt but suddenly he broke away, craning his neck to the back of the auditorium.

Rhea followed his gaze but didn't understand.

He handed her the wine bottle, removed his shoulder holster, scooped up his jacket and tie, turned on the flashlight and, motioning to her, led her away from the balcony, out of the box, and down a dark, curving passageway.

"Where are we going?" she said and laughed.

"Watch your step," he answered.

His flashlight landed on a large roll of canvas blocking their path. Keeping the light steady, he helped her over.

He led her halfway around the theater before stopping. His flashlight made an arc around a large, ornate portal.

"Yes," he said, "this must be it."

"Must be what?"

"Where we belong," he answered.

They entered the opening. Through a gold, triple archway, the auditorium once again came into view.

They were in the Royal Box.

# 13

Henry's feverish eyes jerked open to a dark room with an even darker figure standing, quite still, at the foot of his bed. He knew who she was. Her head was slightly cocked—a familiar posture. But why did she hesitate? Was she determining Henry's precise position beneath the covers?

He took a deep breath and whispered, "How did you get in?"

"You're awake," she said, sounding disappointed. "I have a key. I was going to surprise you."

"I'm plenty surprised. What time is it?"

"Shh. It doesn't matter."

He saw her silhouetted arms shoot above her head. He heard the rustle of silky material fall to the floor.

"What are you doing?" he demanded.

"I just took off my blouse. Do you mind? Don't turn on the light."

He reached over and turned on the light.

She froze, shamefaced, her hands clutching the waist of her blue jeans, the fly halfway open. No panties underneath. Her dark breasts. . . .

"Please turn off the light," she said, looking down at the carpet.

"No."

"Please. The moon's out. I'll open the curtains and—"

"No."

She walked around the end of the bed. She reached over and tried to touch his bare chest but he rejected her arm, shoving it away with a brusqueness that almost made her topple onto him. She caught herself and turned away. She moved to the windows shrouded in floor-to-ceiling curtains. She drew them back. She swung open the windows. A cool summer breeze wafted in. "Please turn off the light," she repeated.

He sat up a little. "What are you ashamed of?"

"I didn't do anything wrong. It was you. Don't you think I know that you had Jodie killed? God, why are you acting this way? Aren't you happy to see me?"

"Get out of my room."

"It was my room, too," she said, turning around. Tears streamed down Lisa's face. "I know I've hurt you. Turn off the light, Henry. You want me. I know you do. And I want—"

"What? What do you want? To have it again in Jodie's bed with Jodie's dumbshit brother? What you want!"

Henry tried to laugh as a means of concealing his rising desire. Involuntarily, his eyes dropped to her breasts. Her eyes narrowed in recognition. A sad smile cropped up through her tears, which made Henry turn over on his side. He knew he had lost.

"Turn off the lights."

Henry turned off the lights. Blue moonlight flooded the room.

Lisa kicked off her shoes, peeled out of her jeans, hurried over to the bed. He threw back the covers. She got in, sliding against his tense body. All of his anger and humiliation were instantly dispersed by the extravagant softness of her body pushing against his. He entered her with an urgency that must have hurt her but she submitted willingly, almost imploringly, without making a sound.

A low, guttural curse erupted from the vestibule.

Instinctively, he pushed up and away from Lisa's body but she tightened her armlock around his neck and distracted him with a shiver-inducing kiss.

Again he heard the guttural sound, only now it was closer. He wrenched his neck sideways just in time to see his father at the side of the bed, lifting a *rostro* high above his head. For a split second, its edge glinted in the moonlight like an ax.

"Lisa, let go!"

The blade came down into the center of Henry's back with a force and pain that obliterated all other sensations. His arms and legs jerked helplessly against the weight of the blade.

Henry woke up.

Someone was knocking at his door.

"Who . . . who is it?" he barely managed to ask.

The door opened. The harmless clatter of covered dishes and cutlery on casters stirred him into a sitting position. A man in a starched white uniform wished him a good morning, fussed with the tablecloth for a moment, then backed out of the room.

Henry half crawled, half rolled out of bed and onto the floor. He executed thirty push-ups. He turned over and did sixty sit-ups. For a few moments he lay, naked and motionless on the floor while he caught his breath. The aroma of warm ham and eggs filled his nostrils. His stomach tightened in revulsion.

He lurched to his feet, rolled the table out of the room and into the empty corridor. He slammed the door, secured the chain lock and rushed into the bathroom where, sinking to his knees, he yielded to nausea.

*The process has to be reversed,* he thought to himself, over and over again. He uprighted himself and took a long, cool shower. He dried off and swallowed two tablets of codeine. He padded into the bedroom, searched for his watch, finally found it stretched out over the arm of a chair, plucked it up and checked the time.

It was 7:15 in the morning. What time had he passed out the night before? He had no idea. The important thing was that the process had to be reversed. Things might have been different had Rhea kept her promise the night before—had she called his room after her dinner with Dr. Lago. He could have invited her up and shown her what he had discovered in Jodie's suitcase. Things would have been different this morning. But Rhea had blown him off. Things were the way they were and, goddamn it, the process had to be reversed.

He called the concierge and told him he wanted a reservation for the first flight out of Venice. He dressed and packed his meager selection of clothes.

The concierge called back. "It doesn't look good, Signore Rivers. There's a flight leaving in twenty-five minutes but, unfortunately, there's not enough time for you to make it to the mainland. The only available flight is not until seven o'clock tonight. It's a connecting flight to Rome. But, again, there aren't any available flights to New York from Rome until tomorrow morning."

"You mean, I'm stuck here? Surely, there's another way."

"We are on an island, Signore Rivers, and everything is booked. There are seats still available on tomorrow morning's TWA flight, leaving here at nine fifty-five and stopping briefly in London. Unless it's a case of life and death, that really would be the easiest way."

"Very well. Book me."

Henry slammed the receiver into its cradle, thinking, *is it a matter of life and death? And why hadn't Rhea called him last night as she had promised?*

He tramped to the windows and yanked back the heavy curtains. He gnawed on a neglected cuticle for a moment, staring blankly at the water below him. It was a brilliant morning on the Grand Canal. Barges slogged through the water leaving trenches of quicksilver in their crisscrossing wakes.

He turned away from the view. He rummaged through the disarranged covers of his bed, retrieved Jodie's sketchbook—the sketchbook he had discovered in Jodie's suitcase the night before—the sketchbook he had so wanted to share with Rhea—and stormed out of his room.

Posh emptiness: Why were the passageways always empty? The hotel was full. Great movie set for a murder: Verle Rivers charging down the corridor, sacramental *rostro* raised above his head, slashing through chandeliers . . . no witnesses, of course.

He didn't wait for the elevator. There was something mocking about the rich tapestries, the exuberant flower arrangements, the murky portraits of long dead potentates that punctuated the hallways. Feeling foolish and befuddled, clutching the sketchbook to his breast as if it were a goddamn bible, he raced down the staircase.

He stopped at the concierge's desk and said, "I was to meet my father and his wife at ten o'clock this morning. Can you leave a message that they will have to go on without me? Oh, and could you give me a map of Venice, please? Thank you, and would you mind just putting a little *X* where police headquarters is? Thank you."

"Mr. Darlington is having breakfast in the restaurant," the concierge said, folding, then handing Henry the map. "If you would care to speak to him . . ."

"No thanks. My message is for my father."

"As you wish, sir."

He walked quickly to the revolving door and escaped into the early morning sunlight. He set a rapid pace for himself to discourage the inevitable distractions of Venice's distended architecture. His eyes resolutely focused on the stone pavements and his little map. He negotiated through a series of narrow *calles* and over two bridges and through a deep, dark colonnade . . . and out into the sudden bright vastness of St. Mark's Square.

Henry stopped in his tracks. He couldn't help himself. He had seen St. Mark's before but, still, his mouth flopped open in utter amazement. At the far end of the quadrangle, the outlandish Byzantine basilica stood out in garish relief against a pale blue sky—its jangling domes and clashing mosaics and overpopulated statuary and corrugated spires—all seemed to attack one another with self-importance. The giant edifice reminded him of nothing so much as an antique brass cash register on steroids. It brought out the prude in Henry. Given its ostensible religiosity, St. Mark's seemed carnal.

More pleasing to his eye was the square, itself. He had never seen it at this hour. It was devoid of tourists. The only pedestrians were Venetians, presumably on their way to work. The multitude of doves reigned at this time of morning. Thousands exploded into the air while others gently settled to the ground.

He walked forward. The piazza seemed to expand as he approached its center. Setting his jaw with a snap, he referred to his map, then guided himself toward the left side of the basilica where the square funneled into a narrow street.

He traversed a maze of canals. At a kiosk, he spied and bought *Il*

*Gazzettino,* the newspaper with Lisa's photograph on the front page. To see a treasured photograph printed on pulp for mass consumption made him gasp for air. It was as if the entire world had laid claim to his most private thoughts.

The next thing he knew, he found himself at a table, in a middle-class café, where men stood at the bar—their briefcases at their feet—drinking espressos and smoking their first cigarettes of the morning. Henry ordered hot chocolate but barely tasted it. Suddenly he looked up: Why the hell was he sitting here? And drinking hot chocolate? He never drank hot chocolate.

Jodie, who was sitting across the table from him, answered with a serene smile: "Lunkhead. Don't you remember anything? You were afraid that you might arrive at police headquarters before Dr. Lago came to work. You decided to cool your heels for a little bit, to come in here and give him time to . . ."

Henry started to offer some sort of retort but checked himself. He was being surreptitiously scrutinized by the local clientele.

Henry got up, snatched the sketchbook and map off the table before Jodie could bolt with them, made room for himself at the bar, ordered a glass of red wine (which he drank in one gulp), and paid the bill with a tip of guilty proportions.

But of what was he guilty? It seemed that he had spent his entire life feeling guilty and, now that he thought about it, he didn't know why. He had done nothing to warrant guilt.

He walked the remaining few blocks to police headquarters with growing dread. What was he intending to do once he got there? He didn't know exactly. Maybe it would come to him when he got there?

An *agente* took him up to Dr. Lago's tiny office. Lago was at his desk fiddling with his ugly cobra ashtray, sipping a Diet Coke and talking on the telephone all at the same time. Was he surprised to see Henry? If he were, he didn't let on. He simply nodded and motioned for him to take a seat. When he got off the telephone, he said something in Italian.

*Christ!* Henry admonished himself. *How am I going to talk to this guy? I don't speak his fucking language. What was I thinking of?*

"Translator," Henry blurted out. "No speak Italian."

Lago called for an underling who arrived minutes later. The translator was a young lady; not much more than a kid, really, and in civilian clothes. She introduced herself as Rosa, an attendant at the bar.

"What bar?" Henry asked.

"The bar in the basement," she replied. "But I studied English in school and sometimes, when it's needed, I'm called to help out."

"Wait a minute. Are you telling me there's a bar—a real bar—here, at police headquarters?"

Rosa smiled in affirmation. "Is that strange to you?"

"No," Henry snapped. "Nothing is strange anymore. Tell Dr. Lago that I won't keep him long. I wanted him to see this sketchbook, which I found among Jodie's things—things left at the hotel. I thought he should see it."

Lago made no comment but seemed appreciative as he was handed the sketchbook. He opened it with care and slowly, page by page, went through the drawings: a partial view of the basin from Jodie's hotel window; several drawings of lions, the symbol of Venice; a portrait of Verle Rivers as a lion; a *rostro,* another *rostro,* another *rostro;* a nude woman with *rostros* for eyes; another portrait of Verle— this time, brushing his teeth with a *rostro;* the nude backside of a black woman facing a three-panelled mirror; a bride and a giant rooster (with a *rostro* for a coxcomb), taking the rites in an empty, Baroque theater; several views of the theater's ornate interior; more sketches of a bride with pursed lips. . . .

How long did Lago take to thumb through the drawings in a kind of awful, stonefaced reverie? It seemed an eternity. When he finished, he turned back to the drawings of the theater, sighed and finally looked up.

"The commissario says he would like to keep this for a while," the young woman translated. "He's particularly interested in the drawings of the theater and wonders if you have an explanation for them?"

"No," Henry answered, out of patience. "I don't know what the hell he was drawing a theater for. It's the *rostros*—the repetition of *rostros* and their affiliation with my father that's important. Tell Dr. Lago that this sketchbook is like a diary. It chronicles Jodie's week here in Venice. It has nothing to do with drugs and it has everything to do with my father."

Lago listened with interest then asked what was it, precisely, that Henry inferred from the chronicle.

"It's rather obvious, isn't it? The preponderance of portraits of my father indicate that he was bearing down very hard on Jodie. In the week that Jodie was here, Dad's presence became increasingly suffocating and ominous. The *rostro* is a weapon and my father was the one wielding it."

"You're accusing your father of murder?" Lago asked.

"Yes."

Lago laughed. "In the week that Jodie was here, your father's presence was practically nonexistent. During five of the seven days that your brother was in Venice, your father was in Geneva. Did you know that?"

Henry went slack-jawed. "No. No one told me that."

Lago nodded and suggested that Jodie's obsession with his father was self-induced. Then he tapped his index finger on one of the drawings of La Fenice. "What," he asked, "is the importance of the theater sketches?"

"I don't know," Henry shrugged. "It could be a reference to my mother who is still, after twenty-five years in the grave, an audience to my father's fraudulent actions."

That explanation took time to translate. The more he repeated words, the more he was convinced that Rosa was scrambling and undermining his meaning.

"Not you?" Lago asked.

"What?"

"You're the one in the family involved with theater, aren't you? Why couldn't this be a reference to you?"

Henry's face reddened. "You're turning this whole thing around because my father is a powerful man."

"I would like your father's motive for strangling his own son."

"Maybe it has to do with Dad's business? Jodie came to extort money from Dad. He got—or was going to get—thirty thousand dollars out of him. And once he touched you, he'd come back for more and more until the money was gone or he was banished. Well, Jodie got banished in a big way. Maybe he found out something about my dad's business operations that he wasn't supposed to. Maybe he aced into a business conversation that wasn't meant for his ears. Maybe he decided to try out a little blackmail. . . ."

Henry swallowed hard. He suddenly realized how lame and vague and floundering his accusations seemed when spoken aloud. And the stop-and-go of the translating didn't help. He was beginning to regret coming. Everything he said this morning sounded like so many words deposited into quicksand. It was as if there were some sort of sluggish, residual effect from the nightmare. . . .

Lago slid open a drawer. He pulled out a brown file and offered it to Henry.

Henry held it in his hand for a moment, staring at his brother's name typed on the tab label.

Inside, were black-and-white, eight-by-ten photographs taken by the forensic department.

*Shot:* close-up of an open palm, cut and bruised from the imprint of the *rostro* prong, clutched during the moment of death.

*Shot:* contents of Jodie's pockets: passport, small change, two casino chips, two dark nuggets (presumably, hashish), a tiny pipe, a lighter and a felt-tip pen.

*Shot:* *rostro* prong posed next to a ruler that indicated, in millimeters, the length of the sawn-off object.

*Shot:* naked corpse in morgue with red-inked arrows pointing to clearly visible bruises about the neck, wrists, groin, and one leg.

*Shot:* exterior photo of Jodie lying prostrate under the high awning of the back entrance to La Fenice.

*Shot:* close-up of Jodie: tongue swollen, black and protruding; eyes bulging and glazed; left leg slightly off the landing and hanging down the stone stairs that disappeared into the murky water.

Henry could take no more. As if in slow motion, he closed the folder and set it on Lago's desk. Was Lago waiting for him to vomit again? Or maybe cry? He stole a glance at Lago who returned his gaze with dark blue inscrutability.

In a throaty voice, Henry said, "Ask Dr. Lago why he has shared this . . . this scrap album with me."

"He wants you to tell him, now that you've seen what it was really like, that you still accuse your father of murder."

Rosa and Lago exchanged a conspiratorial look of . . . of what? Distaste? Suddenly there was something distinctly superior in the air . . . something that told Henry that there was nothing more obscene to these two Italians than to hear an American accusing his own father of murder.

Henry stood up, unsteadily. "I can see that I have been wasting my time."

Lago glanced at his watch. "Yes, if you don't hurry, you're going to be late for your brother's burial. If my sources are correct, the family plan is to leave the Gritti at ten o'clock, to go to the island of San Michele. Am I correct?"

"I'm not going," Henry answered, glaring at the handsome chief of police. "My presence is of no consequence . . . anywhere in this town . . . including this office, as you've so clearly shown. Good-day, Dr. Lago."

Henry stormed out.

Lago lighted a cigarette and called in an out-of-uniform subordinate. "When you were tailing him from the Gritti, did he come straight here or did he go someplace else?"

"He stopped at St. Mark's Square, sir. I mean really stopped. He stood in the middle of the Piazza for over ten minutes just kind of rocking back and forth—like he was on drugs or something. And then he started waving at the sky or the pigeons or . . . who knows? I don't know what he was waving at. Next, he stopped at a café, sir, for a hot chocolate and a wine."

"That's an odd combination," Lago mumbled.

"Yes, and there was something unusual about his behavior too. While he was at his table, he was talking to himself. But it was more than that. He was talking across the table."

"What do you mean?"

"As if he were talking to another, specific person. In fact, it looked like he was having an argument with an imaginary person. Shall I keep following him?"

"No," Lago answered. "Marcello has instructions to follow him from here on out. You boat on over to San Michele and see who, in this backstabbing family, can bring themselves to pay their final respects."

# 14

*"Pronto?"*

*"Madame Buerklin, s'il vous plaît."*

For a moment, Rhea forgot what country she was in. Why was someone addressing her in French? She switched on the light, checked the time—11:30 A.M.—and transferred the receiver to her other ear.

*"Oui. Qui est là?"*

"This is Marina," a thin, clearly shaken voice answered in a French burdened by a German accent. "Marina Heidinger—Lisa's friend? I've been out of town. I just got the message. If this is some sort of joke . . ."

"I assure you, it's no joke." Rhea switched to German, asking: "Forgive me, but are you Bavarian?"

"Austrian," she answered, immediately reverting to her native tongue. "Lisa's dead? I can't believe it! She was murdered? What . . . what . . ." Marina's voice collapsed under a barrage of heavy sobs.

Rhea shook back her hair, waited for the crying to subside on the other end. Then—as gently as she knew how—she disclosed the gruesome events to the model. Marina remained silent until Rhea mentioned the suitcase full of hashish.

"No!" Marina interrupted, "that's impossible! Lisa never did drugs. Never."

Rhea paused before continuing. "Nevertheless, it was Lisa's baggage in which the drugs were found."

"Impossible," Marina repeated. "Frau Buerklin . . ."

"Fraulein," Rhea corrected her.

"Fraulein Buerklin, how did you know to contact me? Did Henry Rivers give you my number?"

"No. Lisa called you several times last week. It's in the hotel's records. Henry *is* here in Venice and I *did* know that he called you—"

"But the idiot! He didn't tell me Lisa had been murdered!"

"When he called you, he only knew about his brother's death. Lisa was missing and he was worried sick over her whereabouts."

"Then why didn't he tell me about Jodie's murder?"

"I can't presume to answer for Henry," Rhea said, sighing. "But, when he called, why didn't you tell him that Lisa was on her was to Paris? Lisa told you that she was coming, didn't she?"

"Yes. But I didn't tell Henry that because . . . well, I didn't think it was any of his business and I was fairly certain Lisa didn't want him to know. After all, Lisa *had* dumped him in order to have an affair with Jodie. She described Henry as a case—a nanny goat with no ass. I was just protecting Lisa."

"No ass?"

"You know, slang—no luck."

"And Lisa didn't waste her time on losers?"

"Why should she? And why should I tell Henry anything? I didn't know him. I didn't know that she was . . . she was . . ."

Again, Marina broke into sobs and, again, Rhea waited until the crying abated. "Marina, it was brutal of me to break the news over the answering machine. But I didn't know how else to get in touch with you. I thought you would want to know. I know what you're going through. It's an awful shock to all of us. But we have to do everything we can to get to the bottom of this . . . this double tragedy. And as soon as possible. Did Lisa have any enemies? Was there anyone in her life who would have wanted her murdered?"

"No. Not unless you count all the men who didn't get their way with her. Why don't you ask Henry Rivers?"

"I'm asking you."

There was an uneasy silence on the other end. Finally, Marina asked, "Do the police know about me?"

"I'm not sure."

"You're not with the police?"

"Believe me, my interest is purely personal. And I haven't told the police about you. Is there any reason why I shouldn't?"

"Of course not. I have nothing to hide. It's just that I don't know how I could be of help. . . ."

Rhea furrowed her brow. "I just thought you might be able to shed some light on Lisa's last week."

"Why me? I wasn't in Venice. And I've never met any of the Rivers family."

"Well, what did Lisa say about the Rivers family?"

"Why would she mention the family?"

"I don't know . . . *you* just mentioned the family. She called you five times. What did you talk about?"

"Nothing of importance. Clothes, work schedules, the money she had won and lost at the casino. I think Jodie took her there every night. . . ."

"Did she mention La Fenice?"

"What's that?"

"The opera house, here, in Venice."

"No . . . I don't think so. Is it important?"

"Probably not. How did she sound? Was she having a good time here?"

"Who wouldn't with Verle Rivers footing the bill?"

Rhea cleared her throat. "I thought she didn't mention the family."

"Of course she mentioned them. But only in passing."

"I see. But if she were having such a good time, why did she decide to go to Paris?"

"For work, I suppose."

"Had her agency booked her a job?"

"Yes. She said she had a job."

"With whom?"

"She didn't say."

"When did she tell you that she was coming?"

"That last time I talked to her. She said she had booked passage on the train for the following evening. I was going to be out of town for a day and a half. I told you, I just got back this morning. I had a shoot in Ibiza for *Marie Claire;* Satochi was the photographer— doing one of his typical, out-of-focus numbers. Anyway, Lisa knew where I kept an extra key to the flat and . . . well, she was always free to make herself at home, whether I was here or not."

Rhea rummaged through her brain for a way to proceed without making her questions sound like an interrogation. She failed. The more Marina said—or, more precisely, the more she didn't say—the more Rhea suspected her of throwing out a smoke screen. One thing was certain: Marina was a shamelessly bad liar. So far, the most precise information Rhea had received was about Marina's job in Ibiza; the details were obviously important to her. How likely was it that she wouldn't have known who Lisa was supposedly working for in Paris? Wouldn't that have been an essential exchange between two models? And then that entire "I don't know anything about the family" routine was transparently contradictory.

"Marina, was Lisa in love with Jodie?"

"Lisa was always in love with somebody. And, from what I heard, Jodie knew how to have a good time. Look, Fraulein Buerklin," Marina said, easing into a self-deprecatory tone, "I don't know how I can be of help. It's so horrible, horrible, horrible what has happened, but I really didn't see Lisa all that often and, well and oh . . . God bless her soul . . . I'm just too upset to talk about it . . . to think clearly . . ."

"I understand. I know I've caught you by surprise." Rhea thought for a moment, then decided it was time to pull back. "If you do happen to think of anything . . . anything that might assist the police—"

"I'll call them immediately! I promise." Marina jumped at the idea or, at least, at the sudden opening Rhea had given her to terminate an unpleasant conversation. "Oh, I'm going to cry again and someone's at the door. Oh, God, this is awful. Could I call you back?"

She rang off with Rhea's ears positively burning. Marina had no intention of calling her back.

Marina didn't want to be farmed for information. Was she afraid of getting involved with the police? And, if so, why? Was she Lisa's drug contact in Paris? It didn't seem likely. If Marina had been involved with a drug shipment, wouldn't she have been interested in the details of Lisa's confiscated suitcase? Instead, she had immediately dismissed the topic as patently absurd. So, what was her problem? Something, in addition to the shock over Lisa's death, was affecting her behavior.

Rhea placed a call to John Tennyson in New York.

"Woke you up again, didn't I, John? I'm sorry, but I had to tell you about Lisa's friend."

She reported her choppy conversation with Marina Heidinger.

"Give this information to the local police," was Tennyson's advice. "Let *them* find out what's bugging her."

"I'm afraid they'll queer the whole thing. You have no idea how evasive she became once she weighed the prospects of police involvement."

"All the more reason to tell the police."

"Not if she's basically innocent of any wrongdoing."

"Goddamn it, Rhea, I know where this is leading. You've got it in that goddamn stubborn Kraut mind of yours that you could handle this better than the police."

"I do not!"

"Then how come you're calling me about it? You're trying to dispense with your own guilt in advance of the fact. Why don't you just call your new friend, the chief of police? Speaking of which . . . how did your dinner go last night?"

"Fine."

"Did he manage to keep his hands to himself?"

Rhea swallowed hard. "Dr. Lago doesn't grope. He was a perfect gentleman at dinner."

"And afterward?"

"Afterward, we visited the opera house where Jodie's body was found."

"Why?"

She informed John of Jodie's "phoenix" drawing and its curious implications.

Tennyson grumbled something unintelligible, then asked: "So what are you going to do? Stay there until the case is solved? I have to know."

"No. I'm coming home—either tomorrow or the day after. Have you found out anything new?"

"Last night, I talked to Lisa's father in Nassau. I got his number through Lisa's agency, here, in New York. He'd already been contacted by the Italians. He sounded old, or vague . . . or maybe he was just in shock. He couldn't offer much. Lisa hadn't visited home in over three years. He knew nothing about the Rivers boys. Occasionally, she sent her parents a big wad of money but, other than that, I think she had pretty much severed the family ties. I got the distinct impression that he didn't approve of her association with white men. That may have been the source of their falling out. You sure that you've been a good girl?"

"I didn't say that I had been a good girl," Rhea snapped. "Have you been a good boy?"

"Okay, sugar dumpling, let's move on to areas in which I *can* slap your hand. Tell your Dr. Lago about this Marina woman, fight down the impulse to get any further involved than you already are, book a flight and . . . oh, yes . . . call Anne."

"Why? What's happened at the gallery?"

"The problem's not with the gallery. The problem is with your dog. Anne called me last night from your loft. Apparently, Crunch had adopted Anne's purse as a gnawing implement and, when she tried to retrieve it, he transferred his interest to her right wrist."

"Crunch bit Anne?"

"Dined on Anne, is a better description . . . then backed her into your bedroom, where she was panicked into calling me. I had to go down to the loft and save her from certain death—at least, in her mind."

"Where is he now?"

"At the foot of my bed, happily passing gas at five-minute intervals."

"That's what I get for hiring an anorexic to pet-sit. She never gives him enough food, that's all. He's undernourished."

"I don't see any ribs sticking out. And if you don't get your nosey ass back to New York, he's going to be serving time in a kennel."

"Give me two days, John. I'm coming home."

No sooner had she hung up than the phone rang. It was Lago reporting Henry's surprise visit to police headquarters. "I'd like you to see this sketchbook," he said. "How about lunch?"

"I can't. I'm supposed to have a late lunch with Verle and his wife."

"What time?"

"The time wasn't established . . . just that it would be late. Verle said that they had some business to take care of this morning."

"Business," Lago repeated, then laughed. "They're at San Michele, right now, burying Jodie."

"Why didn't he tell me that?"

"Maybe he wanted it to be just a family ceremony . . . in which case, he's been disappointed. Henry refused to go."

"Where is he?"

"Wandering the streets. One of my men is tailing him. As of ten minutes ago, he was on the north side, pacing up and down the Fondamente, talking to himself or the pelicans or God knows who."

"The Fondamente? You can see San Michele from there, can't you?"

"Best view of the cemetery in town."

"I'm so worried about him."

"Me too. How about dinner?"

"I don't know. I'm sick of sitting at tables. And your dinners turn into other things."

"So let's dispense with dinner and go straight into other things."

"I'll make a deal with you. Got a pencil? I'm going to give you the telephone number of a model in Paris. She's an Austrian and her name is Marina Heidinger."

"What's the deal?"

"You get her address for me and I'll take you out to dinner."

"A friend of Lisa's?"

"I'll explain tonight. Shall we say seven-thirty?"

"You taking advantage of me again?"

"You complaining?"

"I'll see you tonight."

Rhea hung up, took a deep breath, then called the concierge.

"This is Rhea Buerklin. I'd like to make a reservation for a sleeper tomorrow night. That's right. The train bound for Paris."

# 15

Wallace Darlington was waiting, impatiently, for Rhea in the lobby. As always, the diminutive man sported a smile cranked up by invisible pulleys. Not so invisible was his agitation as he limply shook her hand.

"A sad day, a dismal day," he said.

Rhea noticed that the briefcase he was holding was handcuffed to his left wrist.

"Did you go to the burial too?" she asked.

He shook his head.

"Where are they now?"

"We're to meet them at Nardi's."

"Nardi's? There's a jewelry store by that name on the south side of St. Mark's Square."

"That's right."

"I don't understand. I thought I was to have lunch with—"

"Everything's backed up today. You and Mrs. Rivers are to go to lunch after Nardi's."

"Verle's not joining us?"

Darlington shook his head. "Verle and I are taking a meeting with the Japanese at the Danieli. I'm rather pressed for time, actually. Shall we go?"

Rhea, who despised tardiness and was nothing if not punctual, resented the implication that she had been holding things up. She had been waiting by the phone for an hour and had come down immediately. Besides, she was sporting a fairly respectable hangover from the night before—in no mood to be admonished. As a minor reprisal, she set a rapid pace for St. Mark's Square—a gait that forced Darlington's short legs into double-time.

"So," she said over her shoulder, "what's at Nardi's?"

"Mrs. Rivers is in the market for emeralds."

"*Is* she?"

Darlington just managed to stay by her side, but he said nothing. Had there been the slightest hint of resentment in his voice?

"What's Mrs. Rivers like?"

"Her people are from Connecticut," Wallace panted. "The Lowry-Chaberts. Do you know them?" He asked as if everyone should know them. "The hyphenation is an old one. Respected East Coast family . . . belongs to the right country club, charity groups, that sort of thing . . . not terribly rich anymore, though her father manages to remain on two notable boards of directors due to his twenty percent holdings in Chabert Enterprises. Mrs. Rivers's maternal uncle is the one with the real money."

"I didn't ask for a portfolio. I asked what she was like. Babs, isn't it?"

"Her Christian name is Barbara."

"Attractive?"

"We'll be at Nardi's in a few minutes. You may judge for yourself."

"I'm asking you. Is she a looker, is she a dog, is she in-between? Surely, you're allowed an opinion."

"It's none of my business."

"How old is she?"

"Past her first youth."

Rhea groaned. "That can mean anywhere between twenty-five and fifty."

"Yes."

She stopped. "Jesus Christ, Wallace, is Babs classified information?"

"No. And I didn't intend to impart that impression."

"Then take out the wooden stake. I'm not a gossip columnist. I've been invited to lunch with a woman whom I've never met and it would be nice to know a little about her."

For the first time, Darlington looked directly into Rhea's eyes—the unfriendly aspect of his smile never more evident. "I'm sure you'll manage to size things up on your own."

"Oh? Because I'm a nosey bitch or because Babs is that self-evident?"

"Please, Ms. Buerklin, you're putting words in my mouth."

"Someone needs to." Rhea resumed walking, though at a slower pace; the street was becoming more crowded as they neared St. Mark's Square. "How did she meet Verle? Can you tell me that much?"

"Business. She was working for him."

"A secretary?"

"Certainly not. She received her M.B.A. from Harvard. She was working for the Rivers Foundation in Liechtenstein when they met."

"What's the Rivers Foundation?"

"Perhaps you should ask her."

"What is it, Darlington, don't you like her?"

"Ms. Buerklin, I'm not paid to like people. Ah!" he said, with sudden relief, as they approached the deep shadows of a stone arcade—massive Sixteenth Century columns—a boundary that separated the ubiquitous Venetian alleys from the singular expanse of St. Mark's Square. "Nardi's is just on the other side of this."

They emerged into the southwestern corner of the Piazza. The sun was quite intense now. A few steps farther, they stopped at a door with a glass panel. Darlington rapped the pane with his knuckle. Osmar could be seen inside, near the entrance, but another large, well dressed man approached and unlocked the door. Wallace and Rhea entered the small establishment.

Few jewels were actually on display. There were richly upholstered taborets posed before transparent tabletops where serious buyers could be attended to in style. As if to verify this, at the far end of the narrow room, Verle and Babs were seated before an array of black velvet trays.

Verle immediately stood up and approached Rhea in a slow stiff gait. The events of the day had obviously taken their toll. It was as though his sorrow prevented him from standing up straight. He wore his sunglasses; his smile was bold but crumpled. He gave Rhea a peck on the cheek and she could smell whiskey on his breath.

"You look beautiful, Rhea. Hope Wallace, here, didn't talk your ear off."

Rhea shook her head. "He restrained himself."

"Ha! Come and meet the wife. Babs, this is Rhea."

Barbara Lowry-Chabert Rivers remained seated but extended her right hand in greeting: faultlessly manicured nails—not too long, clear polish—supporting on her ring finger the largest emerald Rhea had ever seen: a fiery green gem that, in spite of its dark brilliance, looked as soft as butter.

"Nice to meet you, Rhea." Babs pointed to the ring. "What do you think?"

"Very . . . big."

"Yes," Babs frowned, "but what about the color? Is it the right green?"

Rhea took a closer look.

"Green as poison ivy," she offered.

Babs smiled to herself and said in a low-registered voice: "At last, someone to talk to. You know, you and I have a mutual friend, if you can call Ornella Saltzman a friend."

"How do you know Ornella?"

"Well, I knew her when she was Ornella Williams. My first husband and Ornella's third husband were business partners. We had to attend the same boring dinner parties. I can't say I ever liked her, but it does tickle me to know that she's still pursuing the younger men . . . with industry, if not discretion."

"Jodie told you that they were having an affair?"

"Not in so many words. He described her as a patron. Well, you and I both know that the only 'causes' she supports look good in blue jeans." Babs looked back down at the ring. "You're right, Rhea. It *is* a vulgar rock. Too big by far. It's like being saddled. Still, I might get away with it, if I don't wear other jewelry. Maybe I should wait until Geneva? The selection is larger at Cartier's but . . . it's the sentiment that concerns us. Perhaps an emerald *should* come from Venice."

"I'd never really thought about it," Rhea answered, thinking to herself, there isn't a sentimental bone in your well-put-together body. Harvard business school? Well, if you're going to snare a rich man, even an old one, marketing and entrepreneurial skills would come in handy. And what cuddly, high-pitched breasts! Braced for any recession.

Beyond the breasts—and it took Rhea a moment to get beyond the breasts—was a woman in crisply tailored pink linen; a woman approaching, not denying, her mid-thirties. Her honey-colored hair was thick, shoulder-length, and naturally wavy. Her face was fine featured and her complexion was pale and translucent. Rhea guessed her eyes to be hazel but she couldn't be sure; they were red and puffy and partially veiled by sturdy, thick, slightly tinted glasses.

Babs suddenly stood up and Rhea was taken aback by her petite stature, which belied her low voice. Even in heels, she couldn't have exceeded five-five.

She walked past Rhea—over to her husband—and, standing on tiptoes, kissed him on the lips. "I'll take it, Verle. Thank you. I know you're trying to cheer me up. . . ."

"It's been a pretty sorry beginnin'," Verle agreed.

"We'll get past it somehow. And the ring is beautiful."

Verle nodded, then motioned to Darlington: "Settle up with these Mediterranean bloodsuckers. Make sure you get the written description and worth of it on Nardi's letterhead in triplicate form. Osmar and I'll meet you at the Danieli. You brought the papers, right? Just remember, I ain't mentionin' the hiring freeze until we get a fist-full of hard numbers to throw back in their faces. Osmar! Get your ass off that squat-box and open the door. Omar, put those goddamn beads away. Rhea, see if you can cheer her up, would ya? It's been a shit-can honeymoon."

Verle gave a tentative "thumbs-up" to his wife, then hurried out the door, closely followed by Osmar.

Babs stared vacantly for a moment. "That man is in hell," she whispered. "Let's get out of this place. I'm suffocating." Babs returned to the table and plucked up her purse.

Leaving Wallace to attend to the actual purchase, the two women emerged into the early-afternoon brilliance of St. Mark's Square— now laden with thousands of tourists. Omar followed two steps behind.

"It must be difficult," Rhea quietly suggested, "having a guard glued to you all the time."

Babs didn't reply. They walked in silence some fifty yards toward the Campanile. Then, suddenly, Babs came to a halt. She turned around to Omar and said: "I'm so stupid! I left my compact at Nardi's. Would you mind going back and getting it?"

Omar hesitated. Politely but firmly, he objected. "Mr. Rivers said I was to stay by your side."

"I don't think Mr. Rivers had in mind that I should have to needlessly trudge back to Nardi's, do you? Don't be a brute. It will only take you a minute and we'll stay right here."

Omar retrieved his worry beads and flipped them maniacally. Rhea was fascinated by the black tufts of hair sprouting from his nostrils. "I don't know," he said.

"Omar, what, in your wildest Lebanese imagination, do you think could occur in that amount of time and in broad daylight? Besides, I have Rhea to protect me, don't I, Rhea."

"Um-hum," Rhea agreed with mounting interest. She had witnessed Babs gathering up her purse in Nardi's and there had been nothing left on the glass tabletop.

Omar shrugged and executed an about-face. Babs carefully studied his diminishing figure. "Well, Rhea, what do you think? Can you make time in heels?"

"I can fly in high heels, if properly motivated. What did you have in mind?"

"You said it yourself: It's a bore having a guard breathing down one's neck—especially a guard as ugly as Omar. How are we ever going to get to know each other with . . . What do you say we make a break for it?"

Rhea hung back. Was Babs fishing for complicity in order to get Rhea into trouble with Verle? Or did she want to prove to Rhea, that she was her own boss—that she did what she wanted, when she wanted? "Look, Babs," Rhea hedged, "I can't argue with the impulse but . . . what about the consequences? Won't Verle be angry?"

"What would you do, in my situation?"

"I'd probably try to ditch Omar as often as I could but—"

"Where's Omar now?" Babs interrupted. "Can you still see him?"

Rhea stood on tiptoe. By bobbing to the left, then right, she just managed to spy Omar's form disappearing into Nardi's.

"He's gone inside."

"Come on!" Babs urged with a nudge in the opposite direction.

They didn't exactly fly, but with Rhea leading the way and clearing a path for her shorter conspirator, they managed to negotiate the endless knots of tourists—past the Campanile, and then, turning right, between the twin columns of the lion of St. Mark and St. Theodore—past the Doge's Palace flanked by crouching, petulant backpackers—and arrived at the gondola station jutting out from the Basin. A dozen or more faces of expectant gondoliers stared back at the out-of-breath women.

"Which one do we choose?" Babs giggled.

"Well," Rhea said, raising an eyebrow, "if we're trying to escape . . . I'd say . . . go with the man with the biggest forearms."

A quick consultation ensued and, in no time, they were sequestered in the stern of a gondola, among myriad fringed pillows, retreating from the quay and heading toward the mouth of the Grand Canal.

Babs kept looking over her shoulder in apprehension. Once the craft had slipped away from view of the Doge's Palace, Babs leaned back a little and stretched her legs.

"That. Felt. Good."

"Yes." Never one for male curtailment, Rhea heartily agreed. "Are you sure Verle won't be angry with us?"

"Why should he be? Can we help it if his meat fleet can't keep up with us? And it's not the first time I've pulled an exit on Omar. What is it that Wallace says about him? Oh yes . . . 'Omar grew up in Beirut; a great playground in which to learn the difference between hazard and real danger.' Well, maybe so. But Omar doesn't know a snip about women. That's why we got away. His days are numbered, I assure you. It's Omar who will catch hell . . . or, if we're lucky, maybe even Wallace will catch hell. He's the one who hires the muscle."

"Wallace is a resourceful man," Rhea observed.

"Too resourceful. And where does he find these goons? Do you suppose there is some sort of international association for retired terrorists? Macho networking is bad enough without Wallace at the helm."

"He doesn't like you, that's for sure."

"He doesn't like you, either."

"Do you think Wallace is gay?" Rhea asked.

Babs sighed and shook her head. "I wish to God that he were. Then he would be human." She leaned toward Rhea. "Just between us, Wallace has alien bodily fluids. You think I'm joking. He's an honest-to-God monster, Rhea . . . don't accept any other explanation . . . and the guards he hires are the worst kind of thugs. I can barely eat when they're around."

"Have you complained to Verle?"

"Cast aspersions on Wallace? Are you kidding? Wallace was here before any of us and he'll be here long after we're gone."

"What's his hold over Verle?"

"His only allegiance is to the business. That makes him special, in Verle's eyes."

"Why?"

"Well . . . Verle makes all of his key people multimillionaires. You can't be more seductive than that. It keeps them loyal to a point and perversely servile, if you see what I mean. But Wallace is different. His love of money is purely theoretical. I mean, it has to be. How could he enjoy it? He buys nothing. And buys nothing because he has no private life. I think that amuses Verle. Wallace's loyalty goes beyond Verle's cult of personality. I don't think he gives a damn who Verle is or isn't. His robot brain doesn't account for personality. His life is numbers . . . and the cold power that accompanies them . . . and as long as Verle can continue to amass numbers, Wallace will be there to protect them, to line them up into neat little columns."

"How did you meet Verle?"

"Same way I met my first husband. Through my work."

"Which is?"

"It's rather complicated, really. Just think of me as an interior designer for chunks of money being drained by taxes or likely to be. I come in where Republicans leave off. I rip down the fusty old damask and put up something hard and shiny in its place. I helped develop the Rivers Foundation."

"Which is?"

"An umbrella organization to shelter Verle's various interests throughout the world."

"A tax dodge?"

"Among other things."

"And Wallace is on the board of directors?"

"I told you. Wallace is on the board of everything and will remain so, even in the event of Verle's death. He will also receive ten percent of the key registered shares of the Rivers Foundation."

"That must be a fortune." Rhea frowned. "But that's what I don't get about him. If Wallace is so important, why is he delegated to the dinky stuff, like hiring bodyguards and buying jewels?"

"Partially because he qualifies as Verle's oldest watchdog. Partially because he wants to. And maybe it's not so dinky. Maybe it's an essential part of the protection of the little columns I was talking about."

"Well, if Verle allows Wallace to hire thugs it's because Verle has powerful enemies, right?"

Babs was very still for a moment. "Yes," she mumbled, "Verle has enemies. A man in his position . . ." Babs touched Rhea's hand. "Rhea, I'm no fool. I've been around long enough to know what people must be saying about me . . . a gold digger, all of that. But try to believe me, *I'm* not Verle's enemy . . . at least I don't want to be."

"Babs, I have no reason not to believe you, and I certainly didn't mean to suggest that. Look, I don't know how much his money has to do with it but—"

"The pre-nup is as follows: a million upon marriage and, for every year I remain with Verle, I receive, theoretically, an additional million."

"Theoretically?"

"In other words, if I divorce him three years from now, or he divorces me, I will receive three million dollars. Period. End of gouging. Verle and I shake hands, go our separate ways. If the marriage last five years, I get five million, and so on."

"And if Verle dies?"

"Same deal. One million per marital year. No more, no less. It's the goose-that-lays-the-golden-egg clause. Keeps everyone's greed within limits."

Rhea looked out the corner of her eye. "Why are you telling me this?"

"It's not you who needs to know. I thought you might pass the information along to Henry. Unlike Verle, I think Henry has a right to know."

"Why don't you tell him?"

"When would that be?" Babs asked, taking off her glasses. Her cheeks, her lips, her nose, her brow—as if released from a dam—rushed together to form an exquisitely proportioned face, swirling around grayish green eyes. The effect sickened Rhea because she knew the extent to which the move, bordering on the erotic, had been calculated to imply softness. It was a weapon, Babs face. A tool of authentic glamour. "Henry," she continued, "is avoiding me like the plague when all I want to do is to be his friend. I'm no threat to him . . . to anyone . . . and I love Verle desperately . . . though no one will ever believe that."

"Oh, I could believe that," Rhea objected. "For what it's worth, I think Verle, in spite of his age, is a very attractive man. And very vital."

Babs nodded. "And very busy. That's the worst part of it, actually. I spend more time with his underlings than I do with him. We haven't been married a month and, already, our meetings seem like official visits. At his age he should be able to slow down. I thought maybe that that was what this marriage was all about . . . slowing down, enjoying his last few years . . . but now, with Jodie murdered . . ."

Babs looked out toward the water. "I've caused him so much pain. It's my fault that Jodie was killed."

Rhea stared at her but carefully refrained from commenting.

Babs yanked a handkerchief from her purse as if to catch the sob that suddenly erupted from her mouth. The tears streamed down her face. "I'm sorry, Rhea," she cried, using her other hand to rub her forehead. "It's been such a wretched morning. If you could have seen Verle out on that . . . that hideous island . . . sinking to the ground in abject sorrow . . . crying like a little boy over his son's ashes . . . and it's all my fault. Oh, I don't mean that I actually strangled Jodie. . . . How could I have? . . . But I might as well have."

The gondolier, hearing the sobs said something from behind. Rhea turned around and motioned for him to continue rowing. She put her arm around Babs and gave her a squeeze. "Now, come on, Babs, quit talking nonsense."

Babs shrugged off the embrace. She pointed to the right while sinking lower into the pillows. She turned back toward Rhea, half sobbing, half laughing. "God! look where we are." They were passing by the terrace of the Gritti Palace. Babs looked the other way and slouched farther. Rhea scanned the half-empty terrace for members of the Rivers's entourage. There was no one she recognized.

"I'm sorry, Rhea. I didn't intend to make a spectacle of myself. If you like, we can pull over somewhere and you can get off—"

"I'm not going to abandon you." She spun around and told the gondolier to head for the Rialto. "Now, what is this nonsense about you being responsible for Jodie's death?"

"It's not nonsense. Verle told you about the thirty thousand dollar loan he made to Jodie . . . with the new paintings as collateral. Did he also tell you that he ordered Jodie to pack his bags?"

"No."

"No, I didn't think so. That's where I came in. I interceded on Jodie's behalf. I asked Verle to let him stay on for a little bit. He and that awful Lisa woman."

"Why?"

"Because . . . bum that he was, I liked Jodie. He made me laugh. Verle's so busy. There was nothing for me to do, especially since Verle was leaving for Geneva for a four-day business trip. . . . Why should I be left here alone with Omar or someone just as dreary as Omar? Jodie broke up the monotony. By comparison, even Lisa, who was unbelievably jealous of me—so unnecessary, so tiresome—started to look good to me. It's not so hard to understand, is it?"

"So you spent a lot of time with them?"

"With Jodie . . . not so much with Lisa. I don't know what her problem was but she sulked in her room a lot."

"You and Jodie went out together?"

"Me and Jodie and the goons."

"So you were never really alone."

"How could we be?"

"Did he ever take you to the opera house?"

"No."

"What did you talk about?"

"Nothing. Everything. He made me laugh. He cut through the ice right away . . . called me 'Mom' from the very beginning. I didn't mind. I even rather liked it. His irony was so good-natured."

"Was it?"

"Yes, I think it was."

"I never knew Jodie to be good-natured."

Babs wiped her eyes one last time then slipped on her black-rimmed glasses. Her lips formed a little pout before saying, "Jodie and I got past the sarcasm."

"You two became close?"

"Considering the short time we were together . . . yes, I'd say so. There was a meeting of minds."

"Did he ever mention his real mother?"

"Oh, Lorna's story: Verle told me about that. Yes. Jodie talked, to some extent, about his new project based on some stories his mother had written. He was very excited about it. He made me promise not to tell Verle."

"Why?"

"Jodie's self-esteem was pretty rocky—particularly around Verle. But Jodie was genuinely proud of his art. In that one category he had managed to achieve something that even his father ought to have recognized."

"But Verle didn't?"

"Not to his face, no."

"And you had taken it upon yourself to do a little redecorating? To streamline the family shambles?"

Babs jerked her head slightly as if she had just thought of something. "Tell me: Is it true you dined with Dr. Lago, last night."

Rhea looked out toward the water. "That's right. Why?"

"Quite a package, Dr. Lago. What's his first name?"

"Giovanni. What's your point?"

Babs leaned back a little. "You don't want to talk about him?"

Rhea exhaled deeply. "You got a couple of hours?"

"I knew it!" Babs clapped her hands. "Good for you, Rhea. At least someone's having a good time in this odious, petrified city. Did he come on to you? Verle said he would."

Rhea held up her hand. "You have to tell me something first."

"Anything."

"Well, I know your cut in Verle's will, I know Wallace's cut in Verle's will. . . ."

"Yes, and I told you, I think the information should be passed on to Henry."

"I'll be glad to . . . but what good does that information do Henry, if he doesn't know the nature of his own inheritance?"

Babs sat back. "What are you talking about? Henry knows quite well the nature of his inheritance. He gets it all, Rhea. With the exception of Wallace's cut, the boys are the sole beneficiaries."

"And now that Jodie is dead?"

A striped shadow slowly traveled over the gondola. They were just passing under the wooden bridge leading to the *Accademia delle Belle Arti*, a former monastery, now a museum.

"It's fairly clear, isn't it?" Babs sniffed. "Henry gets the whole pie. I'll be a poor relation. But that's old news. I've had enough of the Rivers family to last me a . . ."

The boat emerged into the light. Babs frowned and lifted her hand toward the sun—her eyes scouring her new ring for flaws.

"Now," she said, arching one eyebrow. "You promised me, Rhea. What about Giovanni Lago?"

"Well, he's uh . . . into opera."

"Oh? That's nice. And what, particularly, is it that he likes about opera?"

Rhea thought about it for a moment.

"The encores," she answered, then changed the subject.

# 16

Rhea and Babs lunched near the Rialto, then returned a little before 3:00, by foot, to the Gritti Palace. A scowling Osmar was waiting for them in the lobby.

Babs whispered, "Osmar's a bad sign. That must mean Wallace and Verle are back. Time to face the music."

"If you're worried," Rhea suggested, "we could go out on the terrace for a while . . . put the men in the brutish position of coming down to fetch you."

Babs laughed and shook her head. "I'll be fine. Thanks to you, I've had my daily ration of naughtiness. I can cope." Arm in arm, the women walked passed Osmar and entered the tiny elevator. Babs got off on the second floor.

"You sure you don't want some moral support?" Rhea asked.

"I envision crankiness," Babs said with a shrug. "And if it goes beyond that, it wouldn't take long to pack my bags. I wouldn't mind having an excuse to get out of here."

Rhea nodded, then creased her brow. "Babs," Rhea said, holding the elevator open with the side of her leg, "where do you go from here?"

"What?"

"I mean, you and Verle aren't planning on setting up house here, are you? Venice is just a botched honeymoon, right?"

"Understatement."

"So where's the Rivers home?"

"No home. Just other hotels. Verle doesn't believe in real estate. He's too much on the move to. He has long-term rentals of suites in strategic . . . Geneva, Milano, Paris, New York . . . it was a transient arrangement."

"Was?"

"Is."

"You don't want your own place?"

"What for? It's not so bad, Rhea. Of course," Babs added, smiling over her glasses, "it necessitates buying lots of separate wardrobes. I can't be dragging everything around." She pivoted on her heels and leisurely headed down the corridor.

Rhea returned to her room and placed a overseas call to Ornella Saltzman.

"I remember Babs!" Ornella exclaimed. "Of course it's been nearly ten years. She was quite the dish at twenty-five. How does she look now with all those extra miles?"

"She's taken care of herself," Rhea answered.

"Obviously, if she's snagged Verle Rivers. Still, she's too old to be considered a trophy wife. Let's face it, she's not that much younger than Ivana. Do tell me, Rhea, how did she strengthen her position this time?"

"I get the impression that her tactics have been fairly consistent over the years. She's used her M.B.A. from Harvard as a——"

"Ah, yes," Ornella interrupted. "The finishing school for the younger generation: on your back and at your fax—no need to explain further, darling. So she was working for Verle, was she? Isn't she clever? How can I help to bring her down?"

"Ornella, that's not my intention. On one level, I rather liked her. And, believe me, she has all she can handle. It's an adverse environment here. All I wanted to know was: How did Bab's first marriage end? Was she widowed or divorced?"

"Divorced, darling. The dirt was that she was having an affair—I never learned with whom—and got caught. Made a marvelous recovery, though. Got a decent settlement and then turned right around and maneuvered a job as a personal adviser with one of her ex-hubby's business rivals. The last I heard, she was living in the Hotel de Paris in Monte Carlo. And now she's with Verle Rivers!"

"Yes," Rhea wondered to herself as she hung up, "but for how long?"

Being a successful man-trap was feasible for only X number of years and, as Ornella had pointed out, Babs's years were against her—not a healthy situation when one's natural tendency ran toward unfaithfulness.

So what was Babs's game plan? She had repeatedly complained over lunch that being married to Verle was like being married to a corporation. But hadn't her annoyance seemed feigned? She obviously did as she liked and Rhea had come away with the distinct impression that Babs thrived on being married to a corporation—that a corporate setting was her natural milieu. Whatever her ambitions, they didn't arise from a need to be domestic.

What perplexed her most was that Babs seemed resigned to the fact that her marriage was doomed. She hadn't said it in so many words but there had been moments when she spoke of her marriage in the past tense and in a tone that implied a kind of hale pessimism. Her pre-nuptial agreement might explain such an attitude. Given Verle's vast fortune, Babs wouldn't walk away a big winner. But neither would she walk away a loser.

Babs's only real concern seemed focused on Wallace Darlington. When they had returned to the hotel, she had whispered, *Wallace and Verle are back*. Odd. Why hadn't she said, *Verle and Wallace are back*? Wouldn't that be the more natural placement of the names? Why include Darlington's name at all?

These and other Babs-related questions gnawed at Rhea until about 4:00, when there was a knock at her door.

She had no sooner pulled down on the handle than Henry rushed through the opening.

"Why didn't you call us last night?" he whined, passing right by her.

"Us? Who's us?"

"Me and Jodie."

When he turned around, she was shocked by his appearance. The rings under his eyes were darker than ever, his complexion was an unhealthy gray, his hair was disheveled, and his crumpled white shirt was spattered with what Rhea guessed to be tomato sauce. Most disconcerting of all were his arms, clutching his stomach as if assailed by pain.

"Henry, you look horrible. Do you need a doctor?"

"I could go for a quick brain transplant. The old one seems to have lodged itself somewhere in my gastrointestinal tract. Do you have any idea how much of Venetian statuary is devoted to beasts? Lions, especially. It's a very interesting development. Every time I pass a statue it roars inside my guts."

He plopped down in a chair and kicked off his loafers.

"Make yourself at—"

The telephone rang. It was Tennyson:

"I have something that may be of interest to your cop friend. We ran a credit check on Lisa Morris and the woman was heavily in debt . . . to the tune of thirty thousand dollars. It may be just a coincidence but isn't that the amount Jodie hit his father for?"

"Um-hum," Rhea answered, looking nervously over at Henry who was spinning an ashtray on his forefinger while muttering something to himself.

"Um-hum?" Tennyson grumbled. "Is that all you can say: um-hum?"

"Um-hum."

"There's someone in the room with you?"

"Um-hum."

"Henry?"

"Yes . . . and I think we've gone ballistic. Requires some heavy and immediate hand-holding? I appreciate the information, it's duly regis-tered and I'll get back to you, okay?"

Rhea hung up.

"Who was that?" Henry demanded.

"None of your business. And put down that ashtray before you break something."

"You think I'm nuts."

"You look like a possessed pizza maker. What's all over your shirt?"

"I'm not nuts."

"You're driving *me* nuts. Would you please put down the ashtray?"

Henry obeyed with a blistering smile.

"Thank you. Why didn't you go to the burial, Henry?"

"Why should I? Jodie didn't."

Rhea tried a different approach. "Then what have you been doing?"

"Retracing heavily hoed ground." Henry jumped out of the chair and began pacing the room. "Nobody's paying enough attention to Jodie's work. He left a sketchbook. I would have shown it to you last night, had you called me after your date, like you promised. But I was forced to hand it over to Dr. Lago. Not that it will do any good. It's a veritable diary of Jodie's stay in Venice and nobody gives a shit."

"That's not true. Dr. Lago told me about it. I'm to have a look at it this evening."

"Oh? Another date with Dr. Handsome? Becoming an item, are we?"

"Henry, maybe you ought to rethink the codeine. It may soothe your stomach but—"

"Don't blame the codeine. I'm naturally unlikable. Everybody knows that."

He walked over to the French doors and stared at the rooftop gardens across the way. "I saw a photograph today in Lago's office. I saw lots of photographs, actually, taken by the forensic department—grisly, clinical photographs—images that stick, you know? Stick like fucking flypaper. That's what Jodie tried to do, wasn't it? Create images that struck like something unwanted. That was his approach, wasn't it?"

"What's your point, Henry?"

"The forensic photographs. The one that bothered me the most was the picture of the contents of Jodie's pockets: the passport, some coins and casino chips, some hash, a hash pipe, a black felt-tip pen, a lighter. I've walked a hundred fucking miles today trying to decipher what bugged me about that particular photo. It was like a self-portrait by Jodie, you know? As if he had planned it. The itemized ingredients of his twisted personality laid out on a table. Like one of his sick, artistic jokes. Like the portrait he did of me with the spoons and Mylanta bottles . . . cruel . . ."

Henry spun around and approached her with a belligerent expression. "I tell you, nobody is paying enough attention to Jodie's art."

Just as quickly, a strange, disengaged look came over his face. "My mother paid attention. From the very beginning, when Jodie was old enough to hold a crayon, she paid attention . . . saw his potential. God, to know your direction at the age of three! He could draw all day, perfectly content."

Once again, Henry paced the room. "At first, they were just innocuous pictures that any brat might draw . . . cowboys and Indians, that sort of thing. But it soon became apparent that those cowboys weren't doing very nice things to the Indians . . . and vice versa. Beheadings, impalings, scalpings, flayings . . . and the more violent they became, the more fascinated Mother became. She began tacking his work to the walls. Our house had sixteen rooms; every one of them, eventually, became covered with Jodie's heavily populated massacres. He was like a precocious Hieronymus Bosch and she was his curator. I can still see her with that little hammer she'd ordered from Neiman-Marcus—stalking the house with Jimmie Cloudfoot at her heels, looking for a bare space. She made an unwanted house into a museum. Come to think of it, Jodie spent the rest of his life looking for a comparable patroness." Henry laughed. "Anyway, after an extended trip, Dad came home and pulled down all the drawings. He said she was making a mockery of him, which, of course, was . . . was true?"

A wide-eyed expression came across his face as if he had just discovered something.

"You're asking me?" Rhea said carefully.

He rushed back over to the French doors—only this time he disregarded the view. He grabbed a fistful of the heavy drapery that hung from the ceiling.

"The black felt-tip pen! It could be, you know."

"What could be?"

He no longer heard her. He stormed past her and swung open the door.

"What are you doing?"

"Can't thank you enough, Rhea."

"Thank me for what? Would you come back here?"

"Yes, I'll come back, later—"

"That's not what I meant."

"Gotta go talk to Jodie." Laughing, he planted a kiss on her cheek and left.

"Henry!"

He turned around. "What?"

"Idiot," she said, pointing to his bare feet.

He ran back into the room, snatched up his loafers, mumbled something unintelligible, then hurried down the corridor.

Rhea closed the door and called back Tennyson, reporting Henry's whirlwind visit. "It's getting scary. I don't know if it's the pills or . . . maybe he's just trying to be theatrical. He's a theater person. Don't they act that way? Maybe he's just trying to get attention."

"Maybe he's genuinely unhinged."

"No. I just can't resign myself to that idea. Not yet."

Rhea changed subjects. She told Tennyson about her meeting with Babs. ". . . and according to her, Henry is the main beneficiary. That was the most important thing I learned."

"No," Tennyson disagreed. "The most important thing you learned is that Henry *knows* he's the main beneficiary. That, at least, explains Joella's evasiveness when I visited Henry's office. She knew. And she knew that Henry wouldn't want it broadcast. You're going to have to come to terms with all of this, Rhea."

Rhea hung up, hoping to have a little time to catch her breath—to mull over Henry's frenetic visit and John Tennyson's warning.

No such luck. Almost immediately, Henry rang her up from his room.

"Found it," he sang. "Want to come take a gander? We're on the same floor. I'm at the opposite end."

"Found what?"

"Mother's here. Jodie's here. Dad's here. It's a family reunion."

"What?"

"Come see for yourself. Trust me. Just get down here."

Two minutes later, against her better judgement, Rhea was standing in front of Henry's room.

When he opened the door, she took a step backward. His eyes were glazed now—feverish. Sweat was pouring from his brow and his hands were trembling.

"Now you'll see," he said, gritting his teeth. "Now you'll see. What are you waiting for? Come in."

Rhea took a deep breath and entered. Henry slammed the door and locked it with a grin. The television was on at full blast, blaring an Italian news program. Henry's breath was labored and foul smelling. The entire room was charged with a feeling of hostility and Rhea recoiled from the sudden intimacy.

"You said your parents were here. There's no one here. What's the big discovery?" she asked, trying to remain calm.

"Hiding!" he said triumphantly, pointing toward the open windows overlooking the Grand Canal. "Always hiding."

Rhea didn't understand. "Are you talking about the view?"

"No, not the view! What conceals the view. Mom's drapes. They've been gnawing at me ever since I set up camp here. They were my mother's drapes. That's what I didn't get."

Rhea walked over to the television and switched it off. "That's better," she said, turning toward him. "Now, why don't we just start from the beginning—"

"Don't be condescending to me."

"I'm not—"

He rushed to her side. "Here's what we'll do," he said, grabbing her hand. "We'll walk over to the windows, you close your eyes, I'll draw the drapes behind you, then you turn around, and when I say 'now,' open your eyes."

"Like a child's game?" she asked, stealing a glance at the locked door.

"Yes, that's it. Come on."

Rhea pulled back. "I've got a better idea. First, why don't you just tell me what's so important about the drapes?"

"But I've already told you! The black felt-tip pen found on Jodie's person. That's what was bugging me. I didn't realize it until I started reminiscing about Mother and then noticed the drapery in your room."

"You want me to stand if front of the windows?" Rhea stared doubtfully at the open French doors. "You're still not making sense, Henry."

"Trust me. Just come on over," Henry urged, giving her arm another tug.

"Goddamn it," she exclaimed, wrenching away her hand. "Quit grabbing at me. Just tell me what—"

"Why not?"

"What?"

"Why won't you come to the window?"

Rhea hedged: "Maybe I have a fear of heights."

"Really," he said, his eyes narrowing. "I didn't notice any fear of heights when we were on the jet."

"Jets are different."

"Are you afraid of me? Is that it? What do you think I'm going to do—shove you out the window?"

"Of course not. All I know is that you're coming at me with a lot of creepy dramatics. I'm not in the mood, okay?"

"Christ."

Henry retreated to the bed and sat down. All the excitement drained from his face. His drawn features suddenly made him look ten years older. He plucked at a neglected cuticle. "You think I would want to kill you," he said simply, not looking up. Then, he laughed. "At this point, it's almost flattering to be feared. Beats pity."

"Oh, bullshit, Henry. Eliciting pity is your forte." She added quickly: "Look, I don't want to get into this. Just . . . just slow down for a minute and explain to me what you've discovered."

"I could kill you. I'm strong enough to grab you and throw you—"

"Okay, that's it!" Rhea started for the door.

"Wait. I was just kidding."

"No, I can't take this anymore. I'm trying to help but—"

"Okay, I'm sorry! No more creepy stuff, I promise."

"For God's sake, Henry, just tell me what's so important about the drapes."

"The drapes," he intoned, as if rifling his memory. "Oh, yes. The drapes. It was the forensic photo that made me remember. The felt-tip pen found in Jodie's pocket. Back when we were kids—"

"The drapes, Henry."

"I'm getting to the drapes! But remember? I told you that Dad came home and took down all of Jodie's pictures?"

"Yes."

"Well, he and Mother had a terrible fight. They went from room to room screaming at each other. He called her crazy and told her that she was intentionally trying to vandalize his home. She countered by saying that there *was* no home—just a ludicrous pile of stone and glass. She eventually gave in. She raised the white flag and Verle said all was forgiven." Again, Henry laughed. "But Mother never gave in, not really. That was something Dad never figured out: white flags might be held high on the battleground . . . but they were never evident in the trenches, if you see what I mean."

Rhea cast a fresh glance at the open windows. If the fall didn't kill her, the infested water probably would. "Your mother retaliated? Is that what you're trying to say?"

"The minute he left for his next business trip, Lorna supplied Jodie with a black felt-tip pen—the broad-tipped kind, the kind you use to label boxes. She told him: 'From now on, our art gallery will be a secret one. Wouldn't you like that, Jodie? A house full of secret canvases?' She invited him to use the linings of the drapes—throughout the house. Jodie, of course, loved the idea."

"And he drew pictures on your mother's drapes?" she asked.

"On the linings," he corrected. "And it was a pastime he didn't give up as he got older." Henry looked up with a smile. "He did it to my drapes about two years ago. You see, my mother is here. She won't be excluded. All you have to do is go over to the windows and see for yourself."

Rhea crossed her arms. "Just tell me one thing, Henry. Tell me you're not crazy."

Henry crossed his arms in imitation. "The part of me that is not crazy is telling you that I'm not crazy."

Rhea pursed her lips.

She walked over to the open windows. With her back to Henry, she yanked the edge of one curtain and pulled it away from the casement. Black-purplish lines scored the lining but the folds of heavy material distorted and broke up the image.

"See?" he said. "I wasn't making it up."

She turned around.

"Close the curtains on me," she said.

He got up, approached, waved good-bye to her and drew the drapes.

The smell of the fabric close to her face was dusty and saline. Given the size and proximity of the drawings, Rhea would have to lean back out the windows to get a good look. The sound of motorboats filled her ears. She tried to ignore the sounds coming from behind her. She concentrated on the images in front of her. A gasp of recognition came out of her throat.

On the left curtain was a huge rendition of Verle Rivers's face. On top of his mane of hair was a *rostro*—perched like a coxcomb, the symbol of cuckolds. Below the portrait were the words: "Dad I does."

On the right curtain—in a supine and open-legged, pornographic position—was a drawing of a woman, nude, except for a pair of thick-rimmed glasses. In one hand she held a paintbrush. Below her were the words: "Bride does too."

A low, mirthless laugh erupted from the other side of the drapes. "It's a goddamn wedding diptych! You see what it means, don't you, Rhea? Jodie finally found a way to even the score with Dad! I should have figured it out immediately! The only real power my brother ever had was the paintbrush between his legs."

With her shoulders, Rhea created a gap between the curtains and walked past Henry.

"Well, you *do* see it, don't you?" he pursued her.

Rhea didn't answer.

"Do I have to spell it out for you?" he continued. "Jodie was fucking my new mother. It's obvious."

Rhea turned around. "Is it?"

"I think the inference is logical enough. If Jodie wanted to hurt Verle, sex would have been his way. What other method did he have available to him?"

"Henry, you want everything to be systematic—to be traceable to one source—your father. The drawings don't prove that an affair actually occurred. The only thing those curtains prove is that the disgusting idea of making it with Babs crossed Jodie's mind. Maybe it was only wishful thinking on Jodie's part."

"Listen to me. My father would kill any man who tried to fuck his wife. Those curtains read like a death warrant."

"Only if it actually happened, Henry. And how could it have?"

"Lago told me this morning that my father was in Geneva most of last week. They could have found their moment during his absence."

"But Babs is constantly surrounded by bodyguards and. . . ."

Rhea remembered how she and Babs had escaped from Omar. It hadn't been terribly difficult.

"What are you thinking about?"

"What? Oh, nothing. . . ." She tended to agree with Henry's theory. But at this point, channeling her information to the proper people was essential and Henry was too much of a wild card to be trusted. Rhea assumed an expression of skepticism. "Don't forget Lisa, Henry. Where was she during this alleged affair?"

"The waiter at the restaurant said Jodie's and Lisa's last dinner together was unpleasantly silent. They barely looked at one another."

*Lisa sulked in her room a lot,* had been Babs's explanation in the gondola. Rhea tried to remain impassive: "Henry, I was around Babs and Verle this afternoon. There was no distrust in the air. Verle seemed extremely solicitous, very concerned for his new wife. He was buying her jewelry, for God's sake. If you father knew of an affair, would he buy her jewels? Your father's no fool. I'm sure I would have sensed something. . . ."

Rhea walked over to the bed and sat down.

Henry drew open the curtains and stared out the window.

"Jodie betrayed everyone," Henry said. "You won't disagree with that, will you?"

"No," she answered. "He betrayed me, Ornella, you . . . and this awful drawing of Babs betrays her trust, with or without an affair."

"And if Jodie did make it with her, Verle was betrayed as well." Henry lifted an index finger. "And don't forget Lisa: Left in the dust for my new mother—that couldn't have gone down very well with her."

"Yes," Rhea sighed. "That would make it all neat and tidy: across-the-board treachery."

"Not entirely across-the-board," Henry objected, making a sweeping gesture with his arm. "Don't forget the interior decorator. This room." Henry reached for the hem of the curtain. "You know what I think? I think Jodie was re-creating this hotel . . . transforming it into his home . . . like the only home he had ever known . . . a home of too many rooms, too many ulterior motives, too much silence with an absent father footing the bill. You see? Jodie wasn't totally incapable of loyalty. He remained true to our mother. Even the words on the drapes indicate that."

"Explain."

"Since when did Jodie incorporate the written word into his drawings?"

"Never," Rhea admitted. "He abhorred artists who did that. Jenny Holzer's recent success drove him to distraction."

"So why was he starting now? I'll tell you why. My mother's stories . . . he was planning to do a series of collages incorporating my mother's stories and these drapes were a trial run, Rhea. And just like Lorna, he'd cast Verle as both villain and victim."

Rhea shrugged. "The question remains, did Verle *know* he'd been cast?"

"There's one way to find out." Henry grinned. "Invite Dad and his foxy little wife up here, show them the drawings and see what they say."

"A try-out?"

"A casting person should remain objective until the audition begins."

Rhea looked down to the floor. "You're anything but objective, and your contrivances make me sick, Henry. You long to see his pain."

"Do you wish to protect Dad?"

"I have no interest in protecting him. It's you I'm talking about. Jodie wasn't the only son obsessed with his mother. Your vengeance will eat you up. Just like it ate up Jodie."

"Good God!" Henry's look was incredulous. He put a trembling hand up to his chest. "You sound as if there were something worth salvaging!"

# 17

The police boat was out on the Lagoon, heading for the tiny island of San Giorgio Maggiore. As they approached, the copper-green bell tower of the church stood out in clear relief against a darkening sky. But Lago and Rhea had no intention of visiting the church, nor of stopping at the island. Indeed, Rhea's only desire (and Lago's only order to the driver) was to keep the craft moving. Traveling through the water, removed from the population, soothed by the droning vibration of the boat and the constant jostling of the wind, the two were content to keep a vigil on the progress of dusk.

They had finished a half a bottle of wine before Rhea was willing to talk, in detail, about the afternoon: How she and Henry had reversed the curtains so the linings could be witnessed from any part of the room; how they had called Verle and urged the newlyweds to join them; how Verle and Babs had complied but not without the additional presence of Wallace Darlington. . . .

"Almost immediately, Babs burst into tears," Rhea explained, "so, of course, she was the main focus. She kept repeating the word 'cruel' and 'Why would Jodie do this?' and 'I thought he was my friend.' It was awful. She was as helpless as she was humiliated. And when I tried to console her she pushed me away . . . looked at me with utter hatred. I know what she was thinking: that I was conspiring with Henry to break up her marriage. My mere presence in the room was enough to prove my guilt. And it's true, Giovanni. I could have persuaded Henry not to invite them up. But I went along."

Lago clasped her hand. "And Verle? What was his reaction?"

"Strange. A little shocked, perhaps. But not shaken. He remained calm. His concern was for Babs. It was clear that nothing else, no one else mattered. He put his arm around her and begged her not to give Jodie the satisfaction of seeing her so upset."

"Jodie?"

"Well, that was what was strange. When Verle said that, he was looking directly at Henry, but he said 'Jodie' and, to tell you the truth, for a moment it seemed quite natural . . . as if Jodie and Henry had become one and the same person. I don't know . . . it was just an odd little moment that came and, just as quickly, evaporated . . . like when a computer speeds into a glitch and gets temporarily locked into a different sequence that you are powerless to keep up with.

"Anyway, Verle did calm Babs down. She was so openly relieved to see his loyalty to her . . . his trust in her. Verle never entertained, not for a moment, the possibility that she and Jodie might have been lovers. . . .

"But here's the really weird part: The minute Babs calmed down, Wallace Darlington took up the slack."

"Darlington? What do you mean?"

"He became . . . emotional. I know that sounds absurd but there's really no other word for it. I never would have thought it possible. His face got all red. He cursed. He cursed Jodie, he cursed Henry, and he cursed me. Even more astonishing, he actually vented his anger on Verle. 'This is how your kindness is paid back!' he told him. 'Maybe now you'll listen to reason,' he said.

"And Verle did listen. He nodded his head very slowly. He went over to Wallace and patted him on the shoulder. He came back to me, cleared his throat and said, 'Rhea, the deal's off. I know we discussed mounting a big retrospective of Jodie's work. Yesterday, I wanted to do something in his memory. Not after this obscenity. Let the little bastard and his mother rot.'

"He didn't say a word to Henry. Acted like his son was invisible. He took Babs's hand and urged her toward the door. They left, neither one of them looking back. Wallace shot us a victorious smile as he walked out the door. Bam. And then they were all gone."

"Henry's reaction?"

"Fury. He said that Babs was lying. He called her performance Obie material. But he conceded one thing. Right then and there, he cleared his father of any wrongdoing . . . swore that Verle had known nothing of the affair until he saw the drapes."

"But he still believes that something was going on between Jodie and Babs."

"Yes."

"And you?"

Rhea took another swig from the wine bottle. "I don't know what to think . . . or even if it matters. In any case, any effectiveness I might have had is now gone. No more girlie talk with Babs and no more benevolence from the great Verle Rivers. I'm shut off at the source. It's just as well that I'm clearing out tomorrow night. I blew it."

"You give up?"

Rhea shook her head. "I didn't say that. Marina Heidinger: Did you get Marina's address in Paris for me?"

"I have her address," Lago answered, his blue eyes catching and holding Rhea's evasive gaze. "Why do you want it?"

"I'd like to confront her."

"Now, Rhea—"

"It's the last venue open to me in which I might be of some help."

Lago smiled. "Confront?"

"Confront was a poor choice of words. I promise, there will be no theatrics like this afternoon. This afternoon was Henry's brainstorm. I was caught up in the moment and . . . I just want to talk to Marina."

Lago put his arm around her. "Why don't you let us handle Marina?"

"But that's the worse possible idea! I told you, Marina acted very paranoid about the police. She didn't want any part of them. She's holding back on something, and I know she wants to talk. Just promise me I can have first shot at her. If it doesn't work, then your goons can come in and do anything they want. Shake her down . . . put her on the rack for all I care."

"Give me one good reason why I should let you have first shot."

"Because I'm the one who made the connection. I'm the one who checked out the phone calls placed from Jodie's and Lisa's room. Because I'm the one who tracked Marina down, who talked to her. Where were your police then?"

Lago frowned. "Our investigation hasn't been top-notch," he admitted. "The sketchbook found among Jodie's things should have been brought to my attention. The phone calls should have been investigated. Perhaps the *rostro* and its symbolic importance should have been considered. Your hunch that the *rostro* might have erotic implications seems to be a sound one: Verle as the cuckold—at least, in Jodie's mind. But when drugs are involved—and don't forget, Rhea, drugs *are* involved here—there is every reason why the investigation of that particular illegality should be pursued first. I have done that and I haven't come up empty-handed."

Rhea cocked her head. "You've found something out?"

"While you and Henry were window-dressing," Lago said, casting a wry smile, "I was interrogating a local pusher, brought in this afternoon on a tip that was unrelated to the Rivers-Morris case. His apartment was searched, sizable amounts of drugs were confiscated from the premises—hashish among them. But of even more interest was an envelope discovered in his bathroom: an envelope with the gold Gritti Palace logo. Forensic had a look and Jodie's fingerprints were all over it. Well, the assumption is that Jodie used it to hold the money for a drug purchase. Why else would the pusher have it in his possession? Incidentally, the man's apartment is not far from La Fenice."

"And what did the men find in La Fenice? Any trace of Jodie?"

"Several things: a used matchbook with his fingerprints, several cigarette stubs . . . but there's still no indication as to why he was there . . . and we still don't know how he got into the theater."

Rhea snatched back the bottle and took a drink. "This pusher: Has the man confessed to knowing Jodie?"

"No, not yet. But if the hash he was peddling matches the hash found on Jodie and in Lisa's suitcase, the connection will be just that much stronger. I think it's only a matter of time before he helps us out."

"You think he could have killed Jodie?"

Lago heaved a sigh. "That's a problem. The guy's a runt. He would have had to stand on tiptoe to reach Jodie's neck. Guardia di Finanza is seeing if any of his shoes match the footprints taken from the steps of La Fenice but I'm not counting on that. There's probably other people involved but, in any case, this is our first good lead." Lago gave Rhea a little squeeze. "And my lead is not based upon Gothic interpretations of a *rostro.*"

Rhea said nothing.

Once again, Lago took her hand. "Look, I'm not discounting some sort of family involvement. I've tried to absorb as much of the Rivers's idiosyncracies as I can . . . right down to Jodie's apparent obsession with his mother but . . ."

"But?"

"The Riverses are leaving tomorrow. Babs, Verle, Henry, Wallace, bodyguards, the whole circus . . . have arranged to check out of the Gritti Palace by noon."

"Where are they going?"

"Geneva. All except for Henry. He's booked passage on a commercial airline for New York. Oh . . . and there's Verle's team of private detectives: They're staying for a few days."

"Where are they? I haven't seen them around the hotel."

"They're around . . . though they're not being put up in the Gritti."

"But the main players are leaving. Just like that. And you're not going to stop them?"

"On what grounds? I can't detain them against their will. Besides, Verle's not entirely abandoning Venice. His hundred-thousand-dollar reward is still in effect."

"It's pretty sudden, isn't it? They just fold up camp like a traveling show—"

"Come on, Rhea, what's to keep them here? Jodie has been buried. None of them give a damn about Lisa. Venice can't have very pleasant connotations for them anymore. And I wouldn't be surprised if the drape episode sped things up. It may be time for you to let go of this, Rhea. You and Henry tried to force the issue this afternoon and—"

"And it backfired," Rhea answered with turned-down lips.

Lago kissed her. "No, it didn't. Not entirely. At least it eliminated one suspect: Verle Rivers. If Babs was having an affair with Jodie, Verle didn't know about it until now. You described his behavior as of a man not knowingly wronged. Even Henry absolved him. There's no reason for him to have orchestrated Jodie's death." As an afterthought, he added: "It's only now that he would like to introduce vengeance against his son."

"What do you mean?"

"He's cancelled any participation in Jodie's show. He wants him to die in obscurity."

The sky was quite dark now, the air cooler. Lago tightened his embrace and pointed back toward the glow of St. Mark's Square.

"Shall we go back . . . find a restaurant?" he suggested.

"Not yet." Rhea sighed. There was anything but resignation in her eyes. "It's going to drive me crazy, Giovanni . . . leaving Venice with so many unanswered questions. What was Jodie doing in La Fenice? Henry's the theater person . . . and the footprints on the steps . . . whose shoes were they—?"

"Rhea, there's no use getting into this now."

"It's not a matter of getting into it. It's a matter of getting out. When I'm propelled into a mess, I can't just pick myself up and walk away from it. I've come too far and I don't see any magical stop signs out there that impel my curiosity to comply."

"What *do* you see?"

Rhea consulted the sky—now a mass of scattered stars—before answering: "I see a big fat smirk on Jodie Rivers's face."

Lago laughed. "So what do you want to do? Join the Venice police force?"

"No, damn it. I want a consolation prize. I want Marina Heidinger's address. I want first shot."

"This is our last night, Rhea."

"I know that."

"If I give you Marina's address. . . ."

"Yes?"

"Will you stop talking about the case?"

Rhea reached over and kissed Lago on the lips.

Lago released her and walked up front to speak to the driver.

The boat suddenly came about, slicing through the furrows of its own black wake. A moment later, the craft picked up speed, its nose dead set on the glimmering reflection of the Molo and Riva degli Schiavoni.

Giovanni came up from behind and nuzzled her neck. Rhea shuddered and gave in to his touch.

Why did she so easily, so completely, respond to Lago's passion? Splendid as it was in its own right, there was something else. There was something about the angle of his jaw, the scent of his skin that flirted with the very core of Jodie's murder . . . a perverse kinship . . . a timeless ancestry . . . a sensation that upgraded her tenuous reality of the Rivers family into a logical correlation.

Lago's hands moved to her breasts.

"Let go," he whispered.

Her brooding melted into exhilaration.

# 18

Rhea spent the night at Lago's. Staying at the Gritti Palace was beginning to feel like being an unwanted guest in Verle's personal domain. It was a loathsome sensation, as loathsome as Lago's company was comforting.

Lago's flat—simple and immaculate—was located in the northern section of Venice, next door to what had once been Tintoretto's home. Verrochio had also lived nearby, the sculptor who had created the equestrian statue in front of the hospital—the same statue that, two days before, Henry had likened to his father. Otherwise, the neighborhood's primary charm was that it was rarely penetrated by tourists.

At 7:30 the next morning, they shared a pot of coffee on Lago's roof garden—an *altane,* as it was called locally. Both of them kept referring to their watches. *Only two days ago!* Rhea thought to herself, stirring milk into her cup, remembering her visit to the hospital morgue, feeling as if she had been in Venice for a month. It made her irritable and melancholy at the same time. How much had transpired since her arrival and how much remained to be explained on the day of her departure.

The sad inconclusiveness of the situation spilled over into her feelings for Giovanni. She might have known him all her life. How to say good-bye to this courteous, succinct and deeply passionate man? She passed him his lighter.

As if reading her mind, Lago took her hand and postponed their separation by suggesting that he take her to the train, later that afternoon.

She agreed and they went inside. She took off Lago's bathrobe, which she had been wearing. While he showered and shaved, she donned her crumpled clothes from the night before. She washed and put away the cups and was about to take her leave when Lago's telephone rang. Lago rushed into the living room and picked up the receiver. She started for the door but his forefinger indicated that the call was case-related; he motioned for her to sit down.

"That was Questura," he said, as he hung up. "Verle's reward money is beginning to pay off. The night watchman of La Fenice—the same old man who let us in—has admitted that Jodie bought his way in for a private tour—not once but twice—his last visit being the night of his death."

Rhea frowned. "Jodie didn't speak any Italian. How could he—?"

"Oh, it wasn't hard. He had a crisp fifty dollar bill and he flashed his sketchbook. The old man was impressed by the sketches, took Jodie for some kind of architectural expert and saw no harm in . . . Jodie was alone on both visits."

"Alone? You think the old man's lying?"

"I don't see any reason why he would. He's jeopardized his job in the hopes of reciprocity. The more details he can supply, the better his chance for money. Anyway, the night of his death, Jodie left the theater around three. The old man ushered him to the ticket-office exit . . . even walked outside with Jodie and watched him return to the front of the theater before going back inside. The old man is positive that no one was waiting for Jodie outside."

Rhea looked up. "But the murderer was waiting for him—if not there, then around the corner or in a nearby alleyway."

"Probably, given the coroner's estimated time of death."

"Wait a minute, Giovanni." Rhea stood up. "The night watchman says Jodie had his sketchbook with him?"

"That's right."

"But the sketchbook was discovered in his room by your men! That doesn't make sense . . . not unless he returned to the Gritti after leaving La Fenice, only to leave the hotel again."

"Impossible. In the middle of the night, the doors of the Gritti are locked. You have to ring a bell. The night porter has to let you in and the night porter swears that no one was let in that night."

"So how did the sketchbook find its way back to his room unless the murderer took it back to the Gritti himself . . . someone who had access to Jodie's room . . . someone with the Rivers entourage—"

"Slow down, Rhea," Lago said, shaking his head. He walked over to his coffee table and picked up the sketchbook in question, a flimsy notebook with a black cover. "Students use these. You can buy these in a dozen places in Venice and they cost next to nothing."

"So?"

"You're assuming that Jodie had only *one* sketchbook. What was to prevent him from having purchased two, or three, or four?"

"Yes, but . . . you said that the night watchman was shown drawings. Surely, if you let him look at this sketchbook, he could make a positive identification."

"We'll soon find out," he said, picking up his keys and stuffing them into his pocket. "That's where I'm going right now, to see what he's got to say."

"And if he does identify it as the same one?"

"Then I'll be making an unexpected visit to the Gritti this morning."

"You'd better hurry. They're returning to Geneva at noon. They're probably already packing."

Lago moved to the other side of the room and shut the doors leading out to the *altane*. "Verle and Babs never left the hotel that night," he said, as if working it out for himself. "Darlington was in his room and the two bodyguards were in their room—"

"On the second floor," Rhea reminded him. "Right below my room—overlooking the side entrance to the hotel where no one would see them come or go."

With a smile, Lago grasped an imaginary stick shift, yanked it to the right and then shoved it forward.

They hurried down the four flights of stairs and into the morning light. Lago gave her a perfunctory kiss. "Can you find your way back to the hotel from here?" he asked.

"No problem."

"Good. Stay in your room until you get my call."


The concierge noticed Rhea enter through the revolving door and motioned for her to stop at his counter. He reached back and extracted a sealed envelope from her mail slot.

"From Henry Rivers," he said, handing it to her.

Inside the envelope was a clump of keys and a hastily scribbled note.

Rhea looked up at the concierge. "Mr. Rivers hasn't checked out yet, has he?"

"I'm afraid so. He took the boat to the airport well over an hour ago."

"What was his flight time? Do you know?"

"I made the reservation myself. His plane should have left by now. If you like, I could call the airport and—"

"No, don't bother. It doesn't matter."

She tightened her fist around the keys and read Henry's note.

Dear Rhea,

You engaged yet? Enclosed, please find the keys to Jodie's loft. I found them among the things in his suitcase. You are hereby bequeathed any and all paintings (and anything else, for that matter) that you may find stashed in his loft. I haven't discussed this with Dad but I think he made his position fairly clear, yesterday, in my room. It's amazing, isn't it? At long last, father and son have struck a mutual chord: we both despise the very memory of Jodie. Now that I'm certain Dad didn't kill him, I don't really give a shit who did. As far as I'm concerned,

it was just a convoluted suicide . . . though Babs's
big tits might have helped things along. In any case,
I leave his ghost in your capable hands. I remain
your,

low on codeine Henry


Back at Questura, the night watchman immediately recognized and
identified the sketchbook as the one Jodie had with him on the night
of his murder.

As predicted, Lago, accompanied by three of his men and Rosa, the
translator, made an unexpected visit to the Gritti Palace. He was just
in time. Two stacks of luggage guarded each side of the entrance to
the presidential suite.

It was Verle who opened the door.

Through Rosa, Lago announced the new and unsettling evidence
of the sketchbook. He patiently explained the discrepancy of its
location in light of the night watchman's testimony.

Verle Rivers, though initially nettled, listened carefully and soon
became solicitous. He phoned Wallace's room and told him: "You
and Osmar and Omar get your asses up here double-time! This place
is crawlin' with holsters and I want some answers! No, goddamn it,
not in ten minutes! I said now!"

Babs, newly perfumed, entered from the bedroom. She adjusted
her glasses, looked briefly at each intruder—as if making a head
count—assessed the agitation in Verle's voice, and opted for a low
profile by immediately sitting down at the far end of the room. Her
emerald ring looked like a paperweight as she kept her hands, quite
still, in her lap. She gazed out the window as if to deny the intolerable
presence of her uninvited guests.

Soon after, Darlington and the bodyguards rushed in. Wallace
started for a chair but, noticing that Verle was still standing, thought
better of it. Osmar and Omar stood side by side, their legs spread
apart, their hands folded behind them—like soldiers at ease—their
eyes fixed straight ahead.

Again, Lago explained the new development, adding: "I know you're ready to leave and I really dislike inconveniencing you in this way. But it's very difficult for me to understand how the sketchbook could have returned to the hotel *and* to Jodie's room all by itself—unless, of course, someone in this room put it there."

Darlington immediately stepped forward, his smile an open display of contempt. "Dr. Lago, with all do respect, I don't see anything so terribly difficult to understand. If I were an old man in the process of losing his job, I would probably recognize the sketchbook too—especially if I also saw a reward dangling just out of arm's reach. Your witness is obviously bribeable. He wasn't above taking a fifty-dollar bribe from Jodie. What wouldn't he say for a hundred-thousand-dollar reward?"

Lago nodded appreciatively. "Quite right, Mr. Darlington. But how do you excuse the fact that the night watchman was aware of the existence of the sketchbook?"

"I excuse nothing! It's quite simple. There must have been more than one sketchbook: the one Jodie had with him on the night of his demise—God rest his soul—and the one that remained in his room."

Darlington looked to his boss for approval. Verle merely glared then shifted his attention to the chief of police. "What now, Dr. Lago? Are we under arrest?"

For a moment, Lago glanced down at the bodyguards' shoes. Both pairs were black and with leather soles. He ordered two of his men to search the bodyguards' room for shoes with rubber soles. "If there are any, have them checked against the footprints found at La Fenice." The *ispettori* nodded and left.

Finally, Lago answered Verle. "I have no reason to detain you. I know that you're trying to get to Geneva. You and your wife are free to go whenever you wish. It is essential, of course, that we know where to contact you as long as the case remains—"

"What about me?" Darlington interrupted.

Lago frowned. "I'm sorry?"

"Do you propose to detain me?"

Lago creased his brow and laughed. "On what grounds? For the murder of Jodie Rivers? You were in your room, or don't you remember?"

"Don't laugh at me."

"Forgive me, but it's to your benefit that I do. The idea of you strangling someone is clearly absurd. The police are looking for a strong man."

Babs laughed in the background.

Lago dropped the smile and turned toward Verle. "There is, however, the problem of your bodyguards."

"What problem?"

"Perhaps Mr. Darlington is right: perhaps the night watchman is merely trying to second guess what the police want to hear. That will be discovered soon enough. In the meantime, I'm stuck with the fact that your bodyguards' room was accessible to the street, without any one from the hotel being aware—"

"You're going to detain my bodyguards?" Verle growled.

"I'm sure I won't have to keep them long. They can probably be in Geneva by tomorrow—"

"This is blatant police harassment!" Darlington interjected. "We'll have your badge for this!"

"Shut up, Wallace," Verle snapped.

Lago looked from one man to another. "If it's protection you need," he offered, "I'll be glad to supply policemen to escort you to your plane."

"Goddamn it, Lago!" Verle moved a step toward him, rolling his shoulders as if he was squaring off for a fight. "Why the fuck would my own goddamn bodyguards kill my own goddamn son? It doesn't make any goddamn sense!"

Lago waited for a moment before speaking. He took on an expression of innocent curiosity. "I understand that there was an embarrassing scene in Henry's room yesterday."

"What?"

"Drawings on the drapes that put your wife in a . . . well, in a rather compromising position. . . ."

Babs hand went to her mouth.

"Verle, this is slander!" Darlington sprang forward with all the physical menace his meager frame could muster. "Who told you about that?" he demanded. "Who's spreading that filthy lie? Was it Henry or Rhea Buerklin?"

Before Lago could respond, Verle slowly walked over to Wallace and rested his large hands on the smaller man's shoulders. By exerting the smallest amount of pressure, Verle could have crushed Darlington like an accordion. "Wallace," he asked, barely above a whisper, "why is that important?"

The room fell silent.

The exclusivity of Verle's gaze was extraordinary. Lago and his police force were instantly demoted to the point of non-existence. It was as if no one could penetrate the case unless and until Verle Rivers willed it so.

"What . . . what did I say?" Darlington sputtered.

Babs suddenly broke into sobs.

Verle pretended not to notice, turned away from Darlington, and approached Lago. "Okay," he said with a sneer. "You want my boys? Take my boys."

"I intend to," Lago replied, bristling at the idea that he required Verle's approval but, at the same time, distracted by Babs's outburst.

"Um-hum," Verle laughed. "An Italian with a mission. Well, go on," he added, with an impatient wave of the hand. "Take the bastards away. Get out the electric prods. Yank out their goddamn toenails, for all I care. You won't find out anything. You won't find out *one goddamn thing*."

# 19

The bodyguards' firearms were confiscated and sent to ballistics. The two men were then transported by boat to Questura. They were fingerprinted, and finally brought up to Dr. Lago's office where—tape recorder running—they were interviewed separately.

Osmar, the Brazilian, was first. His responses, related through an English translater, were as concise as they were unhelpful. No elaboration of details were offered. If the questions couldn't be answered by a simple "yes" or "no," Osmar faltered, slack-jawed, and offered up an expression of dim-witted helplessness. Whether or not his stupidity was feigned was beside the point. Osmar was an old pro at interrogation. He knew that a consistent paucity of information was his best defense.

Omar's French was better than his English, so a different translator was brought in for his interrogation. Lago found it tedious work. But after twenty minutes of slow circling, his line of questioning—and, to some extent, Omar's responses—became more interesting:

LAGO:  Let's go back a few days . . . the week before Jodie and Lisa were killed. . . . Verle was gone on a business trip. Osmar went with Verle and you remained here, right?

OMAR: Right.

LAGO: Your assignment?

OMAR: To watch over and protect Mrs. Rivers.

LAGO: Not to protect Jodie?

OMAR: No.

LAGO: So you can account for Mrs. Rivers's whereabouts every moment during that five-day period?

OMAR: That's right.

LAGO: Really? Yesterday, outside of Nardi's, Mrs. Rivers and Rhea Buerklin managed to ditch you. The report I received was that it was a fairly simple maneuver.

OMAR: That won't happen again.

LAGO: I'm more interested in knowing whether or not it happened before.

OMAR: Never before.

LAGO: Rhea Buerklin got the distinct impression that it *had* happened before.

OMAR: Not with me, it hadn't. What does Rhea Buerklin know about it?

LAGO: Did they spend a lot of time together?

OMAR: Who? Mrs. Rivers and Rhea Buerklin?

LAGO: No. Mrs. Rivers and Jodie Rivers.

OMAR: I guess so.

LAGO: You guess. You were with Mrs. Rivers all the time. You don't know?

OMAR: They went out each afternoon.

LAGO: Where did they go?

OMAR:   The sights. Tourist stuff.

LAGO:   And you were with them?

OMAR:   Yes.

LAGO:   And Lisa Morris? Was she included in the group?

OMAR:   A couple of times.

LAGO:   But mostly, it was just you and Jodie and Mrs. Rivers.

OMAR:   Yes.

LAGO:   Why? What was going on between Jodie and Lisa all this time?

OMAR:   I don't know.

LAGO:   They were lovers. How did they act around one another?

OMAR:   I don't know. Normal, I guess.

LAGO:   You never saw them fighting?

OMAR:   No.

LAGO:   It didn't strike you as odd that Jodie was spending more time with Mrs. Rivers than he was with his girlfriend?

OMAR:   That was none of my business.

LAGO:   And what about at night? Did Jodie and Mrs. Rivers spend time together at night, as well?

OMAR:   No. Never. Mrs. Rivers had her dinners alone.

LAGO:   Where?

OMAR:   In her suite.

LAGO:   Jodie never joined her?

OMAR:   I already answered that question.

LAGO:   And where were you during Mrs. Rivers's dinners?

OMAR:   At my post, outside the door.

LAGO:   Outside the presidential suite?

OMAR:   Yes.

LAGO:   I presume that, during those five days, you slept sometimes.

OMAR:   Of course, I did.

LAGO:   But you were her only bodyguard. So when did you manage to sleep?

OMAR:   When *she* slept. At night, after the dishes had been removed from the room. She would open the door when she was ready to retire to her own bedroom.

LAGO:   You spent the nights in her suite?

OMAR:   Yes.

LAGO:   You didn't sleep in your own room?

OMAR:   How could I if I was sleeping in her suite?

LAGO:   Where, exactly, did you sleep?

OMAR:   The hotel provided a roll-away for me . . . in the corner of the salon. You can ask them.

LAGO:   So Jodie never visited her in her suite?

OMAR:   I didn't say that.

LAGO:   Well, did he or didn't he?

OMAR:   He came to her room each morning to have breakfast. Ask the hotel.

LAGO:   Why didn't you tell me that before?

OMAR:   You didn't ask.

LAGO:   These breakfasts: did he come with or without Lisa?

OMAR:   Without.

LAGO: And where were you?

OMAR: I returned to my post outside the suite.

LAGO: How long did these breakfasts last?

OMAR: What do you mean?

LAGO: It's not a difficult question. Did the breakfasts last twenty minutes, thirty minutes, longer?

OMAR: Usually about an hour, I guess.

LAGO: Just an hour?

OMAR: Maybe a little longer.

LAGO: That's a rather long time for breakfast, isn't it?

OMAR: If my boss's wife wants to take her time with her breakfast, what's that to me?

LAGO: And you were always outside.

OMAR: It wasn't my place to be anywhere else.

LAGO: You never thought to check on them?

OMAR: Why should I? Mrs. Rivers is a lady. And Jodie was her husband's son. There was no reason to believe that they might be fooling around.

LAGO: Who said anything about them fooling around?

OMAR: That's what you're getting at, isn't it?

LAGO: Why would it be?

OMAR: This is all about them pictures on the drapes.

LAGO: Oh, yes, the drapes. So what you're telling me is that, each morning, they could have been fucking their eyes out and you wouldn't have known the difference.

OMAR: If Mr. Rivers heard you say that, he'd have your nuts clipped.

~ 234 ~

LAGO: Oh? Would you describe Verle Rivers as a jealous husband?

OMAR: He don't allow no disrespect, that's all.

LAGO: You like Mr. Rivers.

OMAR: They say he's a great man.

LAGO: And what did you tell this great man about his wife, during his absence?

OMAR: Nothing. I never talked to him.

LAGO: You never contacted him? He never contacted you?

OMAR: Never.

LAGO: You were employed to protect his new wife! I find it extraordinary that, during Verle's absence, he wouldn't have called. You were never in contact during those five days, is that right?

OMAR: No, that's wrong. I had to call in a report each day.

LAGO: But you just said that you didn't speak to Verle.

OMAR: I didn't.

LAGO: Then who did you speak to?

OMAR: Mr. Darlington.

LAGO: Mr. Darlington. Why did you report to him?

OMAR: Because he takes care of these things.

LAGO: You answer to Darlington, not to Mr. Rivers?

OMAR: Both, really.

LAGO: But who's your real boss?

OMAR: What do you mean?

LAGO: Who hired you? Darlington or Mr. Rivers?

OMAR: Why is that important?

LAGO: Just answer the question.

OMAR: Mr. Darlington.

LAGO: Who pays you?

OMAR: Mr. Darlington.

LAGO: And you make your reports to Mr. Darlington. Do you like Mr. Darlington?

OMAR: What?

LAGO: Do you like Mr. Darlington?

OMAR: Yes, I like Mr. Darlington. He's a regular sweetheart.

LAGO: You're faithful to him.

OMAR: I don't believe this shit.

LAGO: Neither do I. Why do you like Mr. Darlington?

OMAR: He's as smart as they come. He's what keeps things together. He knows what Mr. Rivers wants . . . what he needs.

LAGO: Give me an example.

OMAR: Well, for one thing, he knows how to keep jerks like you away from Mr. Rivers.

LAGO: He didn't do such a good job this morning, did he?

The report from ballistics was brought into Lago's office. Omar's .45, of German origin, was the same kind as the one used to kill Lisa Morris, but there was no match. Osmar's piece was never in question because it was a different make of pistol, a Glock 9mm semiautomatic, manufactured in the States. More bad news came from the men who had searched the bodyguards' hotel room: No sneakers had been found, thus eliminating a cross check of footprints.

Lago looked up from the reports:

LAGO: Were Mrs. Rivers and Jodie having an affair?

OMAR: Allah, not again.

LAGO: Were they?

OMAR: I already told you, I never saw nothing like that.

LAGO: You never told Mr. Darlington that they were spending a lot of time alone together?

OMAR: No.

LAGO: Why not?

OMAR: Because I didn't see it that way.

LAGO: You didn't see it that way because you were stationed *outside* the presidential suite. Anything could have happened—

OMAR: You don't think I would have picked up on something like that? They were friends, that's all. All they did was talk. They never stopped talking.

LAGO: Talk? What sort of talk?

OMAR: Bullshit talk. Talk that leads nowhere. Just like the talk you and me are having right now.

Yet more bad news came in from forensic: There were innumerable sets of fingerprints found on the sketchbook, but Osmar's and Omar's were conspicuously absent. (The day before, two of the sets had been identified as Jodie's and Lisa's. Remaining prints no doubt belonged to Rhea and Henry and Wallace Darlington, who had returned the sketchbook to Henry's room—not to mention the prints of the policemen who had originally discovered and dismissed the sketchbook as unimportant.)

Reluctantly, Lago switched off the tape recorder. What was the point of continuing? If either one of the bodyguards had been involved with Jodie's death, they had long since had the opportunity to cover their tracks—and with considerable help from the Venetian police force.

Lago ordered Osmar removed from his office with instructions that both men be detained until Interpol's records of the bodyguards (if there were any) came in. But his voice was leached of conviction as he gave the order. Even if they proved to be convicted murderers, how would that help? Unless some unknown witness came forward within the next twenty-four hours, someone who could positively identify the men as having been near the scene of the crime on the night of Jodie's murder, Lago would have to release the bodyguards.

It wasn't going to happen. Lago fiddled with his cobra ashtray, increasingly convinced that *nothing* was going to happen.

More bad news (in the form of a transcript) found its way to his desk.

Jacopo Pittalis, the drug pusher who had been brought in for questioning the day before, had struck a deal with Guardia-di-Finanza: In exchange for immunity, he admitted having sold Jodie the hash. But this news neither surprised nor improved Lago's discouraged disposition. Jacopo swore that the transaction had taken place three nights *before* Jodie's death; he adamantly denied any connection with the murders. Lago didn't doubt this. Jacopo was a local punk, a hash-head himself, a student still living at home, a small-time schemer whose felonious potential didn't extend much further than supplying venturesome foreigners with "soft" highs. Besides, the kid had an ironclad alibi on the night of Jodie's murder: He was on the mainland, visiting his grandparents in the village of Noale.

One section of the transcript particularly interested him. Jacopo had encountered Jodie twice: the first night, when they set up the deal; and the second night, when the deal was actually transacted. Both meetings had taken place in front of La Fenice.

GUARDIA-DI-FINANZA:   Why La Fenice?

JOCOPO PITTALIS:   That's where I first ran into him.

GDF:   Do you often do business there?

JP:   No, never. It's too close to my home . . . in my neighborhood. Besides, at that time of night, there's never any action around La Fenice. Not a soul in sight.

GDF:   What was Jodie Rivers doing there?

JP:   I'm not sure.

GDF:   He was alone?

JP:   That's right. At first, I thought he might be looking for a hooker. Sometimes tourists don't know where to go. He asked me for a light. Then he started talking about the opera house.

GDF:   What sort of questions? Jodie Rivers didn't speak Italian.

JP:   I took three years of English in school. I can get by with the tourists. It's enough for . . .

GDF:   For your business?

JP:   I get by. He was upset that the opera was closed to the public. I told him that there probably wasn't much to see . . . that it was just a mess inside. He didn't care. He even said, "All the better." He told me he had been reading about La Fenice in a tourist guide. He was especially fascinated that Verdi's *La Traviata* had had its premiere there.

GDF:   Why?

JP:   Because the premiere was a flop. He went on and on about how the audience had booed. "The humiliation!" he kept repeating. He said he wanted to get in there so that he could . . .

GDF:   Could what?

JP:   Could laugh.

GDF:   Laugh? He said that? He used that word?

JP:   Yes.

GDF:   Laugh about what?

JP:   Don't ask me. I thought it was a pretty screwy thing to say, so I didn't exactly pursue the topic. I did suggest that he might be able to bribe the night watchman. And then, he brought up the subject of drugs.

GDF:   And that's when you struck a deal?

JP:   Yeah, only he wanted a larger quantity than I had so we made arrangements to meet again the following night.

GDF:   At La Fenice?

JP:   Yes.

GDF:   Your second meeting: did Jodie mention the opera house?

JP:   No. And I didn't bring it up.

Lago put down the transcript and lighted a cigarette in disgust.

Frequently, there was an element of stupidity involved with murder cases. Wrong place at the right time. So often, victims compromised their own safety for the most ludicrous reasons. *So that he could laugh.* Jodie died at La Fenice because he had been attracted to a site where he could vent his cynicism? To laugh? To laugh about what? A long-dead composer's artistic failure? The failure of artists, in general? Or had his attraction to the place been even more perverse? Jodie died with the prong of a *rostro* in his hand—symbol of the coxcomb—his father's virility sawed off and retained as a contemptuous reference. Was his laughter spite-induced? Was Jodie savoring his ultimate betrayal of the filial role? A laugh of vindication for Verle Rivers's new marriage? A long-overdue retaliation? A laugh of ridicule?

Stupid! Jodie's cruelty had vindicated no one. Not Verdi. Not his crazed, ill-willed mother. Not himself. No, someone's strong, capable hands had seen to that!

Large capable hands.

Stubbing out his cigarette, Lago remembered the moment, earlier in the day, in the presidential suite, when Verle Rivers had rested his hands on Wallace Darlington's shoulders.

Why had that moment possessed such resonance for Lago? Why did the entire case seem to center around that one, salient gesture and Lago's simultaneous sense of utter exclusion?

Lago picked up the phone and placed a call to Geneva. Several years before, he had helped a Swiss detective track down and arrest a murderer who had unwittingly fled to Venetian waters. It was time for his associate to return the favor. Lago gave the detective a quick run-down of the case, informed him of the imminent arrival of the Rivers entourage and asked him if he would keep an eye on them.

"You got it," the detective responded. "I'd be happy to help, old man. Just tell me what to look for."

"I'm not asking you to put tails on all of them," Lago explained, "but just let me know if anything exceptional happens in the next few days. I'm particularly interested in Verle Rivers's bodyguards, who I'll have to release by tomorrow. Unless something breaks through here—and I doubt it—they'll be in Geneva by tomorrow night."

Dr. Lago hung up the phone with a sigh.

A group of people come to Venice. An artist is strangled. A model is killed by gunshot. A cremation. A burial. A once-beautiful woman is shipped off to the Bahamas in a body bag. And the group of people? They pack their suitcases, pay their bills, return their hotel keys like good tourists should. . . .

With both hands, he picked up his coiled, turquoise snake. He stroked its smooth ceramic hood for a moment, then carefully returned it to the desktop. His head turned toward the window—his nostrils flaring—as if some malodorous waft had just invaded his tiny office.

"Dead end," he whispered.

And then he closed his eyes.

He would have been hard pressed to explain what, exactly, a dead end smelled like, but an emanation, suspended with the spoors of mockery, was all around him. A cloying and musty scent. Overwrought. Dark and artificially illuminated. Not unlike the sweltering, echoic interior of La Fenice . . . all trussed up for grand passion . . . suitable for kings and whores alike . . . like spent sex, arousing and post-coital at the same time. . . .

# 20

At 4:00, Lago returned to the Gritti by police boat. He gave the driver instructions to secure the *volente* to the moorings, informing him that they would be escorting Signora Buerklin to the train station.

He turned around and realized that Rhea had been watching him from the terrace. She stood up by her corner table. In her hand was a very tall Dewar's and water. He approached, devouring her with his look. She wore a black T-shirt stuffed into skin-tight black jeans. Emblazoned across her breasts, in dark green letters, were the words NO WHINING.

"You've grown taller," he said.

With a shrug, she pointed to her black lizard cowboy boots and returned to her seat. "You're early," she said. "My train doesn't leave for another two hours. Do you want a drink, or are you on duty?"

"I'm on duty," he said, reaching over and taking a long drink of her scotch.

"Rough afternoon?" she asked.

"The Verle Rivers faction. Most of the day, I've been banging my head against the wall . . . brooding about their escape from my jurisdiction."

"You've said all along that, unless you came up with some hard evidence, you couldn't keep them here against their will."

"Until this morning, I didn't *want* to keep them here. Now that they've left, I realize that the odds are against my ever concluding this case . . . at least, officially. The evidence keeps transferring itself from one person to another. It's like a virus, mutating from one moment to the next. How do you trace it back to the original strain? There's no use denying it now: The proof in this case has been buried by an excess of wrong-doers . . . and almost certainly irretrievable."

Rhea frowned. "Have you given up?"

"Give up?" Lago laughed. "Far from it, Rhea. I have newfound hope. I have every reason to believe that this case will be solved. It's just that . . . well . . . I won't be around when justice is served. People more resourceful than I will have that satisfaction."

"My God," Rhea said, setting down her drink and suddenly understanding his buoyant mood. "Do you know who killed Jodie?"

Slowly, almost imperceptibly, Lago nodded. "As I say, I can't prove it and I probably never *will* be able to prove it but, yes, I think I've learned the truth."

"One of the bodyguards?" Rhea guessed.

"Almost certainly Omar. He had easy access out of the hotel. He was strong enough to strangle Jodie. And though the gun that killed Lisa was not the one found on Omar, both guns were the same make . . . thugs have their preferences. It probably pained him to have to dispose of the second gun. None of this is terribly surprising. Among the Rivers's delegation, he was always the most likely candidate. Omar doesn't interest me."

Lago helped himself to another drink from Rhea's glass.

"What *does* interest me," he continued, "is the person who not only managed to secure Omar's services, but had a motive for doing so."

Lago leaned over and whispered a name into Rhea's ear.

Rhea closed her eyes.

"When?" she asked. "When did you realize it was—"

"Oh, this morning in the presidential suite. There was a moment, a very weird moment when an extraordinary silence pervaded the room. Verle held command, as always . . . but his appropriation of the moment was quite chilling to witness. It was if he were sucking the very oxygen out of the room. This horrible realization washed across his face . . . followed by a deadly calm.

"But it was only *after* I had interviewed Omar that I realized the true importance of that moment. What I had witnessed was the act of the great Verle Rivers learning the truth."

"But this is all intuition. How can you be so sure Verle has finally discovered—?"

"He knows all right," Lago smiled. "The first thing that Verle did, once I had left his suite, was to call the Hotel Serenissima, where his private detectives were lodged. Without explanation, he terminated their services. They'll be flying back to Washington, first thing in the morning."

"And the reward he offered?"

"There's no reason why he shouldn't let it stand. He knows better than anyone that no one will ever be able to claim it."

Rhea was visibly shaken. She had to clear her throat before asking, "So . . . what do we do now?"

"You go to Paris as planned. See if you can get anything out of this Marina Heidinger person. If she *is* willing to talk, it will merely verify what I've already told you. As for me: I wait and watch. Verle Rivers has never backed down from a situation in his life. It's only a matter of time before he makes his move. And when he does, the case will be over."

"What do you think Verle will do?"

"An eye for an eye? Or maybe he'll opt for a more subtle retribution. Who knows? Time will tell."

"You're willing to sit back and allow Verle to take the law into his own hands?"

Again, Lago laughed. "You've got to be joking. What law, Rhea? The law that governs Venice? That man has created a universe so vast, so protected, so exclusively his own that he *is* the law. Mother of God, what would you have me do? What can I do that I haven't already done? I'm the Fiat, Verle's the Ferarri. I can either choke on his exhaust fumes or fill up his tank."

"I know, but—"

"Let go, Rhea. Do you want justice, or do you want procedural ethics?"

"I want justice. You know I do."

"Then don't try to yank the wheel away from Verle. It's not within our reach anyway."

"Then what is within our reach?"

Lago looked out toward the water. "From where I'm sitting?" He turned back toward Rhea and took her hand. "We still have two hours before you leave."

It took Rhea a moment before she realized his proposal. She shook her head. "I've already checked out of my room. I had to. Some horrible Scandinavian couple was waiting for it."

"It doesn't matter. Where are your bags?"

"You walked right past them. Over there, on the landing."

"You've paid your bill?"

"Yes. Paid, tipped the concierges—"

"Then what are we waiting for?"

Rhea smiled, in spite of herself. "You mean? . . ."

"You booked a sleeper, didn't you?"

Minutes later, the couple was seated at the stern of the *volente*. The general manager, who had rushed out upon learning of Rhea's departure, personally pushed the boat away from the moorings and blew her a kiss. The pilot nosed the craft to the left, then, picking up speed, headed into the sun and the ancient embrace of the palazzo-laden Grand Canal.


At 6:15, the porter knocked on the door of Rhea's compartment.

"Forgive me, Dr. Lago," he called, "but you really must deboard now. The train has been ready to leave for over—"

Lago unlocked the door and poked his head through the opening. "This is official business," he growled.

"But the passengers are beginning to complain."

"Tell the engineer that the *Commissario Capo* requires a few more minutes. Do I make myself clear?"

"Yes, sir," the porter said to an already shut door. He checked his watch, shook his head and retreated down the corridor.

When Lago turned back around, Rhea was standing at the window. "Official business," she muttered, raising the blind and letting in the sunset.

"It's not so far from the truth, is it?"

"Our relationship has been part of your job?"

Lago shook his head and took her into his arms. "You said it yourself—the other night at La Fenice: that this case was more about desire than it was about death. When are you coming back?"

"I don't know, Giovanni. I always come back to Venice. You had better go. The mob grows restless."

Rhea kissed him. He put on his jacket and left the train.


Rhea arrived in Paris the next morning at eight. She hailed a taxi outside the train station and gave the driver Marina Heidinger's address, 32 rue Cler. It was slow going. It was rush hour and her cab had to traverse—from east to west—the very core of the city.

Rhea knew the seventh arrondissement fairly well but she wasn't familiar with rue Cler. It was a narrow, one-way street lined with unremarkable apartment buildings that ended at Marina's corner. Beyond this, the pavement has been cordoned off for pedestrian use only—it was the neighborhood's open markets, and the fruit stands were piled high with colorful spheres.

Suitcase in hand, Rhea walked into a stone courtyard, conferred with a truculent concierge (a Spanish woman to judge from her accent) and walked the four flights of stairs to Marina's apartment.

Rhea had to ring the bell three times before the handle turned and the door opened up just a crack.

"Who is it?" came the voice.

"Rhea Buerklin."

The door opened further. A six foot tall woman with blond tousled hair clutched at her dark blue kimono and peered down with open hatred.

"What time is it?" she asked, rubbing one eye.

"Time to talk."

"I told you the other day that, if I had anything else to say, I would contact the police."

"If you don't talk to me, you won't *have* to contact the police. They'll be breaking down your door."

Marina noticed Rhea's luggage. "Planning on moving in?"

"If I can get to de Gaulle in time, I'll return to New York today. Are you going to let me in or not?"

"Yes, all right, just be quiet, Okay? My man is still asleep."

The door opened into a large room with a window that gave view to tile rooftops and, beyond, the higher stories of the Eiffel Tower. Marina rushed to the bedroom door and carefully secured it shut, then motioned Rhea to follow her into the kitchen, which wasn't much larger than a closet. "At least let me have some coffee first," she mumbled as she began washing out the coffeepot.

Rhea used the interval to scrutinize the hundreds of photographs that were taped to the cabinets and refrigerator door. Professional and amateur photos alike shared equal billing in this collage-tribute to Marina's beauty. Marina alone, Marina with other beautiful women, Marina with beautiful men—in short, Marina with Marina. Included in this montage, were several snapshots of Lisa Morris and Marina— arm in arm on a beach somewhere in the south of France.

"It'll be ready in five minutes," Marina said over her shoulder as she opened what could only be described as an undernourished refrigerator: a couple of yogurts and a bottle of milk were the sole contents.

Rhea nodded and asked for directions to the bathroom.

Like the kitchen, Marina's bathroom was devoted (though on a more practical scale) to beauty. Glass shelves, floor to ceiling, lined one wall—all laden with a veritable library of cosmetic preparations. Rhea ferreted through the medicine cabinet and, among other things, found a dusty bottle of mouthwash with a few marijuana seeds stuck to the base.

How innocent—and almost touching—this would have seemed had Rhea been snooping through a twenty year old's apartment. The feminine vanity of the place would have seemed spontaneous and newly applied . . . a girl's first apartment away from home . . . a girl just discovering the double power-punch of youth and beauty.

But Rhea wasn't in a twenty year old's flat. Marina Heidinger was over thirty. Like Lisa Morris, Marina had been in the business for over a decade. The newness had worn off. The hot glamorous excitement of strobe flashes, of self-discovery and quick money had long since lost their pop. Marina's beauty had become a job, like any other—though, more of an uphill climb as the years attached themselves to her face.

No: What Rhea saw in this apartment (and in Marina's eyes) was a selfishness grown thick with age . . . a torpidity with no happy endings in sight.

Coffee was served, in mismatched cups, in the living room. Discarded clothes and an open suitcase had to be removed from the couch before Rhea could sit down.

Rhea came straight to the point: "Are you modeling illegally in this country? Is that why you don't want to get involved with the police?"

"We all do it," Marina answered. "I can't get work in Austria any more. My face was over-used there. Naturally, I have to keep moving. We all do it," she repeated.

"I know that. And I have no desire to interfere with your means of support. Just tell me what you know about Lisa's stay in Venice—and tell me the truth—and I can guarantee you that, even if the police question you, they'll stay off your back."

"You told me you weren't with the police. How can I be sure they'll leave me alone?"

"Because I have the Venetian chief of police's word for it."

Marina raised her eyebrows. "Oh? And how can you be so sure of his word?"

"Because I'm fucking the man."

Marina almost choked on her coffee. "Are you serious?" she said with a wry smile.

"Do I look like the type to kid around?"

"No . . . no, you don't. This chief of police: is he good-looking?"

"Not if he's trying to nail your ass."

Marina dropped the smile.

"I'm dead serious, Marina, he'll have this place torn to shreds if you don't cooperate. He strikes fast. He'll have you booted out of this country so fast you won't know what hit you. Is that what you want?"

Marina set down her coffee. "Are you threatening me?"

"Um-hum. I'm going to be thoroughly pissed if I can't catch a plane this morning. When I get pissed, I tattle. Are we going to talk about Lisa, or not?"

Marina's eyes darted nervously about the room. "What do you want to know?"

"I know that Lisa was up to her neck in debt back in New York. My guess is that—in some way or another—her debt, or more specifically, her desire to get *out* of debt, is inextricably connected to her death. What do you know about that?"

For the longest time, Marina said nothing. Then her eyes suddenly became moist, her cheeks flushed. "I tried to talk her out of it!" she blurted out.

"Talk her out of what?"

"The whole idiotic scene . . . you can't imagine . . . it sounded too incredibly sick and I told her to . . . just leave!"

"But she wouldn't listen?"

Marina stole a glance at the closed bedroom door. In a lower voice, she said, "I don't even *begin* to know where to start."

Rhea leaned forward. "It had to do with Babs, didn't it?"

Marina looked down and nodded her head.

"She hated Babs."

Marina nodded.

"Jodie had seduced Babs, hadn't he?"

Another nod. "Lisa was not the type to be spurned. She was thinking of a way to get even—with Babs, with Jodie, with the entire whitebread family. She was going to blow the affair wide open, the minute Verle Rivers returned to Venice."

"What happened? Why didn't she?

Marina bit her lip and brushed the hair away from her face. "The day Verle Rivers returned—she was going to tell him . . . but . . . but she couldn't get to him."

"What do you mean?"

"Well, I guess he has this kind of maze of people she had to go through before she could get an interview with him and . . . she didn't have any luck."

Rhea reached over and touched Marina's trembling hand. "So she gave up?"

"I wish to God she had. No, Lisa opted for a different approach. She decided on more serious tactics."

"What tactics?"

"I told her not to. I told her she was way over her head. She decided to attach a little economic leverage to her vengeance. She needed the money. She was in debt and the jobs weren't coming in like they once had. For a while, she had flirted with the idea of going into acting. That's when she hitched up with Henry. But when she realized that Henry wasn't going to help her, she dumped him for the younger brother. He was so cute, she told me, and he was fun and, most important, he had the same father as Henry Rivers. By then, she had a fairly good idea of who Verle Rivers was. Then this trip to Venice: Jodie puts the make on Babs—Lisa can't get to Verle—it was clearly time to cash in. Her intention was to blackmail."

# 21

Rhea sped to the airport from rue Cler. All the New York-bound flights that day were booked, save one economy-class seat in one plane: last row, smoking section. Even more fortuitous was the fact that the plane didn't take off for another hour and a half, giving Rhea ample time to get in touch with Lago.

"So that's it," she said over the phone. "Marina's admissions conform with your theory. Well . . . mostly conform," she amended her statement. "The hash in Lisa's suitcase remains unexplained. Marina denied knowing anything about that."

"She might be protecting herself on that point," Lago responded. "But there's two other possibilities. One: Having threatened to tell Verle of the affair, Lisa might have extorted the hash from Jodie as a kind of slap-dash, temporary pay-off."

"You mean, you think she was blackmailing Jodie too?"

"Why not? At the end, she was swinging wide."

"Okay. What's the other possibility?"

"Two: Lisa may have simply appropriated the hash, at the last minute before leaving for the train station. She was still staying in Jodie's room . . . no doubt she knew where his stash was hidden. And, as we know, she wasn't above theft: Remember, there was also a silver-plated teapot of the Gritti's, found in her suitcase."

"So what happens to Marina?"

"Nothing much. She's been helpful. The French force will get a signed deposition from her. Other than that, I'll see to it that they leave her alone."

"What happens to the deposition?"

"It will make the rounds. The Rivers delegation will get an opportunity to respond to it. It will have virtually no impact—at least, in Verle's eyes. He's already way ahead of Marina: what she didn't know was *who* Lisa intended to blackmail. The wheels—or, more precisely—Verle's wheels of justice are already turning."

"What do you mean?"

"This morning, Babs got on a plane bound for Boston. Looks like she's going home to Mama."

Rhea paused for a moment. "The day I was with her, she said she wouldn't mind getting away for a while. That doesn't necessarily mean anything, does it?"

"Perfectly understandable," Lago agreed. "Her departure, in and of itself, means nothing. What I do find significant is that she was not given use of the company jet. She took a commercial flight. Not only that, there was no escort. Not a bodyguard in sight. She got into a taxi, just like normal folks, and went to the airport by herself."

"You think she confessed to Verle? You think she admitted to the affair?"

"I think getting involved with Verle Rivers is like investing in bonds with quick dividends. Sometimes it's to your advantage, sometimes it's not."

"Giovanni."

"Yes?"

"Nothing . . . I . . . I've got to go."

Rhea landed in New York in the middle of the afternoon, local time. The customs line was interminable. While waiting, she borrowed a woman's compact and checked her reflection. She looked ten years older. What she needed was three days of uninterrupted sleep—a luxury she could ill afford. Intentionally, she had stayed out of touch with her staff—partly because her whirlwind stay in Venice precluded anything else, and partly because of her detestation of the Press: it was in her interest to keep her staff in the dark about the murders. They couldn't divulge what they didn't know. In any case, from the airport, she took a cab to her gallery, knowing full well that an avalanche of unwanted problems awaited her there.

What she didn't expect, upon arriving at her gallery, was to be immediately confronted by a woman she truly despised: Joan McCabe. Joan McCabe was a reporter from *Manhattanite*, a trendy-sleazy magazine specializing in exposes of New York's social set. When Rhea's partner had been killed, McCabe was the proponent of the theory that Rhea had somehow been responsible.

"Rhea!" McCabe cooed. "You look fabulous!"

"I look like shit."

"Well, of course, considering the shocking news of Jodie's death—"

"What do you want, Joan?" Rhea asked, setting down her suitcase, glaring at the red smear of lipstick on her adversary's front teeth.

"I just popped in to see if your staff had heard from you—ghastly thing about Jodie, isn't it?—and, instead, I get to speak to the source! You've got to deny these rumors for me!"

"What rumors?"

"That the Orloff-Buerklin Gallery is jinxed."

"Deny it?" Given present company, how could she? Rhea rifled her purse for a cigarette. "Got a light, Joan?"

McCabe handed her a book of matches.

"The thing is, Rhea, news is so slow getting over here. So many conflicting reports from Italy. Is it true that you were personally invited by Verle Rivers to investigate the case?"

"Of course not. I went over to discuss Jodie's work and the prospect of upcoming shows. Look, Joan," Rhea said, exhaling smoke in her face and dropping the matches into her own purse. "You want an exclusive? I'll give you an exclusive . . . but it's got to be a short one."

"You're a doll, Rhea."

"You promise you won't be disappointed?"

"I'm sure I can come up with a slant."

Within seconds, McCabe had pad and pencil poised in midair.

"Okay," Rhea sighed. She crossed her arms and, assuming the role of yellow journalist, lied through omission. "This is what I know. Verle Rivers was in Venice on his honeymoon with the former Bostonian, Babs Lowry-Chaberts. I'm not up on Babs's lineage but I'm sure, if you squeeze real hard, it's worth a couple of oozy paragraphs. Footnote: this is her second marriage."

"Love it!" McCabe scribbled madly. "Lowry-Chaberts. . . . Yes, go on."

"Anyway, Jodie, who was head-over-heels in love with the glamorous model, Lisa Morris—"

"Black, wasn't she?"

Rhea nodded. "Unlike your readers, Jodie was color-blind. Anyway, the interracial lovebirds flew to Venice to offer the newlyweds their congratulations. Everyone was happily ensconced in the rarified walls of the Gritti Palace—"

"Good, good—"

"Then, things took a sinister turn."

"Marvelous."

"Jodie got involved with a local drug dealer, bought a sizable amount of high-grade hashish, got strangled at the very same place where he bought the drugs, the Venetian opera house, and Lisa, whose only mistake was probably being with Jodie, was taken out by gunshot. That's about it. Jodie's ashes were interred on the island of San Michele, resting place of Sergei Pavlovich Diaghilev and other assorted dignitaries. Lisa's body was returned to her home in the Bahamas. Verle and Babs, utterly grief-stricken, returned to Geneva where they make their home, among other places."

"And what about Henry Rivers? Isn't it true that he had had an affair with Lisa?"

"I don't know anything about that."

"But I've been told that Henry and Jodie were not on speaking terms."

Thinking of Jodie's postmortem visits with Henry, Rhea laughed in spite of herself. "Nothing could be further from the truth! Jodie and Henry were constantly in touch—especially at the end."

"Do the police have a suspect?"

"Not yet, but I'm sure it's only a matter of time. Verle has helped the cause by offering a one-hundred-thousand-dollar reward."

"But they think that the murder was drug-related?"

"It would appear that way. Now . . . really, Joan, I'm dead on my feet. I've given you the facts. There's nothing else I can add. If I find out anything, you'll be the first to know."

Rhea picked up her suitcase and started to walk past her but Joan held up a finger.

"One more question, Rhea."

"What?"

"Well, you've mentioned everyone but yourself."

"What do I have to do with it?"

"Jodie is scheduled to have a show next month, isn't he?"

"That's right."

"Well, given the fact that he's now dead—and we all know that a dead artist's work is blue chip investment—can the public expect his prices to be significantly higher?"

Rhea shifted her suitcase to the other hand.

Until that moment, she had only vaguely considered how or if to capitalize on Jodie's work. Now, looking into Joan McCabe's revoltingly avaricious countenance, she made a split-second decision. She set down her bag and announced:

"There will be no show in October. At least, not a Jodie Rivers show."

"Why not?"

"Well, for one thing, I'm not sure how many new pieces he had actually finished before he died. I've only seen a few of them. I'll have to go through his studio and . . . maybe I'll mount a retrospective in the spring . . . when things have cooled down a bit . . . when people can be more objective in viewing his work—"

"Oooh, that *is* clever: making the public wait for a half a year. Why, the anticipation, alone, will make his price soar!"

Rhea set her jaw: "That's not what I meant. Good-bye, Joan."

As she walked into her office, a wave of helplessness overcame her. Time and space and Joan McCabe had conspired to play an unwanted trick on her. The sensual mist that had enfolded her in Venice had been replaced by smog. She looked up at the expectant faces of her employees and knew she was in for a tough transition.

That evening, John Tennyson returned Crunch to Rhea's apartment.

It was a dismal reunion. Whatever else he was or was not, John was her friend. She couldn't bring herself to lie to him about Lago. How could she? There was no way she could relate her *sense* of the case without including her involvement with Giovanni. In her mind, lust had been a governing force, or—as Henry might have put it—the leading lady.

Tennyson listened quietly.

"Aren't you going to say anything?" she asked.

John stood up.

"I guess you had to be there to appreciate it."

He slammed the door as he left.

The timeless, collective experience of Venice was further compressed into an intangible, unreal flashpoint. Had she even been to Venice? The mossy, battered palazzos were still fresh in her mind. But the reflections they cast in the canals—where were they? The embossment of details, of sensations, had completely abandoned her—banished her to a mirrorless island called Manhattan.

Crunch tried to offer solace by jumping up on her lap. His coat was filthy and he smelled to high hell.


She went to work each day, but her heart wasn't in it. Her depression deepened.

She called Henry four times: twice at his apartment, where she got his answering machine and twice at his office, where she got excuses from Joella, his secretary. Henry never returned her calls.

One day, Ornella visited the gallery.

"When am I going to get to see Jodie's work?" she badgered. "There's no reason why I shouldn't get first pick of the litter. Darling, I was one of his first patrons—"

"And most ardent!" Rhea interjected. "And you were going to let him dump me without telling me first."

"That's not fair, Rhea. Remember, you got your brooch back but I'm still missing my Redon . . . not to mention the half-finished powder room in Martha's Vineyard. How am I to be recompensed for that?"

"Ornella, I don't give a shit."

Day by day, she retreated further into her shell. She turned forty without telling anyone. Her staff knew only too well—especially in her present taciturn state—to let the event pass unnoticed.

A week after her return from Venice, Lago called. Their conversation was short and confined to the case. There were no new developments. Babs was still maintaining a low profile in Boston.

"The waiting is horrible," she said.

"You must be patient," he kept reminding her. "Verle will find his moment."

"And what if that moment involves more blood?"

"You know as well as I that there is nothing, at this point, that I can do to stop it."

"Would you want to stop it, Giovanni, if you could?"

"My official answer is yes."

Unable to deal with clients, Rhea began to spend a great deal of time in Jodie's loft on N. Moore Street. She began to rely on it as a kind of added insulation.

Each afternoon she and Crunch would take a cab to TriBeCa, climb the four floors to Jodie's studio, unlock the heavy metal door, and enter a huge open space with the barest of amenities . . . a platform bed, an open bathroom, a hot-plate, a refrigerator, a sink choking on dirty dishes and oily paintbrushes, a phone that never rang . . . that was about it. The rest of the ex-warehouse was devoted to Jodie's art. In every direction were canvases, some finished, some mere hints of what they might have become. The saddest canvases were the ones that had never been touched: pure white rectangles of silence.

She came upon the box of Lorna's short stories. Some were calculated to inflate Jodie's ego. Some were to assure him that self-destruction was a foregone conclusion in life. Some were odes to resilience. All were discourses on the importance of undermining Verle Rivers's control.

She even grew to like the smell of the place, which was quite toxic: an unhealthy mixture of acrylic paint, venomous solvents and dust. Sometimes, when the odors became too much for her, she would retreat to the west side of the loft where a series of grimy, double-hung windows looked down over the Hudson River. She would lean out the windows and inhale deeply, just as she knew Jodie must have done on innumerable occasions—after brooding about his father—or mother—after temporarily appeasing his insatiable libido with some nameless woman.

In this space alone, Jodie had made something good out of life. He should have been locked up here. The dead bolts should have been placed on the outside of the door. She could have been his warden. She could have brought him his daily ration of food and booze and drugs and cigarettes and women . . . and come back the next day with a new supply, taking away the spent ones. . . .

On September 20, Rhea received a letter, postmarked from Frankfurt, Germany. It read:

> Dear Ms. Buerklin:
>
> At Mr. Rivers's request, I am writing to you concerning Jodie's estate. As you will recall, all paintings and any items you may deem related to Jodie's career have been given to you to do with as you see fit. Both Verle and Henry Rivers have relinquished all rights to the aforementioned. (See enclosed signed statement.)
>
> Jodie's loft, however, is to be put up for sale on October 1st, of this year. Therefore, any items that you wish removed from the loft should be done so before the end of this month.
>
> Sincerely,
> Wallace Darlington

It was a typed letter but the signature was handwritten. For the first time since her return to New York, something actually fascinated her:

Darlington's calligraphy. Never had she seen such perfect, steady, school-text penmanship. Every letter, every space between each letter was a tribute to equanimity.

Often, during the next few weeks, she would return to that signature as if, by staring at it long enough, one minute quiver of the hand would reveal itself. It never did. His spinelessness never betrayed itself. If Wallace Darlington had a noose around his neck, he still didn't know it.

On the twenty-ninth of September, when she could put it off no longer, she brought in the men who would crate and empty the loft of its life. As they were pulling away from the wall a stack of empty canvases, Ornella's precious Redon fell to the floor. It was a beautiful little piece. So soft, so unlike anything Jodie ever did. . . .

Rhea picked it up and dusted off the frame.

"No need to box this one," she told the men. "I'll be responsible for it. It belongs to someone else."

The packers left at the end of the day. She took one more look around, closed the windows, walked down the stairs for the last time and dropped Jodie's keys into the nearest garbage can.

Crunch anointed the can with a polite little squirt of urine.

The three of them—Rhea, Crunch, Redon—walked home in the twilight.


It was the thirteenth of October.

She was in her office, finalizing a deal with two important clients, when she got the phone call from Lago. The news she had been waiting for—sometimes hoping for, sometimes dreading—nevertheless shocked her. During the long wait, she had envisioned a hundred different scenarios. But the form in which Verle took his revenge was—even for Verle—magnificently exhibitionistic.

Verle's BAC-1-11 had detonated just off the coast of England, on route to New York. Offshore fisherman had seen the explosion and had recounted how a million and one shiny parts, like a universe of silvery fish, had slowly drifted—as if in slow motion—down, down, down into the Atlantic.

For such a large aircraft, the passenger list was remarkably small. Beside the pilot, co-pilot, and the steward, Matteo, there were but two other people aboard: Wallace Darlington and a Lebanese bodyguard by the name of Omar.

"Revenge?" Rhea asked Lago. "That's not revenge. That's mass murder."

She hung up the phone, informed the clients that an emergency had arisen, flipped through her address book, jotted down a street number, walked out of her office, told her staff that she didn't know when she would be back, left the gallery, caught a cab at the corner of Prince and West Broadway, and directed the driver to a place she had never been before: "Nineteenth Street, please—between Fifth and Sixth."

She tipped the cabbie handsomely. She entered the building, entered the elevator, and got off on the twelfth floor. She asked for directions from the glassed-in receptionist, walked down the corridor—past a waiting area where a group of black actors pored over scripts—arrived at the door she was looking for and, without bothering to knock, opened the door.

Henry was standing at his desk packing books and papers into moving boxes. A woman with jangling charm-bracelets was doing likewise at the other end of the room.

"Going somewhere?" Rhea asked.

"That's right," he answered, not appearing to be in the least perturbed, nor surprised at her intrusion. "I've had it with New York. I should have gone to California a long time ago."

"Let me guess," Rhea said. "You're going to start your own production company—financed, of course, by your father."

Henry shrugged but said nothing.

"My, how our scruples have changed."

Henry continued packing. "What do you want?"

"I want to talk to you, Henry . . . alone."

Joella put her hands on her hips as if to resist the idea but Henry gestured that it was all right. Reluctantly, Joella left the office.

"Lago called. Wallace and Omar went down in your father's jet."

Henry nodded. "So I heard. Terrible thing."

"Yes," Rhea snarled. "It was such a beautiful plane. I wonder why anyone would have planted a bomb on it?"

"Well, the police suspect some terrorist group, of course. Dad represents the worst aspects of capitalism. And then there's all the enemies that Dad inevitably generates through his deal-makings. This communications conglomerate that he's trying to take over in Italy, for instance. Lots of ill will. It's so fortunate that Dad had to remain in England at the last moment and—"

"Oh, shut the fuck up Henry. I don't expect you to admit the truth."

Henry looked genuinely puzzled. "Then . . . what are you doing here?"

"All I want to know is: When, Henry? When did you realize that it was Wallace who ordered Jodie killed?"

Henry turned the other way. "What are you talking about? That's preposterous."

"Is it? During those five days, when Verle and Wallace had gone to Geneva, Verle knew nothing. But Wallace did. Every day he got the report from Omar: Jodie was putting the make on Babs, they were spending all day together, they were alone each morning . . . sometimes hours on end . . . Lisa was sequestered in her room, pouting . . . Wallace knew perfectly well what was going on.

"But Wallace kept his cool. He knew that Jodie was the last person on earth who would have brought the affair to the attention of his father. Wallace had known Jodie since he was in diapers. In fact, he may have known Jodie as well as anyone because they shared a mutual bond: They were cowards. Wallace disguised his cowardice by turning himself into a machine . . . a disguise in which all personality traits were rendered negligible. Jodie's cowardice was hidden behind contrived aggressiveness. The very fact that Jodie *was* fucking Babs proved to Wallace that Jodie was yellow. If Jodie had been a real man, he would have struck at Verle directly, not through Verle's new wife."

"Bravo, Agatha Christie." Henry clapped his hands three times, then laughed. "You've talked yourself into a corner, Rhea. If Wallace knew that Jodie wouldn't let the cat out of the bag, why would he have had him killed?"

"Because Jodie's habitual malice had taken a new turn. He was getting closer and closer to the source of his hatred. Maybe—just to taunt him—Jodie even shared Lorna's story with Wallace. Wallace knew that something—sooner or later—would have to be done about Jodie . . . and he knew it wouldn't be done by Verle. For years, Darlington had been cast as the fiduciary parent for Verle's two miserable sons. It was in his hands to punish you boys when you misbehaved . . . and Jodie had never been naughtier.

"There was also this about Darlington. You, yourself, were the one who so carefully explained it to me: Darlington derived his identity from the economic inviolability of Verle's empire. Anything that might disturb Verle's clear-headedness would also compromise the security of the organization. He saw himself as the keeper of Verle's flame and Jodie's only remaining goal was to make that flame go out . . . in any way he could.

"Wallace's patience had been severely strained . . . I have no doubt that he was already considering the necessity of, at some point, eliminating Jodie . . . but the time wasn't right yet. And the situation, as he saw it, was still containable.

"What pushed him into action was Lisa. Ambitious, debt-ridden, aging, desperate, vengeful Lisa. She wanted to hurt Jodie and she wanted to destroy Babs. She decided to tell Verle, the moment he returned to Venice. She may have told Jodie about her plans. Knowing Jodie, he would have laughed in her face. Her anger intensified. And then, when she couldn't get to Verle . . . when she failed to penetrate his fortress of isolation . . . when she was left howling on the wrong side of the drawbridge . . . she played her last card. She did the next best thing to telling Verle. She told Wallace instead, hoping that, if she couldn't extract revenge, she could at least get paid for her failure.

"Again, Wallace played it cool. He probably agreed, unconditionally, to whatever payment she demanded. The only problem was that it would take him a few hours to get the money. Knowing that she was to take the night train to Paris, he suggested they make the transaction at the train station. Lisa agreed. She packed her bags, phoned Marina Heidinger to brag about her success and, hoping to make one last dent in the Rivers armor, helped herself to Jodie's hashish.

"She went to the train station, earlier than necessary, just like I did. She went to her assigned compartment, a sleeper, just like the one I traveled on when I went to Paris. And guess what?

"Darlington didn't show. Omar came in his place. It wouldn't have been hard to come up with an excuse. Omar could have told her that there had been a mix-up in the transferral of money . . . that Darlington was waiting for her at the American Express office, or some such place, and that she would have to meet him there . . . that there would still be time for her to get back to her train . . . any excuse to get her off the train and into a boat so that he could put a hole in her gut.

"Unfortunate mess. Darlington hated messes. He could never forgive anyone for creating messes that he would eventually have to clean up. He'd had enough of Jodie's games. Nothing could be allowed to bring down or even compromise the empire. He probably shared all of these misgivings with Omar, who looked up to Darlington, saw him as his boss, as the one man who knew what was best for the empire. What was good for the empire was good for Verle. There's no love lost. Can't you just hear Uncle Wally? 'The kindest thing we could do for Verle, at this point, is to take out his reckless, worthless, stab-in-the-back son.'

"Omar knew Jodie's pattern: every night, out on the streets, over to La Fenice. . . .

" 'But let's not use a gun, shall we, Omar? Too noisy. And too referable to Lisa's death. You're a strong man, Omar. Any suggestions?' "

Rhea stopped. All this time, Henry had continued packing. Finally, he sighed, and looked up.

"Your imitation of Wallace is better than your elaborate theory. In any case, I hope you don't intend to waste your time trying to prove it."

"I don't have to prove it," Rhea said quietly. "Your father has done that for me. Have the divorce papers been served on Babs yet?"

"Why don't you just go, Rhea? You're wasting your time."

"How's your stomach, Henry?"

"What?" The question caught Henry off guard.

"I said, how's your stomach?"

Henry rolled his eyes. "Oh, why, thank you for asking! I haven't had anything to drink since Venice, so it's better. It's still a little tender."

Rhea nodded. "I have a message for your father. Will you see that it gets to him?"

"What's the message?" Henry asked, returning to his packing.

"Taking out Omar, I can understand. Darlington, I can understand. Any father, given the same opportunity, might have done likewise. But two innocent pilots and Matteo, the steward? It was necessary to eliminate three innocent people in order to slake Verle's thirst for revenge? Your father is a thug. Tell him how common I think he really is."

"He'll be shattered."

Rhea made to go.

"Wait a minute," Henry said, "that's not a good exit line."

Rhea turned around.

"You're not playing your part," he explained. "You need to say something devastating about *me*. *Then* you quit the stage before I can respond."

Rhea opened the door and hurried out.

At the far end of the hall, she saw the elevator doors just opening. "Hold it, please!" A sullen, compressed group of black child-actors and their mothers reluctantly made room for her in the lift. Rhea descended, looking down on a restless sea of dark hair.

*Exit line?* Was that how Henry was going to cope with the truth . . . to turn the wreckage of his family into an imaginary stage production?

Henry was his *own* exit line. He wasn't a survivor like his father. His self-loathing alone made him a prime candidate for a variety of stress-related deaths. Already, his hemorrhaging stomach gave him an edge on the competition. Jodie had foreseen it: the spoons and Mylanta bottles that fenced in WALL STREET HERE WE COME like a proscenium arch. . . . And if he didn't manage to kill himself, there was always a Lorna or a Jodie waiting in the wings, posthumously offering internecine advice.

Dark hair. . . .

*But Jodie had been a blond.*

Rhea got off the elevator, consumed by a sudden revelation and barely aware of the children trying to get past her. Dark hair: Jodie had painted both boys' hair a dark brown. At last, Rhea had decoded the sad iconography of WALL STREET HERE WE COME. The older boy in the picture was definitely Henry. But what about the younger boy—the lifeless, dark-haired figure who Henry carried in his arms? Was it, as she had thought until now, a self-portrait of Jodie?

Of course not. She should have known a long time ago. Jodie never allowed his imagery to be that obvious. Jodie had transformed a real childhood experience into a cruel character study.

Like the double frame surrounding the canvas, Jodie had painted a double Henry.

Henry was slogging through life carrying his own corpse.


The next day, a short item was run in the *Times* about Verle Rivers's jet. Several subversive European groups were already taking the credit for the explosion.

Tennyson called around noon.

"I'm over my tantrum. I'm getting so old that it's hard for me to remember what my tantrums are about. How about dinner tonight?"

"Why?" Rhea asked and laughed. "Because you've forgiven me or because you've read the *Times* and want the low-down on the explosion?"

"Tough question," John replied. "Do I have to figure that out this very minute?"

"I still think about my cop in Venice. I mean, it wasn't just a moment of promiscuity over there."

Tennyson was silent a moment. "Hell, Rhea, I've accumulated too many memories of my own to be jealous of someone else's. Could you transplant him?"

"What do you mean?"

"Would Dr. Lago survive, if you brought him to New York?"

"No, probably not."

"Well then, goddamn it, I'll pick you up at eight."

~

In mid-November, returning from lunch, Rhea found a parcel on her desk. It was postmarked from Venice. She called for Anne:

"When did this package arrive?"

"About an hour ago. Why?"

"Was there a letter with it?"

"No, just the package. It's marked PERSONAL, so I didn't open it."

Rhea tore open the box and extracted a turquoise object.

"Good Lord!" Annie exclaimed. "What is *that* supposed to be?"

Rhea didn't answer. She emptied the butts from her Hermès ashtray and relegated it to the bottom left-hand drawer of her desk. In its former place, she carefully set down a garish ceramic cobra.

Anne stood wide-eyed. "You've got to be kidding!" she said with a giggle. "You're not going to actually display that thing? What will clients think?"

Rhea closed her eyes. In her mind, she saw herself seated in a gondola. Lago was next to her. Neither one was saying anything. There was anticipation in their expressions . . . anticipation of something simple yet glorious. Threading its way out of the dark backwaters, the boat finally, deftly, turned into the Grand Canal and glided into a sun-spangled waterscape.

"Anne," Rhea murmured, her eyes still closed. "You've been such a help to this gallery. Don't let it turn you into a small-time snob. Life is blurry enough. . . ."